THE HISTORY ROOM

THE HISTORY ROOM

ELIZA GRAHAM

ISIS
LARGE PRINT
Oxford

First published in Great Britain 2012
by
Pan Books
An imprint of Pan Macmillan
A division of Macmillan Publishers Ltd.

Published in Large Print 2012 by ISIS Publishing Ltd.,
7 Centremead, Osney Mead, Oxford OX2 0ES
by arrangement with
Macmillan Publishers Ltd.

British Library Cataloguing in Publication Data
Graham, Eliza.
     The history room.
     1. Large type books.
     I. Title
     823.9'2–dc23

          ISBN 978–0–7531–9080–7 (hb)
          ISBN 978–0–7531–9081–4 (pb)

     Printed and bound in Great Britain by
     T. J. International Ltd., Padstow, Cornwall

For Matthew Day

CHAPTER
ONE

Meredith

We didn't mean to vandalize the mural. The thrill of scraping away the paint and seeing the image underneath intoxicated me. I should have stopped. I couldn't stop. I didn't know what I was exposing.

We were ten and eleven so it must have been the autumn of 1991. A wet Saturday morning. Dad was showing prospective parents around the school. Mum was covering a domestic science lesson for a sick teacher. At that time everyone at Letchford had Saturday morning lessons, boarders and day pupils alike. Clara and I, too young to be pupils here, had done the homework set by the village school. We'd finished our piano practice as well, even the scales. Hours and hours to fill until Saturday school finished at lunchtime. Too wet to ride our bikes around on the drive, even if it had been allowed during school hours. I'd read all my library books. Clara never was much of a reader. We tried to play a game of Snakes and Ladders but both of us kept sliding down the snakes and we started to squabble, accusing one another of nudging the board.

It was ages until we could go and buy Wagon Wheels or cheese and onion crisps from the school tuck shop at break.

So we drank the milk and ate the biscuits Mum had left out for us. Still only ten o'clock.

"We could paint something." Clara screwed her face into a hopeful expression.

"I hate painting." In fact I loved it, but my efforts were never as good as my sister's so I avoided putting brush to paper when she was around.

"I am soooo bored."

"Me too." It wouldn't be much better when Mum and Dad returned at lunchtime, I decided. Dad was up to his ears in managing the building project. He'd spend all afternoon in his office, going through paperwork, muttering about delays and paying bills. Mum would be trying to help him. Then they'd need to walk around the new boarding houses and gym to make sure everything looked right. They wouldn't let us go with them as the building sites were supposed to be dangerous for people our age.

Clara stood on a chair and put her ear to the clock to make sure it hadn't stopped. She said it was still ticking. Half an hour until morning break, when Mum would come back to see how we were. On Saturday mornings in term time we dropped down the priority list like pebbles in a pond. Sometimes I hated sharing Letchford with everyone else; sharing my parents, too. Mum and Dad were always quick to remind us that we had the holidays to ourselves, give or take the odd student or teacher who couldn't make it home to the

2

other side of the world. "And this house would have been sold decades ago if we hadn't turned it into a school," Mum reminded us, with a quick glance around the oak-panelled rooms we lived in. "This is the price we pay."

"You don't know how lucky you are to have this stability," my father would say, a faraway look in his eyes.

Sometimes I wished we lived in a semi in the village like my friend Janet at primary school. TV always on. Just the four of us. No other children. A mother who was either in the kitchen or out in the garden. No strange teachers creeping around at night with their mothball-smelling tweeds and reading glasses. No sharing of our parents with three hundred other youngsters. And now Dad was going to take boarders. Great. Even less time for us.

"You wouldn't make us board, would you?" I'd asked my mother.

"No." The answer came back swiftly and firmly.

"So why do you let those other parents leave their children?"

She put down the pile of washing she was carrying. "It's not that simple." She spoke slowly now. "Some of them work abroad. Or they have long working days. They have no choice."

"Their children could go to school in the other countries. They'd learn foreign languages. That would be good for them. Or the parents could work shorter days."

She made low demurring noises but I could tell her heart wasn't in the rebuttal.

"Won't the boarders miss home?" I knew I would.

"I don't know." She'd held out a bundle of socks and I'd known the subject was closed. "Pair these for me, darling."

"Mum and Dad are always so busy, busy, busy," I complained now to my sister.

Clara gave me a sidelong look. "Something's going on." She drew a circle with her finger on the kitchen table.

"Have the builders done something silly?" Only last night, I'd heard Dad exclaiming over the stupidity of anyone who thought that a door frame could be built a half-inch too narrow and expect to get away with it.

She shrugged. "Not sure. It's to do with Mr Collins."

Mr Collins was the bursar. I never knew what a bursar did. Something to do with counting money. Mr Collins gave us chocolate digestive biscuits and let us write *ShELLOIL* on his calculator using the numbers. I'd noticed my father going into the bursar's office last night with Mr Andrews. Mr Andrews was Dad's old friend, almost a father to him, Dad said. He'd helped Dad when Dad had left Czechoslovakia. Mr Andrews and Dad sat together in the evenings and examined sheets of figures, muttering about the cost of tiles and bricks.

"Perhaps the adding up was wrong," I suggested.

"Perhaps." Clara contemplated her invisible circle. "Mr Collins's new baby is poorly. I heard him talking to his wife on the phone about him." She yawned.

Minutes passed; plodding eternities. Clara suggested creeping downstairs with the scooters and whizzing round the marbled-floored hallway, another pastime forbidden during term time, but there was nobody around to see us now.

We'd invented a game that was a cross between polo and ice hockey. It involved passing one another a rolled-up sock, using brooms as sticks. We were proud of our skill; it wasn't easy to steer a scooter with just one hand. The hall housed the famous Letchford Mural, doubly special to our family because Dad was the painter and Mum his model. He'd painted her in an old-fashioned long blue velvet dress with the house behind her, hair tied in a ribbon with one piece falling over her neck. She was as beautiful as Michelle Pfeiffer. Dad was a good painter. Sometimes visitors came here specially to look at the mural. Some of them said it was a shame that Dad hadn't stayed an artist. He'd ruffle his hair and smile his funny, almost shy smile, that made him look sad rather than happy.

Clara knocked an ace towards me, which I saved, nearly falling sideways off the scooter as I did so. I hurled my broom at the sock and sent it flying towards the mural. Clara was already hard on it. She intercepted the sock before it hit the wall but leaned too far forward, only saving herself from going over the handlebars by slamming a hand against the wall. The scooter fell, its rubber handle scoring the wall with a red mark. And not just any old part of the wall, either. It had scraped our mother's image, making her look as though a knife had cut her from her neck downwards.

We looked at one another. The bell would ring for break within minutes. Mum would come to check on us. I remembered the dishcloth by our kitchen sink and bounded upstairs, leaving Clara still standing staring at the wall. She probably thought I'd abandoned her. I grabbed a bottle of Harpic from the cupboard under the sink and dampened the cloth. I was back with Clara in seconds.

"Here." I took a stab at the red mark. It seemed to lift very quickly. Clara's expression lifted, too.

"That bit's still marked." She pointed at the impact point where the scooter handle had left a crimson gash. I squirted more Harpic onto the cloth and applied it to the wall with vigour. A citrus smell permeated the hall.

The bell trilled.

"Quick!" Clara hissed. "One more go. Here." She grabbed the cloth. "Let me." She attacked the wall. The last bit of the red mark from the handlebars came away. As did the top layer of paint.

"Oh." The single word seemed the only one suitable for expressing my surprise. I looked more closely at what Clara had exposed. "Oh," I said again. Beneath the dark blue of our mother's dress I could make out a white undercoat. And something else. Brighter tones.

"What is it?" Clara asked. "What's under there?"

We could have stepped away from the wall then. It was only a small patch of damaged paint; it could have been overlooked. Or explained away as an accident. But something about that vivid hue had caught my imagination.

"Give me that." I reclaimed the cloth from Clara and scrubbed at my mother's blue dress. More of the white paint appeared. I attacked it. Little flecks of purple and orange appeared. Even then I could have stopped, made some excuse for what I'd done, used the falling scooter as the excuse. But I couldn't stop now.

"Merry," said my sister. "What are you doing?"

I shook my head, not really knowing myself, possessed by a demon that insisted I find out what was underneath the surface. On I rubbed, revealing flesh-coloured tints.

"Arms," said Clara, sounding fascinated despite her earlier caution. "And look, those bits are hair." She sounded almost awestruck. "It's another lady — a girl."

Behind me I heard footsteps. Heels clattered over the stones. The prospective parents coming back inside with Dad. Someone drew in a sharp breath.

"Meredith." My father's voice could have frozen a boiling kettle. "What have you done?"

CHAPTER
TWO

Twenty years later

A Letchford late-September day. Light the colour of
champagne. Leaves turning amber and bronze.

I sat in the window seat of the staffroom on the
second floor feeling so cut off from the bright scene
outside that I might have been wearing a sign round my
neck saying *Outsider*. Even a homesick first-year
boarder couldn't have felt more separated from the
general cheeriness outside. But I couldn't be homesick
because this was still my home.

I was watching my father escort a small group of
parents around the school grounds. They passed a bed
of gold roses and I heard one of the mothers exclaim at
the scent. Pupils, newly returned from Turkey, Thailand
and the South of France, showed off tanned faces and
limbs lithe in games shorts as they escorted parents to
the gymnasium, squash courts and indoor swimming
pool. At that age I'd never felt as at ease in my skin as
these sleek teenagers. Out on the hockey pitch a match
was in progress. A hand punched the air in triumph and
a cheer erupted, the players framed by the green curve
of the Downs to the south.

My father was wearing his light-grey Italian summer-weight suit. I was looking for my mother, who ought to be beside him in her blue linen shift dress, simple and perfectly cut, with an ivory cashmere cardigan over it. A pair of models for a life insurance policy or pension plan. Middle England: playing fields and nice manners. But of course my mother wasn't here. She'd died in the summer holidays. I blinked several times and forced myself to look at the sixth-formers in the group: a boy and girl, each of them gilded by the soft light. The mothers were darting looks at the boy. Probably wondering whether their own sons would gain that poise, that feline sleekness, if they sent them to Letchford, The fathers were trying not to gawp at the slender sixth-form girl with her mane of hair and long golden legs. Perhaps we should insist that girls wore tracksuits on open days.

They were all coming inside now, the mothers' heels clattering up the stone steps into the marble-floored, white-stuccoed hall, an anomaly in the Elizabethan manor house with its oak-panelled rooms. The group would stop in front of the famous Letchford mural. Everyone always wanted to see the painted wall with its gowned chatelaine standing outside the tree-surrounded house. Normally at this point my mother Susan would have given her quick commentary, explaining that the artist was the headmaster himself. If pushed, she'd have admitted to being the model for the serene Edwardian-looking woman. There'd be murmured acclaim.

Normally, by this stage, Dad would have found an excuse for moving swiftly out of the hall, perhaps muttering about checking on the coffee and biscuits in his study upstairs. Today he'd have to talk about the mural himself. He'd hate it, preferring to deflect conversation towards the wall's earlier fate, during the Second World War when the army had been billeted here.

"The soldiers completely covered the wall in graffiti and lewd drawings," he'd tell the group. "And put a dartboard on it. The wall was whitewashed when they left but you could still see the words. And the images." Laughter from the group. "Hence the mural."

This afternoon I was supposed to be marking English essays. They weren't bad. Early in the term so perhaps I'd forgive the first-years the missed apostrophes and erratic understanding of *they're, their* and *there*. I circled errant letters and wrote comments and breathed in air that smelled like Earl Grey tea. On an afternoon like this I could believe I could make my life work. A new academic year. The school smelling of new leather shoes, crisp exercise books and freshly painted walls.

Someone knocked on the staffroom door. Tempting to ignore the knock. I wanted to stay here in the sunny window seat with its view of the grounds and the Downs. Only pupils knocked, so the interruption would probably involve someone being taken ill in class or behaving badly. Or a teacher needing help with a recalcitrant piece of technology. I slipped off the cushioned window seat and walked over the wooden floor to open the door. In front of me stood a third-year girl. "Oh, you're here, Mrs Cordingley. Mr Radcliffe needs a member of staff to go to his classroom straight away, please."

Her wide eyes broadcast excitement. A disciplinary problem? Nope. Simon could have managed a classroom full of chimpanzees. I sighed for my interrupted solitude and followed her. As we walked across the landing to the stairs I saw the rounded grey outline of a Globemaster plane through the window. Taking off from RAF Brize Norton. My muscles stiffened. I hoped the girl hadn't noticed.

Outside the history room third-years clustered, chatting and laughing, eyes bright like magpies.

"It's a stiff," one boy was saying. "Got your iPhone? We'll get a picture." A hand moved towards a pocket.

"Thank you." I held out my own hand for the phone. "You know the rules about mobiles. Collect it from me after assembly." The second boy dropped the phone into my palm with a scowl.

"There've been Satanic rites going on in there," someone else muttered. "That's why Mr Radcliffe wouldn't let us see inside that box."

"Did you see a pentagon in the floor or something?"

"Sometimes they kill chickens. There was that film on in the holidays . . ."

I put the mobile into my pocket and pulled the door handle. It didn't open.

"Mr Radcliffe locked it," someone said helpfully. I knocked and the door opened. Simon stood in front of me, his round, friendly face pale.

"Meredith, thank God." He waved me inside and shut the door on the goggling eyes outside. A cardboard box sat on one of the desks. It was about the size of a large shoebox. "Can you call the police? My mobile's out of battery."

"What's in there?" I approached the desk. He put out a hand to restrain mine from touching the lid of the box.

"Probably best not to look. The police mightn't like it."

I moved my hand away but not before I'd nudged the lid so that it opened a little. "What do you mean, the police? What's in there, Simon?"

He turned to me. "A baby."

"What?"

"A dead baby, Meredith. Oh God." And he put a hand to his mouth and coughed. I peered at the gap left by the displaced lid and thought I could detect something light and delicate in the box, shaped like a curling shell. Or an infant's hand. I stared at the vague outline. Something else metallic glinted inside the box. Simon had placed the little coffin on one of the girls' desks and it sat beside a fluffy fluorescent-green pencil case; pens, compasses and rulers exposed.

"Where did you find it?" I could barely speak.

"In the cupboard." He nodded at the large oak piece in the corner. "I went to look for textbooks. I saw the box and wondered what it was." His eyes were still wide, remembering. "Wish I hadn't peeped inside during the lesson. When I saw what was in it I closed it immediately and sent the children out of the room. I don't think any of them saw the . . . what was in it." He swallowed. "Perhaps I should have left the box inside the cupboard. Hope I haven't disturbed the crime scene or something."

"I'm sure you haven't. And you were right to send the kids outside."

"Go and call the police, Meredith," he said again. "And tell your father, too. I'll lock the room until they get here."

CHAPTER
THREE

Normally the minutes leading up to a staff meeting were filled with gossip and complaints that someone had used up all the milk or pinched the last chocolate biscuits. This room was oak panelled like most of the Letchford rooms apart from the entrance hall. Once the staffroom had been a library to which Edwardian males retired for post-dinner conversations about racehorses, gun dogs and mistresses. You could still smell the cigars smoked there over the last century or so, even if the aroma of musty textbooks and the PE department's damp trainers had insinuated themselves into the scent.

Only my father was yet to arrive. I was still keeping half an eye open for my mother. She'd normally been the first to appear, with a quick smile for everyone. Often I'd seen her in a corner talking quietly to someone. Mum would be nodding, eyes fixed on the person addressing her. And the teacher or lab assistant would sit up straighter. They might even smile. She'd been the perfect foil for my father, who, for all his cultivation of a genial English gentleman's persona, had never discarded his central-European seriousness.

Growing restless, people were checking mobiles for messages and jumping up to peer out of the windows.

One or two pulled exercise books out of bags and began marking work. Others huddled in groups, whispering and shrugging. Emily Fleming bit her lip and looked intently at the chair on which my father would sit when he came in. Emily was the young New Zealander Dad had taken on as a gappy, as pupils called them: a school leaver who wanted a year's work experience in a school before university. Gappies helped organize games lessons and after-school activities. Usually they were cheerful, sporty young men and women, half nostalgic for the cricket pitches and tennis courts they'd only just forsaken themselves. Emily Fleming looked like the kind of girl who'd prefer to stay indoors. This afternoon she sat with one foot wound around the opposite leg, biting her lip and hugging her mug of tea to herself. Her long light-brown hair fell over her face, obscuring her features. She'd only been in England a few weeks. Staff meetings were new to her. Everything was new to her. God knows what she'd made of the police cars. She was as pale as the white mug in her hands.

"Did you notice," Deidre Hamilton, head of languages, whispered to Simon and me from behind her hand, "that the police didn't take anything away with them? No body or anything?" Her eyes glinted.

I hadn't mentioned the contents of the cardboard box to anyone, telling the children milling outside Simon's classroom to go outside immediately for an early break. One or two had hung around, reluctant to sever themselves from the excitement, and I'd threatened them with demerits. I'd gone straight to find my father, catching him in the front hall as he was saying goodbye to a group of parents who'd finished their tour of the school. He'd listened to what I'd told him, betraying his concern only by the twitching of a nerve beside his eye, and insisted on calling the police himself. As we were talking, Emily Fleming had come inside from the garden. Her eyes widened as she watched him rush upstairs to his telephone. Dad never carried a mobile with him. "Is everything all right?" she'd asked me. "Has there been an accident?" Her voice quivered slightly.

"We found . . . something in Simon's room," I told her.

"What?" She bit her lower lip.

"I'd better not say any more just now. There'll probably be a staff meeting later." As I walked upstairs I felt her stare on my back and felt the urge to turn to ask her if she was all right. But Simon had been waiting.

The pupils in Simon's disturbed history lesson would have babbled to their friends about something going on. There'd have been texting, tweeting and Facebooking. And they'd certainly have seen the police cars pulling up outside. And now Deidre knew about the little body within the box.

"Are you sure?" I asked Deidre. "Perhaps they've already taken away . . . whatever it was." I tried to remember how they carried out these procedures in television dramas. My husband Hugh had been a fan of anything involving onscreen mortuaries. He'd have known the order in which these things occurred.

"I'm certain." Her head bobbed towards ours. "And I haven't seen a pathologist or what-do-you-call-them, SOCOs."

"Hanging out of the window, were we, Deidre?" Simon tutted. "You're worse than the kids. You've been watching too many forensic dramas." His voice was jovial but I still detected a note of strain.

What would things be like by now in the boarding houses? Most of the children here were day pupils but some were weekly and termly boarders. The sixth-formers would have a job keeping the kids' minds on their prep while we held this emergency meeting.

Dad was coming in now, carrying a plastic bag, his eyes slightly narrowed. People nudged each other. Some gave me quick sideways glances. The headmaster's daughter: the one who'd slouched home because her life had fallen apart. The one who couldn't be entirely on their side because of her family loyalties. *Careful what you say in front of her, it might get passed back to Charles. What's she like in the classroom, anyway? Lucky for her there happened to be a maternity leave to cover here. Anyone know where she was before? Ah, a comprehensive. She'll be great at crowd control.*

Dad had presence, the kind that can't be learned or taught. People sat up straighter when he entered a room. Men fiddled with the top button of their shirts and adjusted ties. Women teachers swept imaginary creases from their trousers or skirts. He was pale this evening, his mouth set. He looked round the room, probably seeking out my mother, too. He'd always liked her to be here. I saw him give himself a mental shake.

She will never come to another staff meeting. He walked to the table where we served coffee and biscuits each morning break, his Lobb shoes shining, his summer suit still uncreased. Nobody said a word.

"Good evening, everyone. There is something I need to show you." He pulled the cardboard box out of the bag, took off the lid and tipped the box over. I stood, couldn't help myself, wanted to shout at him to stop, not to expose to us whatever was in there.

A small body toppled onto the table. Metal clinked against wood. Someone repressed a scream. "My God," Simon said. I heard myself make a sound like a muffled warning.

The baby lay on the wooden surface, one arm hanging loose, the other curled up towards its face as though it were about to suck its thumb. It wore a long white linen gown and lace cap. Its hands were motionless; its pale-blue eyes gazed at us calmly. From its chest protruded the handle of a silver paperknife. I blinked and looked again and there was the baby, still lying on the oak staffroom table, beside the pile of geography exercise books and a single unwashed coffee cup.

"Dad . . ."

"A prank." His hands were trembling. "Someone placed this, this . . . doll in the box in the history room cupboard."

"Doll?" I said, stupidly.

Simon was rising to his feet. "I'm telling you it looked like a real baby, it . . ." He choked on his words.

"I wouldn't concern yourself about having been gulled." Dad's lips formed a forced smile. "Even the police were convinced. For just the one single moment." He was feeling the strain; reverting to over-precise, stilted English, with a hint of foreign intonation. I wondered if the others had noticed.

Emily stared at him. I noticed how she clenched her thin hands together so that the knuckles showed white. She seemed to retreat beneath the folds of the silky cardigan she wore as though she were trying to hide herself away. It was just a prank, I reminded myself. Horrible and macabre, but nothing more than a prank.

Deidre had risen from her seat. "It looks incredibly lifelike." She approached the table and put out a hand, looking at my father inquiringly.

He shrugged. "Go ahead."

"What about fingerprints?" someone asked.

"The police didn't take them."

"Why on earth not?" burst out Simon.

"No crime has been committed. Other than wasting police time."

"But . . ." Simon pointed at the paperknife.

"This" — my father nodded at the stabbed doll — "is merely a toy. There is no known crime of stabbing a toy, unpleasant though we have found it."

"Pretty weird toy." Simon spoke through gritted teeth. "What kind of person would want something like that?"

"I've read about those dolls. I can't remember what they're called." Deidre bit her lip, considering.

"You mean there are more of them?" Simon sounded revolted. We were all craning our necks towards the table now, the staffroom resembling a dark repainting of a Nativity scene: the onlookers scared and repulsed by the infant at the centre of the tableau.

"Reborn dolls, that's their name. I remember now." Deidre ran her fingers over the baby's face.

"Reborn?" I asked.

"There was an article about them. They're designed to be as lifelike as possible. There have been cases of people calling the police because they've seen the dolls in cars and been worried that they were real babies who might overheat." She must have seen incredulity on our faces. "People push them round in prams and buggies," she insisted.

"Women, you mean." Jeremy Warner, head of PE, crossed his tracksuited arms as though he were trying to ward off the doll's influence.

"There have been some very sad cases where women have lost children through miscarriage or cot death," Deidre said, with acid in her tone. "They buy these dolls, sometimes even commission them to look like their lost babies."

She pulled out the knife. I found myself holding my breath, half expecting blood to flow from the cut. The blade had left a slit about half an inch long in the linen.

"There, it looks better already, doesn't it?" My father gave an approving nod. Deidre examined the paperknife. "Nothing special. Not silver, anyway."

Emily unwound her legs and recrossed them. I felt another pang of sympathy for her.

20

Deidre gave Jeremy a little smile with a challenge written into it. "Come on, Jeremy. You're the family man. You pick it up and tell us whether it feels lifelike or not." On his desk, along with his referee's whistle and team sheets, Jeremy kept a photograph of his two small daughters, both in pink pinafores and sun hats.

He looked as though he wanted to sprint out of the room, but masculine pride propelled him out of his seat towards the doll on the table. He scooped it into his arms. Surprise flashed across his face.

"It's like holding a real baby, even the way the head feels heavy. But it's cold, not warm." He gazed down at the doll, and the desire to fling it across the room was clear in his expression. Deidre held out her arms for it and he passed it over with evident relief. "Just weird."

Her shoulders dropped as she cradled the doll. Deidre's two boys were teenagers now, but her body obviously remembered how to cradle a newborn. There was something familiar about the baby's costume: the long ivory gown and lace cap; they pulled at my memory. I couldn't recall where I'd seen them. The doll gazed at us with its blank but detailed features.

"It feels too real." Deidre put it down on the table again, carefully, as though it were a real baby. "Apart from the coldness, as Jeremy said. Rather disturbing, in fact. I wonder if this is more than just a prank."

"What do you mean?" Dad peered at her.

She took her time in answering. "The women who use these dolls have psychological issues. According to what I read." She looked directly at my father. "And stabbing it with the knife like that . . . We need to approach this very carefully."

"Do you think a girl here might have been . . . in trouble?" Even my father flushed at the old-fashioned term. I could see him filing a note of his mistake for future reference. "I mean, she might be or have been pregnant?"

"It's a possibility." She shrugged. "One for Cathy, perhaps."

Cathy Jordan was the school nurse.

"I want you all to talk to your tutor groups or classes." Dad sounded as he might have done following a long academic year, but we were only weeks into the new term. The benefits of the Greek holiday he and Mum had taken before her death had already been wiped out. "And the prefects. But above all, let's try and keep this low-key. It's just a silly joke gone wrong." He seemed to push his weariness aside for a second to produce his calm and confident headmaster's smile.

Most people nodded. Only Deidre looked uncertain. I knew she was thinking what I was: that the two activities Dad had prescribed were incompatible. If we talked to the pupils they'd know that something was bothering us. They'd speculate. That was a polite way of putting it. And then the social messaging would start in earnest.

Jeremy seemed to recover his nerve and picked up the doll again. "Its head's filled with something." He sounded disgusted. "That's what makes it heavy, just like a real baby's head." He shoved it back on the table.

Simon shuddered visibly again.

"I recognize the costume," Deidre said, fingering the ivory linen. "Isn't it one from the play, Jenny?"

Of course, *The Crucible*. One of the girls in this term's play carried a baby in her arms in a courtroom scene. But that was a traditional baby doll once belonging to my sister, obviously plastic, with eyes that shut with a slight flap when you laid it down.

Jenny Hall, head of drama, came closer and fingered the ivory robe. "Looks like our costume, all right. We've had them all out in the drama department. I haven't missed it but we haven't got far in sorting out costumes and props yet." She grimaced at the cut the knife had made in the linen. "Hope this will be easy to mend."

"I can fix that for you." It was the first thing Emily had said this evening.

"Thanks." Jenny looked surprised at the offer but relieved.

"I'll make the mend invisible," Emily went on. "Nobody'll ever know." There was still a quiver in her voice. I smiled at her, trying to convey encouragement.

"If that's all." Jeremy tugged down his tracksuit top. "It's lower school basketball club in ten minutes. I need to set up the hall." A few of us rose as well. It was my turn to supervise prep in Gavin House, across the lawn. I needed to liberate the sixth-former left to keep the kids quiet, and answer queries about geometry and French verbs taking *être* in the perfect.

My father glanced at his watch. Checking I wouldn't be late. Only a few days ago I'd found a printout of my own timetable sitting on top of his desk. He'd taken a risk, giving me the English job here. And there'd been that week, that bad week, that week we didn't talk about. Once again I felt myself look round the room for Mum. If she was here this evening she'd be packing up her sewing things now, chatting as she wound threads round bobbins and folded fabric.

She was always making curtains and cushion covers, had quite a talent for it. The long William Morris curtains in the hall and at each landing casement were ones she'd sewn, and the striking brick-red paint on the drawing-room walls, which most people would have shied away from, had been her choice. The colour always drew compliments from parents when they visited. Over the summer she'd re-covered the staffroom window-seat cushions in bold geometric prints. Anyone else would have worried that they'd be too overpowering for an Elizabethan room. But even an ageing classics teacher had been spotted stroking them as though they were kittens. Mum's brain haemorrhage had struck just hours after she'd sewn the last zip into those cushion covers. She'd had the headaches for a few weeks before then but had attributed them to too much time at the sewing machine during the hot weather.

The evening air was only now turning cool. The summer didn't want to die this year and low golden rays bathed the lawn. I walked across to Gavin. Dad had built four boarding houses in the late eighties. He'd never intended Letchford to become a boarding school proper, just as he'd never intended to become a teacher at all. He'd agreed to take boarders with some reluctance, accepting that changing work patterns meant that parents were working late.

"It's better for children to be brought up by their parents than by other adults, no matter how well-intentioned and qualified," he'd always said. "The family should be the child's best refuge." The premature rupture of his own family life had perhaps reinforced this belief. Dad had come to England in 1968 as a boy the same age as the sixth-form boys loafing around on the lawn as they waited for the late buses home.

Twenty years of weathering had softened Gavin House's bricks so that they were now the muted red of a Cox's apple. I let myself slow down. I was retracing steps I'd been taking for decades. Any moment now I might meet myself as an eight-year-old, riding my bike while my mother deadheaded the late roses. I might come across myself playing croquet with Hugh on an August weekend while he was on leave. I might hear the clop-clop of tennis balls from the courts where my sister had practised her strokes with meticulous accuracy. This evening the ghosts were hanging all around the fringes and if I turned my head quickly enough I'd glimpse them. The reborn doll had set my nerves on edge.

I went inside Gavin and brushed my sleeves as though to remove the shreds of memory. The reassuring scent of damp pupils and freshly made toast met me. No ghosts here. I opened the door of the room where the younger pupils were doing their prep. They dipped their heads like cranes towards their books as I came in.

The perpetrator of this afternoon's prank might be in this room now. He or she could have slipped the box into the cupboard while Simon was fiddling with his whiteboard, back to the class.

The sixth-former supervising was so caught up in his laptop screen he didn't hear me approach. He closed the lid but not before I'd seen what he was reading. There on his Facebook page I read the words *OMG, Dead Baby at Letchford!!!* He turned puce.

"You'd better delete that and tell your friends to do the same. It's just a doll." He looked doubtful. "I saw it myself." He shrugged. "You wouldn't want to look as though you'd fallen for a kid's joke, would you?"

CHAPTER
FOUR

My outside-work world had shrunk to the simply furnished rooms of my apartment. I liked to think of it as minimalist, though I was probably too untidy ever to fall into that school. I made another mental note to myself to sort out the pile of bills and admin awaiting my attention.

A year or so ago my mother had converted the old stable block into a retirement home for her and my father, in case it were ever needed. They'd probably never dreamed that their twenty-nine-year-old daughter would drag herself back to fill it. I appreciated its winter-white walls and restored wooden floors and beams. One of these days I'd even get round to putting up some of the paintings I'd brought with me from Wiltshire, still stowed in the loft above. I could pull out the rugs Hugh'd brought me back from Middle Eastern bazaars and display them. But I wasn't sure I was ready to live with their jewel-coloured patterns. Sometimes I'd even longed to pull down the blinds to block the view of the green sweep of Downs to the south. As autumn progressed and the slopes turned to muted khaki I found the sight more bearable.

My dog met me as I opened the door and it took a few moments to disentangle myself from his greeting. Samson was a leggy mixture of retriever and spaniel plus a few other breeds thrown in for interest. It was only recently I'd started thinking of him as my dog instead of Hugh's dog or *our* dog. He was quietening now he'd reached the age of two, just as Hugh had predicted.

A quick morning turn through the woods behind the school, followed by a longer walk at lunchtime or in the evening, kept Samson happy. At weekends I took him up to the Ridgeway on top of the Downs for a good run. I knew that if I sat down now my muscles would refuse to propel me out of the apartment again so I pulled on my wellingtons and found the lead. A very brisk walk in what my mother had always called the gloaming would shake out the tensions of the afternoon.

The dog carved long circles round me, tail up, ears back. I threw his ball for him and watched him shoot after it. I wondered whether he missed Hugh now or even still remembered him. If Hugh reappeared, would Samson tear towards him in ecstasy or consider him with pricked ears and cocked head?

I walked faster through the increasing dark. My brain gave up its efforts to think about Hugh or about the stabbed doll in Simon's classroom. The history room, we called it. It had once been a bedroom housing a four-poster with velvet hangings. Nobody had slept in it since the sixties. Before Simon's time it had been the bursar's office. The bursary was now housed in its own purpose-built premises at the rear of the house. In the large oak cupboard in the history room resided not only Simon's teaching materials but also photograph albums and documents relating to the house's past. During the school holidays Simon was putting together a history of Letchford.

I turned back. I had marking to do. Not much, though. On an evening like this I could have done with a big stack of exercise books. Long essays on *Macbeth*. Grammar exercises. A trayful of stodgy comprehensions. I was in serious danger of having to sort out my mail if I didn't think of some other distraction.

I needed company. Thank God for Simon, who was single, roughly my age and always made me laugh, regardless of my mood. I thought of ringing him to offer a glass of wine. Or two. Surely he'd want to mull over the discovery of the doll. But he'd already admitted to having a pile of lesson-planning to tackle tonight, something he'd failed to do over the summer.

"I like to get the feel of my classes first," he'd told me. "A sense of their personalities and chemistry. Then I tailor what I have accordingly." He'd responded to my searching look with a burst of laughter. "Nah, you're right. I'm awful at planning. I'll wing it, though." And he would, too. No, leave Simon to his work this evening. I'd ring Hugh's mother, perhaps. It was her birthday tomorrow. I'd sent a card but it would be good to speak to her, to cling to the fragile thread tying me to my husband.

Perhaps I also wanted to cling to her because I'd lost my own mother.

Back in the apartment's kitchen Samson flopped at my feet, tongue hanging out like a small red handkerchief. I boiled water for rice and forced myself to chop peppers, chillies, onions, sweet potato and the beans I'd harvested from my mother's vegetable garden, unable to bear the thought of them unpicked. Hugh had been the cook in our marriage. My skills with knives and pans were limited. When he'd been away on active service I'd subsisted on toasted sandwiches and fruit. Mum had promised to teach me some basic recipes. But now I was on my own.

"Right, you." The frying pan and I were old adversaries. This evening I was going to show it who was boss. I turned up the gas underneath it, heated spices and added chicken strips and vegetables. The results didn't look bad when I'd finished but the chicken strips felt like pencil erasers when I ate them, while the sweet potato pieces were like wood. I pushed my tray away and turned on the Channel 4 news, switching it off when Afghanistan came on. When I'd washed up I found that my marking could be finished in half an hour. Still a whole night to fill.

I ran a bath and lay back in it to let the bubbles do their work. Afterwards I gazed at a programme about a family of meerkats, reflecting on their similarity to a classroom full of chatty third-years that I taught. When it finished I switched off again and stared at the blank screen. Still half an hour before I could reasonably go to bed and tick off another day. I was just about willing myself to sort out the post when the ringing of my mobile roused me.

"Meredith?" Clara. An urgent tone to her voice. "What's all this about a stabbed baby and why didn't anyone tell me?"

"It only happened this afternoon and it wasn't a dead —"

"I am a governor."

"It was only a doll."

Silence.

"A prank, Clara."

"How could it possibly be a doll? Surely even Simon wouldn't be that easily taken in?" She'd never rated him much.

"It wasn't just any old doll." I told her about the reborn, how it had seemed as though it might at any moment wave its tiny fist or start to cry.

"How very peculiar."

"You'd have to see it to believe it." I could hear her tapping on the keyboard as we spoke. She'd be searching the Internet for the dolls. My sister never believed in wasting time.

"What did you say they were called?"

I told her again. "How did you find out, anyway?"

"A friend's got a girl in the sixth form. She texted her mother."

Naturally.

"My God." She'd obviously found an image of one of the dolls on the Internet. "How extraordinary. Who

31

on earth would buy one of those? And who would stab it like that?"

"We have no idea."

"Well, I hope you're going to find out and discipline them for it."

"It was probably just teenagers doing it for a dare." But then I remembered what Deidre had said about women with psychological problems turning to the dolls in times of distress. "I really don't think it's anything too serious." I hoped I sounded convincing.

"We're coming down at the weekend."

"That's really good of you, but you're busy and —"

"Don't try and put me off, Meredith. I have a responsibility to the other governors."

I'd never been allowed to forget it.

"And besides," she went on, in softer tones. "I want to see you. And Dad." I felt my eyes film over. "We both do. So do the boys. I was wondering if they could stay with you?"

At some point over the summer a tradition had been established whereby Rory and Sam, aged six and eight, stayed in the stable block with their Aunt Merry and Samson, and had, as their mother put it, a riot. They stayed up late and ate and drank things normally banished from their Clapham home-cooked diets. I suspected that these visits were designed as much to distract me as for the convenience of my sister. It would have been entirely possible for the boys to sleep in the main house. But whatever the motive, it worked. While the children were with me I almost forgot Hugh. And Mum.

"Oh yes." I heard the enthusiasm in my voice. I was already mentally shopping for ingredients to make them their favourite breakfast of pancakes and milkshakes. I only had one lesson on Saturday mornings. I'd take the boys swimming at the local leisure centre. Then make them monster sandwiches. And perhaps we could hire a DVD and make popcorn in the evening.

"That's so kind." She sounded pleased. My affection for her sons made up for many of my deficiencies. Even if I was incapable of cooking them a wholesome supper of shepherd's pie and apple crumble. Clara and I had been close as young children but from teenagerhood onwards Clara had drifted away from me. Or perhaps I'd started the drift. She'd always seemed so sure of herself, of what she wanted to do, who she wanted to be with, where she wanted to live, how many children she wanted, and when. And everything had happened according to plan.

Only when I'd heard the news about my husband and the explosive device in Afghanistan had I grown closer to Clara again. After I'd taken the phone call from the field hospital in Camp Bastion she'd sat beside me for hours, holding my hand, saying nothing but letting me talk or stay silent as I preferred. Those quiet times together had washed away memories of teenage spats: the time she'd accused me of ruining her new jeans, the time I'd thought she'd made a play for the sixth-form boy here I had my teenage eye on. Then Mum had died so suddenly and we'd found ourselves clinging to one another again like two young girls.

I went to bed feeling that at least there was one thing I was good at being: an aunt. It mightn't sound like much, but it was a start. One day I might make a good teacher, too. Then there'd be two things.

CHAPTER
FIVE

I must have forgotten to set the alarm. I woke with light streaming round the edges of the blinds. Muttering swearwords to myself I dashed for the shower. No time for breakfast. I fed the dog and pulled his lead off the hook by the door. He performed his usual happy dance. The morning was cool, reminding me that it really was autumn now. My still-damp hair felt cold against my head.

I grabbed a beige baseball cap. "Bliss" was written on the front, superimposed upon a palm tree. Hugh had bought it on a holiday to the Great Barrier Reef a few years back.

I was due in assembly in twenty minutes. Unlike me to oversleep. But I'd spent a night haunted by strange images: a baby in a cupboard cried at me. I'd opened a wardrobe to rescue it and found Hugh's bloody severed leg sitting on a shelf. My husband had appeared, shouting that I'd stolen his limb and ruined his life. Then my mother had walked in and told us to stop our fighting: we were disturbing a Latin lesson. I'd woken and sat bolt upright, pulse racing. I hadn't slept properly again after that.

I increased my pace to try and force the dreams from my mind. Samson, pleased at the acceleration, broke into a run, nose down to the dewy grass, zigzagging, picking up the scent of rabbits.

My hair was almost dry now. I stuffed the baseball cap into my jacket pocket, hoping my bob wouldn't be completely squashed flat. Sometimes, standing in front of a group of teenagers, I'd feel their eyes sweeping my appearance: appraising, judging, sometimes — rarely — approving. "You should be so lucky," Deidre had told me. "When they don't even bother checking you over, you know you're just an old bat in their eyes."

We reached the fence bordering the road, the boundary of the school grounds. I turned back. Seven minutes to drop the dog back home and change into something smarter. I started to jog, shouting to Samson to keep up.

I was almost at the stable block when I all but bumped into someone standing with their back to me, staring out across the flowerbeds. Emily Fleming.

"Hi," I said.

She turned. "I was just taking an early morning stroll." Her unusually light blue eyes moved from side to side. There was nothing banning staff from hanging around in this part of the gardens, no signs saying it was private, but it was almost a given that this side of the house was for the family's personal use. How could this young New Zealander know this if she hadn't been told? I didn't blame her for wanting to spend precious minutes among the last asters and roses of the season. Winter would soon be here and the blooms would just

36

be memories. I felt nauseous, remembering the flowers at Mum's funeral. Clara and I had bound sweet peas from the garden into a wreath. They'd been her favourite flowers, the chocolatey-brown ones particularly. The day of the service had been warm and the scent had washed over us as we sat in the church. After that I'd let the sweet peas go to seed on their trellis. Emily fixed her watery gaze on me with an expression I couldn't decipher. Probably my squashed hair.

"Are you all right?" she asked. Memories of the sweet peas must have twisted themselves over my face.

"Fine." I looked at her more closely. She was very slim, with long hair and those interesting eyes. She ought to have been very pretty, but "striking" was more the adjective that came to mind. But even that was too strong a word to describe her. "Thank you. What about you, Emily? Settling in OK?" Something about her presence had disturbed me. She must be homesick. Or unsettled by the silliness yesterday afternoon. Poor kid.

"I'm good, thanks." Her voice gave nothing away. She flicked her hair off her face. She was wearing the same silky cardigan I'd admired yesterday. For a gappy, Emily was certainly well dressed. Usually they arrived at the start of the school year apparently straight from the beach and had to be gently advised on a working wardrobe.

"Best time of the day," I said. "Everything so fresh."

She nodded very gravely. "I can see why it would be hard to leave this school." She was implying that I'd found it impossible to stay away from my childhood home. Perhaps she was right.

"I don't know, there are other places in the world worth seeing." I sounded over-bright, forced. "I expect you'll want to do some travelling while you're over here."

"Nowhere else could be like this." She fiddled with the petals of a purple aster. "No other school could be so beautiful."

I thought of all the other beautiful old schools in their acres of grounds. But I wasn't going to argue with Emily if she thought that Letchford was the most blessed. It was only what I believed myself.

"You've just arrived," I told her. "You won't have to say goodbye until July next year. Plenty of time to grow sick and tired of Letchford. And of us."

"Perhaps." She gave me her curious half-smile. It didn't make her thin face look any more cheerful. "Better make a dash for assembly, I guess."

CHAPTER
SIX

"Utterly bizarre." My sister finished her decaffeinated coffee and signalled with a nod to her husband that it was time to go. Clara and Marcus were staying in the spare room in Dad's apartment in the main house. Marcus had just finished blowing up the air-bed in my own guest room for Sam. Rory was to sleep on the sofa-bed.

"Your father knows there's nothing really to worry about." Marcus still spoke in the breathless tones of one who'd expended litres of air blowing up a large inflatable object. "This doll business is just kids mucking around."

Clara snorted. "I wish he'd calm down." Her features softened. She reminded me again of the big sister I'd grown up with. "What do you think, Meredith? Should we be worried? I just don't know why it's bugging him so much."

I shrugged. I could have mentioned that she herself had reacted strongly to the news of the doll. But I didn't. "Perhaps we're still on edge. After Mum." For a few seconds I didn't trust myself to say more. "I know I am."

She shifted her position on my small sofa so that she was sitting nearer to me. Her warmth was comforting. I was drawn to move even closer to my sister but restrained myself. "I wish he'd put the blasted doll away," I said. The box was sitting on Dad's desk, though the drama department had reclaimed the costume.

Marcus shuffled in his armchair. "It's getting late. The boys probably need to turn in."

I jumped up. "Of course. I'll bring them over to you in the morning when they've had breakfast."

"Ah." Clara looked indulgent. "The traditional Aunt Meredith breakfast."

"The eggs are all ready. Pancakes and milkshakes, my only two culinary successes." I stopped, thinking about the maple syrup that was to go with the pancakes, a present from a Canadian officer Hugh had befriended on a Defence Academy course. I wondered whether Hugh still liked to cook himself something special on Saturday mornings and hoped my face didn't betray this thought. Apparently my husband was spending every minute at the physio or in the gym, building up his wasted muscles. Probably monitoring his diet carefully to make every bite count.

My sister shook her head in mock despair. "Just as well I keep them on porridge the rest of the week."

Marcus caught my arm as Clara gave the boys their final orders. "You must look after yourself, Meredith."

I looked at him sharply. But his eyes were only full of kindness. "It sounds silly now, but perhaps I can see why Dad was bugged by it. And . . ."

"And?" He looked at me.

"Nothing."

He continued to look at me.

"Perhaps I'm more bothered by it than I want to admit. It's just . . . I . . . I miss them both, I suppose. Mum, I mean, particularly." The words toppled out of my mouth. "Obviously Hugh's not actually dead." I let out a high-pitched laugh. "And who knows what'll happen. Perhaps he . . . well . . ." I'd said too much, embarrassed Marcus. But he reached for me and hugged me. It was strange to feel a man's body holding me again, even if it were that of my brother-in-law. A man's body with all its limbs. Whole. For a second I wanted to prolong the embrace, just for the feeling of being held.

"Tough times." He spoke with feeling. "You'll get through, Meredith." He released me.

I realized I hadn't asked him about his own job. "How's the world of property law?"

"Let's just say nothing much is moving at the moment." He spoke quietly.

I thought of the large house in Clapham, the expensive prep school for the boys. "I'm sorry."

He gave a shrug. "We'll get through."

CHAPTER
SEVEN

Sunday teatime. The remains of summer had abruptly packed their bags and shipped off. The school-uniform-grey sky might have belonged to December.

Even Samson gave the air an initial cautious sniff as I took him out for a quick turn through the trees. We reached the edge of the wood and strode along the fence beside the road. Samson's energy began to fizz through his body. He bounded from one scent to another. Tempting to take him for a run on the hockey pitch. But dogs were out of favour on school property.

"Risks, risks, everywhere," my father muttered as he read yet another health and safety recommendation. "This house was once a training base for boys barely older than the sixth form who landed on the beaches to liberate Europe. Many of them were dead before they were out of the water. But we are not allowed to risk a bruise."

I was not a risk-taker. Hugh found my desire to preserve my limbs amusing. "Live dangerously," he'd yell from the bottom of an icy mogul field in the French Alps, as I cowered at the top. But then he really had lived dangerously. The blast in Helmand Province had wrenched off one of the lower legs that had carried

42

him so swiftly and effortlessly down the slope. Two of the fingers on the hand waving a ski pole at me had been severed at the same time. And Hugh's blood, red as his ski jacket, had poured onto the dusty earth beside the road.

They'd told me how it had happened. At the same time as my husband was haemorrhaging into the dirt I'd probably been getting ready for work: cursing the dog for mucking around and not coming in from the garden when I called him. Lamenting the state of my freshly washed hair. Wondering whether I had time to cycle to school or whether I could cop out and drive. Mundane, silly preoccupations.

If I'd been more organized perhaps I'd have found a moment that early morning to think about my husband. Perhaps that moment's thought could have transmitted itself to him. Perhaps he'd have decided they'd gone far enough. "We were about to radio in and say we were turning round," his driver had told me in the email he'd sent a week after the explosion. "We were just driving round the next bend. Then we were going to call it a day."

I'd wanted to ask why they'd chosen that bend and not another, earlier, bend, but I didn't. I studied the maps of the area, looking at the Internet for satellite images so I could work out where in Helmand Province the patrol had been to within a ten-mile or so radius. A country the colour of this baseball cap when seen from above. Hard to imagine anyone living in those dun fields and villages. Impossible to trace the logic of the events that had brought my husband to that dusty track at that particular time on that particular day.

"Just go, Meredith," Hugh had told me the last time I'd visited him. "You can't help me now. Don't waste more of your energy on me."

"Tell me what to do, how to be with you." I focused hard on the get-well cards adorning the bedside table.

He stared down at the hand that had lost the fingers. "There's nothing you can do. It's not fair on you. For God's sake, you've been through enough."

"But you're making real progress. They're going to fit the cosmetic leg soon." The new leg would look like a real one, unlike the prosthesis he was wearing now. "They might give you a running leg, you said. And your hand's healing too."

"This wasn't how I imagined our marriage." A pause. "And seeing you makes it worse for me."

"It won't always be like that. Once you've got used to the leg, you —"

He held out his right hand in admonition, the one that still had all its fingers. "Please leave now." He sounded as though he were addressing one of his soldiers. "I don't want to say these things, I don't want to hurt you. God knows, you've had enough pain."

"Is it true?" I'd asked the male nurse who'd comforted me as I'd staggered away, still clutching the paper bag of fruit and the biography of Wellington I hadn't had time to give him. "Am I making it harder for him?" We sat in a small office, undrunk mugs of tea between us on the table.

The nurse hadn't responded at first. He'd removed his hand from mine, resting it on the table. "He's angry at the moment. He's lost a leg. His life will never be the same again. Some men turn the anger on themselves; that's what Hugh's doing." He looked directly at me. "And we don't really know what bomb blast does to the brain." He opened the paper bag, took out an orange and banged it against the table. "Imagine this is the brain bouncing against the skull as the force of the explosion hits it. Nobody knows exactly what's happened to those cells."

"He might be . . ." I swallowed. "Brain-damaged?"

"His ability to respond to stress might be affected. His concentration. His self-control. And then bear in mind all the drugs he's been on and off in the last months. Some of those can cause short-term personality changes. That may be what's making him so" — he gave an apologetic grin — "bloody insufferable. To you. He controls himself when he's with us. That's good, by the way."

"Is it?"

"Perhaps it shows that he still trusts you enough to let you see him at his angriest and most vulnerable. But at the same time it's unbearable for him."

So I was to be punished, sent away.

"Hugh simply needs to conserve some emotional energy, channel it into learning to walk again. We work them hard. Four or five hours of physical activity a day. While he's here he's got all the banter from the others. They're rude to him when he sounds off and that makes him feel safe. Accepted." He gave a shrug. "I know it sounds strange but that's how it is. They understand him. Eventually they'll all start going out together to pubs and cafes and local swimming pools. That'll help get them back into real life again."

"He told me that he had no bloody intention of being a being a fuc . . . a burden on anyone." I heard my voice tremble.

"He does need you, Meredith." He put the orange back in the bag and scribbled a note on a pad. "I'll talk to the doctors about his drug regime. And the occupational therapist will have some ideas, too."

"What should I do?" I sounded like a frightened little girl rather than a professional woman who kept unruly classes under control. I reminded myself that it was my husband who'd been wounded, not me. But when that explosive device had gone off it had blasted both our lives into shards.

"Only you can really decide. But if it was me I'd give it some time before I came to visit again. Weeks. Perhaps even months."

"Months?" I heard desperation in my voice.

He nodded. "Let him get through the next lot of rehab. It'll be tough. Painful. He's set his heart on skiing again."

Had he?

"He'll need every ounce of courage to get there. As he gets used to the prosthesis he'll be like a mother learning how to manage life with a newborn." He shook his head. "They'd kill me if they heard me say that."

I could imagine. "I'm abandoning him."

"You're doing what he wants."

I slid the biography of Wellington and the fruit across the table. "Someone else might like these." And I'd walked out of the centre without looking back at the window of Hugh's ward.

My father had already told me that he'd have a vacancy for an English teacher at Letchford after Easter; a teacher was going on maternity leave. Fate had nudged me back to my old home with its honey-stoned walls and mature gardens, to my mother with her sewing basket and her vegetable garden. And to my father with his obsessive concern for the school and the pupils. All this had been waiting for me, quietly accepting and welcoming.

I knew from Hugh's mother that he was now living independently in a small flat near the rehabilitation unit and was training hard to become strong on his new prosthetic leg. He was still planning a ski trip at Christmas. "Perhaps he'll be more like the old Hugh if he goes off to the Alps," she said, voice breaking. It seemed as though my heart was bleeding into my chest, spurting acid through my veins. Perhaps Hugh hadn't encouraged his mother's visits either. But at least he hadn't told her to stay away. Every time the post arrived I expected to see a large white envelope from a law firm telling me my husband wanted a divorce.

I needed to sort myself out. I was back at the family home, surrounded by hundreds of children and two dozen teachers. I wasn't exactly banished to a hermit's cave. But since my mother's death it had felt lonely at Letchford.

My mother herself must have felt lonely when both her parents had died and she'd inherited the large house with its acres of grounds.

After her funeral, when all the guests had gone home, Clara and I had gone downstairs and stood in front of the mural, looking at her image. Following my attack with the Harpic, Dad had painted Mum back in all her glory, covering up that other woman. I wondered again about the identity of this person but today was not the day to think about her. Let her stay buried under my mother's radiant image.

"Mum was tough." Clara had sounded proud. "Tough enough to train as a teacher and do all she could to start this school so she could keep the family house." Mum had been a county girl by birth; pearls and hunters. But she'd chosen something else.

"She had Dad to help her." Starting the school had really been his idea. That's what she'd always told us.

They'd met at teacher training college. Both had been young people fired up with the desire to shake things up in the educational world. I couldn't imagine myself at that age with the self-confidence to set such a high bar. My mother had acquired her teaching certificate and completed a few years in a girls' school in Bristol. My father had taught in London. Their friendship would probably have fizzled out if it hadn't been for a chance meeting in a bookshop on Charing Cross Road in London. She'd told him about the old family house she'd inherited. "It's hundreds of years old and it's decaying away," she'd said. "A nursing home has made me an offer but I'm not sure. I don't know what to do."

She'd looked amused as she'd related the story to me. "Your father thought it would make a good school, Merry. We must have been a pair of naive fools. In our twenties and thinking we knew enough to start a school. You'd never be allowed to do it these days."

"Do you ever regret having done this?" I'd asked her only weeks before her death.

She'd looked past me, towards the front door leading to the gardens and grounds. "It would all have gone if it hadn't become a school. But perhaps our family life would have been easier, Merry. We'd have been less on display all the time."

I'd thought about that quite a bit. Bringing up a family, having a relationship with your husband, all under the scrutiny of three hundred pairs of young eyes, plus teachers. It couldn't have been easy. Perhaps she'd regretted it. She'd never have admitted this was the case, but sometimes I wondered. My father could be very hard to deflect once he'd decided on something.

"Sometimes I think the England your father thought he was taking a stake in was an England that never really existed." She'd spoken in a quiet, almost dreamy, voice. "He had such high expectations, as though he was hoping it would make up for everything he'd left behind."

CHAPTER
EIGHT

Karel, 1973

"I can almost smell this place falling apart," Susan said.
They were sitting on the chaise longue in the entrance
hall, cool and marbled, smelling of beeswax and the
flowers outside in the garden. But something undercut
the aroma: an over-sweetness that lingered at the back
of his nose.

She'd come straight here when term had finished
and spent days cleaning. Shadows under her eyes told
him how hard she'd worked. But what needed doing
here was more than cleaning: it was the stripping away
of old wallpaper, rewiring, fitting new window frames,
moving old furniture away from walls to air damp
patches. Karel had watched his mother struggle to do
all these things in the old house in Bohemia after they'd
taken his father away. She hadn't managed. There
hadn't been the materials in post-war Czechoslovakia.
The past and its humiliations had hung round them
like the cobwebs. Eventually strangers had been sent to
live with them — really to keep an eye on them, his
mother had muttered, make sure they were reliable.
The newcomers had put down lino on the wooden

floors and painted over the wallpaper and wooden panels. The house had died.

"I still think you should turn Letchworth into a school." He looked around, almost expecting to see a third person who'd spoken the words. "You've got the space. You're a teacher." He imagined kids running around and shouting, clearing out the ghosts. He imagined himself showing them how to make wonderful things with paint and paper.

She blinked. "A pretty inexperienced teacher."

"So? Employ people who are more experienced to run it for you. Start small." He sounded quite the capitalist these days.

"Suppose so." Susan had already told him that her parents had left her money. But most of it was blowing out of the badly insulated windows, or oozing into damp walls.

"My father might have liked the place to become a school." She sounded dreamy. "He and I talked about education quite a bit before he died. They were surprised when I said I wanted to become a teacher. It wasn't what people from my family were supposed to do."

So many aspects of English social structure baffled him. His friend John Andrews had done his best to explain the nuances but Karel hadn't been here long enough to pick it all up.

She must have picked up his bafflement, and smiled. "I was supposed to go to finishing school in Switzerland and then find a husband." She was frowning slightly. "You look disapproving."

"It's so different from what young women did where I grew up." Unbidden, *she*, the other one, came into his mind. He couldn't help smiling at the thought of *her* being sent to learn how to scoop up a husband. An afternoon in Prague flittered into his mind. She'd lain in her aunt's apartment on the colourful rug she'd woven herself. Her Aunt Maria was out queuing for meat. She'd been completely naked and the sun had gilded her skin.

"Perhaps I'll never bother about marriage," she'd said. "Perhaps we could just live like this for the rest of our lives." Ever since the spring it had been like this in Prague. The shadows were there, massing just out of sight. But for the moment it was just her, naked, on the bright rug with its folk print. Longing for her burned through Karel's veins.

Go away, he told her again. Not now, not here, not in this English house where I am learning how to be an Englishman for this English girl.

Susan was restless. Got up from the chaise longue. Strode around. Fingered the pitted wall in the front hall. Someone had attempted to whitewash over the crude paintings left by the GIs but the paint they'd used had been too thin and watery. He could still make out the outlines of inflated female body parts and attendant annotations. His English was now good enough for him to grin at the latter. The soldiers had mis-aimed darts at a board on the wall and the surface was pockmarked.

He studied the light falling on its surface. It would be almost constant, emanating both from the windows halfway up the stairs and from those looking onto the gardens. At the moment the dirty white wall seemed to sum up the hopelessness of Susan's situation.

"You need something here in the front hall," he said. "To signify a fresh start. A mural." The idea was taking shape in his mind now. "You need to set the tone for your new school."

She blinked. "I haven't decided that I am starting a new school yet."

He smiled.

"You don't understand."

"You don't want to sell your house. What else are you going to do with this place?"

She still looked unsure.

"You should tidy up that wall, anyway."

"I do like the idea of a mural. Would you paint it for me?"

He thought about it. Hadn't painted much these last years. Apart from during a primary school placement, and that had been more about keeping paint off the floor and clothes and directing some of it to the paper.

"Yes. But I'd need you," he said.

"You want me in the mural?"

He walked towards her and looked her up and down, as though he were going to paint a still life. "But not in that dress." If she was going to run a new school she needed to look the part. This lunchtime she was dressed in a thin-strapped sundress. Her posture was very straight, very correct. You could tell she was the daughter of the house, but the frock was all wrong. "Do you have anything else you could wear?"

She shook her head. "I don't dress up much." Why should she? It was 1973. No young and idealistic teacher wore formal fitted dress.

"Are there any other clothes here?" He pictured her in something long, hair tied back. Not too constrained, but dignified.

"There's an old trunk up in one of the attics." She sounded doubtful.

"Shall we look?" He was up the three flights of stairs almost in a single bound, suddenly thrilled at the thought of what he wanted to do. He'd paint her on the wall with an image of the house itself behind her.

In the attic they found dresses from every decade going back to the late Victorians. "They're all so fusty and moth-eaten."

He held up a blue velvet evening gown that looked as though it had last been worn before the First World War. Perhaps it hadn't been worn at all. Karel thought of a girl ordering the dress for a dance and then finding out her brother or fiancé had died in the trenches. Telling the maid to pack the dress away; she never wanted to see it again. "You'd look right in this."

Susan wasn't looking at the dress; she was looking at him.

"What is it?"

"You've learned to speak English so quickly and so well. How long's it been now?"

"Five years since I arrived in England."

"Your accent is getting better and better."

"I am working upon it."

"*On* it." She made the correction lightly. He listened to conversations in pubs, on trains, in the school corridors. At night he practised putting the muscles of his mouth into the strange positions English required. He repeated pronunciations over and over again.

"Milk and no sugar, please. Half of best. A return to Paddington. A pound on number five in the three-thirty."

Susan was looking at the silk gown again. "I suppose it might do."

"Put it on and come downstairs." He sounded abrupt when he asked people to do things in English. He made a mental note to himself to remedy that.

When she came downstairs she'd tied back her hair with a black velvet ribbon. A single lock fell over her right shoulder. She looked very beautiful in that proper English way. Only now was he seeing her as someone he might possibly be interested in. Something about this realization made homesickness strike him cold in the stomach. He didn't want this old house, this English girl with the pale skin and the good manners. He wanted what he'd left behind.

"I'll need to buy paints in Oxford. Then we'll start tonight. While I'm gone you should start washing down the wall."

Surprise flickered across her face.

"Sorry," he added. "I become — what's the word? — bossy, when I am excited by an idea."

On his return to Letchford with the paints and brushes on the back seat of the Mini he'd saved up to buy, he reminded himself of all that he had. A job. A car. A girl, perhaps. Susan, it seemed likely, would probably allow him to sleep with her tonight. There was no reason for him to pine. He'd had word from his mother, sent via a friend in Switzerland. She was well but was moving to the north of the country, near the Polish border. More work up there. And she needed to work. There was no longer a place for her in the commune established in her own house. He'd tried not to worry about the kind of work she'd be doing now.

His mother hadn't mentioned anyone else in her letter. He hadn't told her what had happened as he'd left Czechoslovakia. It was all gone. *Forget it. Concentrate on this. Become the perfect Englishman.*

John Andrews, who'd taken him in when he'd arrived in 'sixty-eight, had advised him to become a teacher. "They always need good language teachers over here," he'd said. "They're bloody useless at speaking other people's languages. I'd go for German if I were you, Charlie." Karel — Charlie — spoke the language fluently; it was his mother's language, though she hadn't spoken it for years. Earlier on, before they'd driven him off to the uranium mine, his father had taught him English, too, shutting the windows so that no passers-by could overhear.

"I never think I end up teaching German," he told John.

"I never *thought* I'd end up teaching German . . ." he corrected him. "Art is all well and good but you can always do that kind of thing in your spare time."

Something deep inside Karel rebelled at that but he'd quashed the sentiment. "I know you know best. I

56

do as you say." Besides, he had no real wish to take up the brush again. Karel Stastny, artist, would metamorphose into Charles Statton, teacher.

As he'd watched the assistant put the paints, white spirit and brushes into the paper bag Karel had felt the old pull. He almost wished that Susan wasn't going to be in the house on his return and that he could be alone with the blank wall: a silent, uncritical, welcoming repository. But of course he needed Susan as his model. He'd already painted the mural in his mind. He'd place her in front of the house and the oaks.

Susan met him on the steps. She wore navy overalls, rolled up at the legs. "I've already sanded the wall," she said, looking pleased with herself. "I filled in the holes with plaster, too. We'll be able to put the white coat on."

She'd done a good job. When they'd painted the wall its white undercoat was as smooth as the sides of one of those wedding cakes the English liked. Even the obscene images seemed to have faded. They cooked omelettes in the kitchen while they waited for the paint to dry. Susan changed back into the velvet dress and he drew half a dozen sketches of her sitting outside on one of the stone lions beside the door.

"I look like Britannia," she said, peeping over his shoulder at the pad. "All I need is a helmet." She pushed her damp fringe off her forehead. "Won't you get some sleep now? I could make up a bed for you." A pause. "Or you could share with me?" She let the question unfold in a way that seemed quite natural. He hadn't slept with her before. His skin prickled in anticipation.

"I'd like to sleep with you," he said in his blunt, central-European manner. His body throbbed at the thought of her slender form next to his. "I'll come up soon." He ran his finger down her soft cheek. She smelled of warm, clean girl. The other one had smelled of something more dangerous: bubbling sugar, or spice. "I just want to finish the plan for tomorrow."

A note of doubt flashed over her face, gone almost before he could register it. She didn't find him attractive. No, it wasn't that. She was wondering why this mural was so important when the whole house needed attention. And if they were serious about turning it into a school they needed to be talking about teaching staff, equipment, books. How to explain to her why the painting mattered?

"I feel it's like, what's the word? An emblem. A symbol of a new start."

Something seemed to shift in her expression. She nodded. "I'll be waiting for you, Charlie."

Charlie. He heard the other girl's mocking laugh. *You're not Charlie. You're still Karel. And you'll never be an Englishman.*

To drive her away he went back to the kitchen and found the remains of the Chianti they'd drunk with the omelettes. The wall was nearly dry now, the last remaining streaks growing thinner by the second. Karel had always found it soothing to watch paint dry, despite what people said. The grandfather clock in the corner chimed midnight. Upstairs all was quiet. His hand went into his trouser pocket and he extracted three coins. Valuable coins, they were. So the collector in Charing Cross Road had told him. He could have sold them but they'd become lucky charms. He jiggled them in his palm and put them back in his pocket. Through the still-open front door came the scent of stocks and roses from the overgrown garden. His eyes were on the blank wall. Images started to paint themselves over the pristine surface. Not Susan with her pale English face. Another girl. Chestnut hair. Hazel eyes. *Draw me*, she demanded. His hands were moving, mixing paints, selecting brushes. Then he was standing in front of the wall.

Each sweep and dab of the brush across the white surface filled her with more life. First the outline of her slim body, then the reddish-brown rush of hair, the pink of her lips. He could hear her sigh. Karel took time over her face. Those eyes, that full mouth, they were hard to capture. He stood back for a few minutes until he saw them in front of him. The rest was easy; she might have been standing there, displaying herself, encouraging him. Her face was complete now. He wanted to paint the print on her tunic dress now. But it was intricate, one she'd hand-blocked herself. He strained his memory for the details of the print and thought he remembered. Above him, somewhere in the bedroom with its four-poster bed, Susan waited for him to go to her. But how could he when this other girl stood so close to him he could almost feel her breath on his skin, feel the silky swish of her hair against his chest, her voice murmuring to him? She pulled him back to her and he picked up the brush again.

It was all happening so quickly. He'd never worked this fast before. It was as though he'd been working on this image in his head without realizing, long before he'd suggested a mural to Susan.

The years apart hadn't meant a thing. An owl hooted outside in the garden, warning him that these summer nights were short; he needed to hurry. He felt himself emerge from his trance. With a critic's eye he surveyed his work. Probably the best thing he had ever done. He knew it without vanity or even particular pride. Vivid. Unusual. Disturbing, almost, in the way it juxtaposed such a modern-looking young woman in front of the smooth honey walls of an English country house. It wasn't finished; it couldn't be in such a short time. The dress was incomplete. There was no background. But the essence of the girl was all there.

The owl hooted again. If it hooted a third time he'd know what he had to do. It was cockerels, wasn't it, with St Peter? *Before the cock crows three* — or was it two? — *times you will have betrayed me thrice*. It was a long time since Karel Stastny had attended Mass. Religion had not been encouraged in his previous life.

He sat on the faded chaise longue and looked at her. There was reproach in her eyes. *You left me*. Not impossible to find her again. Difficult, perhaps. Dangerous, too. A labour camp at worst; menial work

60

for the rest of his life at best. But not impossible. It wasn't a large country. *Don't betray me again, Karel.*

The owl hooted for the third time. He knew he'd have to paint over the girl on the wall.

CHAPTER
NINE

Meredith

I spent the rest of Sunday afternoon finishing lesson plans, taking my time, trying to parcel out each lesson into ten-minute slots, even though I knew I'd never want to stick to such rigid timetabling when I stood in front of my classes. I managed to drag out the task until it was time to go over and play backgammon with Simon. We'd established the Sunday evening tradition last school year, abandoning it over the summer months in favour of croquet and a jug of Pimm's. But I was almost pleased it was well and truly autumn now and I could bury myself in Simon's little living room with the curtains drawn against the darkness outside. He'd light his fire and make us a huge pot of tea, to be replaced at an undefined but discernible hour with a bottle of red wine. I'd laugh and argue in favour of books and films I liked and Simon didn't; be the woman I'd once been.

I walked across the lawn to the drive, feeling a sense of release at the same time as I felt guilt. My father would be alone in his office tonight, dealing with admin, trying not to think of my mother, who used to sit sewing in the sitting room, just visible through the open door, ready to offer advice if it was requested, or to dissect the psyches of teachers or pupils.

Simon lived in a small cottage rented by the school just off the school grounds down the lane leading to the village. The sun had all but set now. On the ridge of the Downs to the south a line of trees was backlit by an orange slash of light, dark clouds massed above. Almost enough to make me wish I could paint. My attempts were always so pitiful in comparison to my sister's work that I'd given up.

This evening Simon looked tired, even if his grin when he opened the door to me was as warm as usual. Perhaps it had been his turn to accompany a team to an outlying school for rugby yesterday. Some of those coaches hadn't returned until seven because of a motorway hold-up.

As we walked into the living room his laptop gave a bleep. "Ignore it," he said. "It's the instant messenger. I forgot to sign out." He pushed down the lid. "I was doing some work on the history of the house." He'd been researching Letchford's past for a book he hoped to publish.

I hadn't thought of Simon using an instant messenger. He gave the impression of being the kind who'd handwrite postcards from interesting art galleries. I couldn't even remember the slick new laptop being a feature of his life before this summer. He'd written his lesson plans by hand, to the mirth of his colleagues.

"Still on for a run over to Burford to look at bookshops and antique shops?"

Only six months ago the prospect would not have appealed. "Definitely," I replied. "But why Burford?"

"Lots of shops. And tea rooms. I've been looking on the net."

I eyed the sleek laptop. "May I have a peep?"

"Help yourself. I saved what I found in a folder. The kettle's still boiling."

I found the folder and browsed the antiquarian bookshops. I hadn't been near my email this afternoon. Sunday night. There was a chance that ... But I probably shouldn't be too hopeful. "OK for me to check my email?" I called.

"Feel free."

Nothing for me. I felt a mixture of relief and disappointment. Simon brought over the tray with the teapot and cups set out on it. I showed him the list of bookshops I'd found.

"Great. I'll just pull the set out."

My mobile trilled as he bent down to retrieve the backgammon box from the cupboard beneath his television set. "Can you come and talk to Tracey Johnson in the kitchen?" my father asked me. "I'm not sure what the problem is but she sounds worried. I'd go myself but I need to call a parent."

Sunday night was Dad's night for ringing round parents who needed reassurance about exam grades. Or a warning that their offspring were in danger of flunking GCSEs or being suspended. There always seemed to be a student or two each year who found

64

alcopops to consume behind the cricket pavilion. My mother would have been the one who'd go to the kitchens to talk to Tracey. Housekeeping and catering were her domain. I blinked hard.

At least Dad credited me with enough common sense to resolve this problem; I should be grateful for his trust. It showed he'd put the memory of my lost week behind him. All the same, I looked at the tea tray and the backgammon set and sighed. "I'll be about ten minutes." I pulled on my jacket.

"I'll put the tea cosy on, then." I'd always mocked Simon's crocheted tea cosy and I rolled my eyes at him now as he pulled it over the china teapot.

"I won't be long," I said. "It's just to see Tracey in the kitchens." The teapot rattled in Simon's hands. "Don't worry, there'll be plenty of time left."

Tracey Johnson was one of the chef's assistants. She was about the age of the oldest sixth-formers but looked older. And more beautiful than most of them. Despite the lack of holidays in the sun and hours of healthy sport, her skin was clear and flawless. She wore heavy eye make-up and her mouth was usually turned down into a near-scowl. My mother had once told me that Tracey had won a scholarship to the school at thirteen. "Your father offered her a full bursary. But she went to the high school instead." At sixteen she'd come to work part-time here in the kitchens, attending technical college for part of the week. Although we had a fully qualified cook Tracey had taken on an increasing amount of the work at Letchford.

I was used to seeing her in whites so her appearance, in skinny black jeans and a jersey tunic top, was a surprise. Something about the air at Letchford made it hard to imagine people here having an existence outside the school. It was as though we were sealed underneath a glass dome, breathing some rarefied air. Occasionally I ran into day pupils in the town on Sundays or in the holidays. Dressed in their own clothes they seemed quite separate from the boys and girls I taught in schooltime.

Tracey gave a little start when she saw me. "I wasn't expecting it to be you." She always addressed me with a near-bluntness. With my parents she'd always been polite, almost warm. Something about me seemed to make her uncomfortable. Perhaps she was resentful at how my job and comfortable accommodation had been laid on by my family. Or she knew about my broken husband. I'd failed to fulfil some basic biological female role: I couldn't nurture my man.

"My father's busy with a call."

She put a hand to the back of her head and pulled at her hair, neatly done up in a bun, plucking at the strands until the whole mass came down over her shoulders. She looked like a girl in a Pre-Raphaelite painting. Once again I admired Tracey's glossy hair and fine-boned features.

"What's up?" I asked, sounding almost as terse as she did.

"It's the oven again. Loose wire. Keeps taking out the circuit."

"Have you called the electrician?"

66

"He can't come out until nine tomorrow. Which means no cooked breakfasts."

"What about the hobs?" I nodded at the stove.

"They're on the same circuit. It's all down."

"Could we bring up that portable hob we use at the summer fete?"

She nodded. "I'll need the key to the cellar."

I went upstairs to my father's office. Dad was on the phone. On his desk lay a lumpy long shape, covered with a tea towel. The reborn doll. In the white shroud it looked even more like a small corpse. I resisted the temptation to pull back the tea towel and meet its blue gaze. It was only plastic and enamel paint, I reminded myself.

". . . if it happens again I can't be quite so lenient . . ." Dad said, raising an eyebrow at me. I made the motion of turning a key and he pointed to his top right-hand drawer. When I opened it, something metallic glinted at me. A small blade. I recognized it as the paperknife stabbed into the reborn doll. Underneath the knife three gold coins sat in a small display box with a perspex cover. Dad had brought the coins with him from Czechoslovakia. I closed the drawer and took the keys back to the kitchen.

"Strange about that reborn doll," Tracey said when I handed the bunch to her, as though she knew what I'd seen in my father's office. She sounded not curious but reflective. "Something like that takes some planning."

"I suppose it does." I made the words as non-committal as I could.

"I mean, finding a time to get into Mr Radcliffe's cupboard."

"What do you mean?"

"He locks the door when he leaves the room."

"Does he?" I thought about it and remembered how he'd always turn a key in the lock after lessons. Some of the books and papers relating to the house were valuable. I wondered how Tracey knew about the lock.

Tracey was twiddling the keys I'd just given her. "Makes you think. Those dolls are expensive."

"Are they?" She seemed to have placed me in the role of hapless questioner.

"Hundreds of pounds, according to what I've heard. There was something on the TV a while back. Wonder who it's based on," Tracey went on.

The question must have been in my face. "Often they give the dolls real babies' features. Especially if a baby's died. It's a way of remembering them."

I swallowed but couldn't clear the moisture in my throat. "Thanks for sorting this out, Tracey. Book the electrician in for as early as you can." I heard something of my father's authoritative tone in my voice.

The wind had picked up and leaves blew around me as I walked back down the lane to Simon's. Another year on the turn. I shivered slightly in the cool air, glad I was going to have company for the rest of the evening. Mention of the doll had made me feel unsettled. Just a prank, I reminded myself, silly teenagers, meaningless. All the same, I wished my father would put the damn thing away.

The pot of Lapsang tea was sitting on Simon's table, clad in its crocheted wool hat. He was sitting on the sofa, laptop on his knees. I could ask him whether he'd left the cupboard door in the history room unlocked. The question didn't seem to want to be asked. Simon closed the laptop. "Let's get cracking, the evening's nearly gone."

I gave him a watery smile and sat down to play backgammon.

CHAPTER
TEN

When I went over to help in the morning Tracey was flipping rashers of bacon, apparently unruffled. A younger girl stood beside her, spooning baked beans onto plates. Tracey acknowledged my arrival with a nod at the newcomer. "My cousin."

"Thanks for coming at such short notice." The girl looked as though she ought to be at school herself.

"She's seventeen," Tracey said, forestalling my question. I wondered about our employee liability insurance and decided not to. Instead I grabbed a laden plate.

"Where are the trays?"

Tracey waved towards a rack, surprise softening her features. She'd probably assumed that I considered myself above helping in the kitchen. "Normally we wheel the food into the hall on the heated trolleys." She flipped two rashers onto a plate. "But there wasn't time to set them up this morning. Anyone who wants cooked gets beans and bacon. No choices."

My father crossed the hall as I carried my laden tray in. He frowned at Tracey's cousin. "That tray looks far too heavy for that girl. But I'm not going to ask any questions." He sounded weary, too weary for early morning at the beginning of the school year. "As long as breakfast is satisfactory." He pulled out the notepad he always carried with him and wrote a few words in the looped and twirled handwriting that gave him away as having been brought up abroad.

I went back to my apartment. The first two periods were free for me. I could fit in a quick dog walk before I returned to school. Teachers were supposed to remain in the staffroom during free periods but a blind eye was usually turned. The answerphone was blinking. Hugh. My heart raced. A message for me. I pressed the play button.

"Meredith," my sister's voice said. "There wasn't a chance to talk at the weekend. But I've been thinking things over. I'm in the office all day. Ring me if you have a free period."

It was already ten past eight. My sister would be in her smart city office with its view of St Paul's, in one of her sharp black suits, laptop switched on, a brought-in espresso on her desk. Nothing frothy and milky for Clara. I dialled her mobile.

"Thanks for getting back to me." She sounded just as you'd imagine a law partner would. "It's about Dad, well, about the school really. Things can't go on like this." She might have been discussing a recalcitrant client.

"What do you mean?"

"Well, things are starting to get to him, aren't they? Even Marcus said so. He's quite flustered."

"It's been quite a week." I wondered if she had any idea how derailing the doll business had been, how much time it had taken up, how unsettling it had been at the beginning of term when things were still fluid.

"It's more than that, Meredith. He hasn't been finding it easy. Every year it's been getting harder to keep the school financed. We've trimmed things back, but there's always more pressure to do this or that. Letchford isn't the school it used to be." Her voice quietened. "Even without Mum's death. We're only just finding out how much she did."

I'd known. Dad had known.

"There's bound to be a period of readjustment." I sounded like something from a self-help booklet.

"I'm talking about more than just the short term. I don't think Dad can carry on like this indefinitely. He's exhausted already and it's not even half-term."

My mouth opened to dispute this. But then I thought about it and my protest died inside me. When we'd been growing up there'd been a relaxed feel to the school. Teachers had seemed to teach pretty well what they wanted or what they felt their pupils ought to know. Judging by the numerous boards on display in the hall, listing scholarships to Oxford and Cambridge, this laissez-faire attitude hadn't done much harm. And my father's role had changed. Twenty years or so back he'd spent a lot of time simply talking to people. Pupils. Parents. Teachers. The groundsmen who mowed and rolled the playing fields. I'd spot him on the move all day long: appearing at classroom doors, standing at the head of the stairs at break to watch pupils streaming out. At hockey and rugby matches he'd pace the sidelines, pleasure radiating from him every time there was a win, even though part of him thought that too much competitive spirit detracted from the liberal atmosphere he wanted for Letchford. He'd been the eyes and ears of the school. Little by little over the last decade a pile of paperwork had kept him in his office for longer.

"He's older, I suppose." It wouldn't be fair to expect him to be as active as he'd been when he was young.

"Exactly. Sixty."

"There's no fixed retirement age for teachers," I reminded her. "He could go on for years yet."

"As head? Would that be best for him, Merry? For the school?"

I pictured my father without the school. What would he do with himself?

Sadness drifted over me. I'd been so caught up in my own grief and anxiety I'd failed to think all this through. "But if Dad stopped being head what would happen to Letchford?" I thought of my apartment and blushed. What would happen to me, I'd meant. Dad might wish to move in here himself, as he and Mum had planned for their retirement years. The thought of more change made me swallow hard. Outside the window chestnuts and oaks blew in the breeze. Soon they'd be shedding copper and gold leaves with each sway. Beyond them the Downs curved like the back of a sleeping brown-and-grey beast.

"I think he should sell the estate to the trust." An educational trust owned the school itself now, as opposed to the buildings and grounds. "Take the money and go and live somewhere away from the school. While Dad's within fifty miles of the place he won't be able to let it go. You know what he's like, he'd always be popping over to tell them they're mowing the games fields wrongly or something."

Dad to leave Letchford. To leave the Cotswold honey-stoned house. And the gardens. The mural. That was a whole different thought from me simply moving on in due course.

"We could never sell it." I sounded furious. "Never." I found myself sitting very upright on my seat, fists curled, ready for a fight.

"Think about it." Clara sounded weary.

"I won't support you in this."

"Don't you think" — she hesitated — "that your reaction to this might be bound up with what's happened in the last six months? Letchford's become very important to you again, understandably."

I felt like shouting at her not to patronize me, But it was true. The place had become a crutch for me. Unfortunate use of a word.

"It's not for us to make decisions for him." I pictured my father leaving the house, my mother's birthplace, her family home for hundreds of years, the gardens still full of the plants she'd propagated, the curtains she'd made hanging at the windows.

"It's something that needs to be discussed with him." She sounded almost mechanical now.

"I don't think we should make him feel he's past it."

"No." She was no longer the law firm partner in the swish office; she was the elder daughter worrying about her family. "I know that. And I don't want to see the

74

place go, either. I love it as much as you do. It would be weird to think of Letchford not belonging to us, of not being able to come back whenever we wanted. The boys would miss it. They're so proud of the house. And the mural, especially."

"Dad's mural," I muttered, clutching the phone so hard my knuckles turned white. "With Mum in it. How could we leave all that behind?"

"Do you remember when we scrubbed at the wall?" She was still talking in the same dreamy way. "What we found?"

I did.

"It was back when there was all that trouble with the bursar."

I didn't really remember the business with the bursar, but I did remember the woman I'd uncovered in the mural. Even my father's tone, angry, clipped and central-European, couldn't tear me away. I'd barely heard the clatter of their shoes over the marble flooring.

I was looking at a girl. But what a girl. She might have been a pop star. Her short purple dress fell to just above her knees. She wore knee-high boots. Her lips were wide and full and her hair fell in an auburn wave to her shoulders. Her large eyes were hazel and seemed to glint with an emotion I couldn't decipher. She seemed to be begging the viewer not to look away. But at the same time the hand we had half exposed was held up in a dismissive wave. *Go away, stay here.* I was only ten but I could spot a riddle when I saw it. "Who painted over you?" I'd asked the girl. "And why?"

My mother's hand was on my shoulder, pulling me away. "What have you done?" she said, sounding almost confused. "That woman . . ." She stopped herself. "How could you do this?"

"Who is she?" I asked. "Why did they paint over her?"

"Upstairs." She pulled me. "Now."

"I only want to know who she is."

"I've no idea."

She was steering me across the hall, my feet slipping on the marble tiles as I tried to resist. A small group of sixth-formers wandered in from the back of the house and stopped to goggle at us. They'd probably never seen my mother in a state before. I hadn't often seen her lose her temper, let alone resort to dragging me around. Clara followed. As we climbed the stairs I turned to catch a glimpse of her face: white. Being good meant a lot to her. I felt a pang for her. Normally I'd almost relish seeing my older sister in trouble.

Mum opened the door to the apartment and pushed me in. Dad appeared behind her. "How dare you?" He spoke so quietly I could barely hear him. "How could you do it, Meredith?" I thought of telling him that Clara had also had a part in the mural defacement, but remembering my sister's stricken face, I said nothing.

"You know how much that mural means to us," my mother said.

"I'm sorry." And I was. Not so much because I'd angered my mother and hurt her but because the painted woman I'd exposed had been so disturbing. I didn't know why. She was just a girl in a really cool dress, barely older-looking than the girls in the sixth form. But something about that expression on her face bothered me. I needed to go and have another look at her.

"Why did you do it?" Mum was leaning against the wall of the little hall into our apartment now, hand on forehead.

"We were playing a game." I explained how the scooter handle had hit the wall and left a mark, how we'd hoped to rub it off.

"So it really was an accident. To start with?" She looked relieved.

I nodded. "But once I saw . . ." Once I'd seen *her*, I meant, but something warned me not to mention that painted woman.

Dad's eyes narrowed. "You don't know what you've done, Meredith."

"Who is she?" I was no longer able to hold back the question.

"Nobody." He moved past me. "I'll see you later." I heard the apartment door close behind him.

"Mum?" I thought she wasn't going to answer.

"I really don't know," she said finally. "Probably someone he made up."

"Why don't we ask Dad who she is?"

"No," she mumbled. "He's distracted enough as it is."

"What do you mean?"

She blinked, seeming to return from a place far away. Her eyes flashed again. "Don't think you can distract me away from punishing you. You two can wait in your bedroom until your father's finished with the parents. Then we'll decide what to do with you."

The girl was only a painted image but she'd changed everything.

CHAPTER
ELEVEN

Clara and I finished our telephone call. She seemed softer by the end of the conversation, as though talking about the mural had reminded her of how much the house meant to us.

"You took all the rap for that incident," she said, sounding sad. "Mum and Dad were so angry. They seemed to blame you more than me. I felt bad about that."

They'd come down harder on me. That's how it had seemed, at least. Perhaps Clara had simply been a better-behaved child.

"Don't worry. I probably made your life hell for weeks after," I told her. After promising to call her again soon I hung up. I found the lead and fastened it to the dog's collar, my mind still on the woman beneath the mural. But as we walked I came alive again, the exercise shaking the past out of me. The air smelled of bonfires this morning and leaves dropped round us as we approached the woods.

Usually when I took Samson out I felt alone. This morning I felt eyes on my back. Once or twice I turned, seeing only oozing dank mist. The world looked as though it had been printed off on a printer that was running out of coloured ink. I shivered. The dog felt the presence of someone, too. He stopped, whined briefly and wagged his tail before continuing his pursuit of rabbits.

Pupils sometimes talked about ghosts at Letchford. I'd never seen any myself. For much of its four- or five-hundred-year history the house seemed to have lived under a blanket of anonymity. The families who'd inherited the house over the centuries seemed to have kept their heads during times of tumult. Even the loyal Simon was finding it hard to dig up anything truly sensational for his history of Letchford. And my mother herself, well, she'd never have wanted to make me feel jittery or uneasy either in life or afterlife. If she'd come back as a ghost it would have been as a most considerate one, hanging around the gardens in full light and rustling a bush in gentle greeting. Thinking about that girl hidden under the paintwork in the front hall had put me on edge, I decided.

I hadn't thought about her for years, that personification of my father's lost life in Central Europe. He'd never told us who she was and my mother had stuck to her story about not knowing.

"She wore nice clothes," Clara said.

"Very striking." Mum's voice was flat.

Clara had nudged me after Mum had left the room. "She was Dad's old girlfriend. Before he came over here."

My eyes had widened. I couldn't imagine Dad with someone who wasn't Mum. "How do you know, Clara?"

She shrugged. "It's obvious. That's why he's been so quick to paint over her again." It was true. The repair job had been done that same day, as soon as school had finished. The house had smelled of white spirit and paint. By morning Mum had been restored.

I still felt I was being observed. A twig cracked and I jumped. "Let's go back," I told the dog.

Don't be a wuss, I heard my husband tell me in his mocking tones.

"Shut up," I told him, silently. "I don't want to hear your voice in my head any more."

I wished I could hear the distant and reassuring shouts of a hockey lesson out on the fields.

I'd reached the iron gate leading to the rose garden when Samson whined again and turned round. This time I felt the hairs rise on the back of my own neck. From the corner of my eye I observed a slight figure step out from behind a bush.

"What are you doing?" I sounded sharp. "This is out of bounds for you." First Emily and now a kid. Nowhere was private.

"I'm sorry, Mrs Cordingley." The girl spoke quietly, her head bowed. I couldn't think of her name. She was a second-year I didn't teach. "I didn't know how else I could see you alone."

"You should be at lessons."

"I didn't feel well. I came out for fresh air."

"What did you want to see me about?" I still sounded sharp. The first person she ought to have gone to was Cathy, the school nurse.

"That baby." She corrected herself. "The reborn doll. The one they found in Mr Radcliffe's room."

"You know something about that? Why didn't you say something at the time?"

She hung her head. "Perhaps I should have. But I heard it was wearing the white gown and cap." Word would have spread quickly. "I've seen those clothes before."

"Are you in the play?"

"*The Crucible*? Yes, I've got a small part."

"So you saw the costumes hanging up in the drama department when you had lessons up there." I sounded impatient. My empty stomach growled and reminded me that, for all the lugging of laden trays from kitchen to hall earlier on, I still hadn't had my own breakfast yet. A bowl of porridge would have been good, but there wouldn't be time for much more than a quick coffee.

She shook her head. "I saw the clothes in Tracey Johnson's bag. In the kitchen."

"What?"

She blushed. "I know we're not allowed in there but I have to have gluten-free bread."

She tugged at the sleeves of her shapeless school jumper. I wondered how anyone could make a piece of uniform look quite so baggy so early in the academic year. She certainly looked like the kind of child who would need a special diet. I shouldn't be judgemental.

"Sometimes they forget to leave it out. So I just get it myself quickly if they're busy."

82

She had very wide hazel eyes. I ought to have told her off for entering the prohibited zone of the kitchen but I couldn't bring myself to do this. The girl had only wanted to grab a slice of bread from the pantry when everyone was too occupied to help her.

"Tracey brings in that basket of hers every day. The baby's outfit was folded up on the top in a bag. A see-through bag."

"When was this?"

"Last Tuesday."

The day before the reborn doll had been discovered in Simon's room.

"Thank you for telling me this."

She nodded and looked as though she was going to scuttle off around the side of the wall.

"Hang on, just one other thing . . . Why did you come to me and not your housemistress or tutor?"

She shrugged and raised a hand to her mouth. The nails were bitten to the quick.

"It's OK, you've done the right thing." I tried to keep my voice level, only mildly interested. "I'm just curious."

She looked down at her scuffed outdoor shoes. "Don't know. You just seem . . ."

"What?"

"Different." She raised her hazel eyes. "Not like the other teachers."

Different because of what had happened to Hugh and my mother, perhaps. I probably wore it on my face, marking me out from the ranks of proper grown-ups.

"I'll go back now." She nodded a farewell.

I watched her as she ran off. My memory managed to fish out a name for her. Olivia Fenton. Her form teacher was Deidre. Deidre had mentioned having a highly strung girl who was finding adapting to boarding school a strain. She was a termly boarder, which was probably just as well, Deidre said, because her family didn't seem to be around most of the time. I felt the unease that occasionally overcame me about the boarders, even these days, when Letchford was apparently such a good example of modern boarding. Some youngsters would simply never be happy away from home and Olivia could well be one of them. Deidre would do her best, as would the housemistress, but they could never really replace Olivia's parents.

But, I reminded myself, Olivia's parents were possibly no longer around. That might be why she had a guardian.

Tracey would be clearing up after breakfast. I could catch her before she went home for the morning. If she'd been on breakfast duty she wouldn't be back at lunchtime because the rota ran dinner — breakfast for three or four days at a time.

I changed into what I thought of as my schoolmarm uniform: black tailored trousers and a smart plum-coloured silk shirt with a steel-grey tank top over it. *You can correct my work any time you want.* Again I heard Hugh's voice in my head. He'd always liked me in work clothes. And in casual weekend clothes. And, most of all, in no clothes at all. Perhaps nobody else would ever look at my naked body. Except the dog, on the occasions when he burst into my bedroom to hurry me out for a walk.

I dropped the dog back to my flat and walked over to the school. A clump of rosemary brushed my leg and its aroma was strong. Rosemary for remembrance. I'd had sprigs of Letchford rosemary in my wedding bouquet. My mother had it in hers, too.

Tracey was still in her chef's whites, taking an inventory of the contents of one of the huge refrigerators. A notepad sat on the table. My mother had always said that Tracey was one of the most thorough members of staff. *Of staff.* Mum had never seen Tracey as beneath her notice.

"Can I have a word?"

She turned round from the fridge. "Hang on." *Two litres semi-skim*, she wrote on the notepad. "If I don't get this down on paper this second I'll forget where I was." She shut the pad. "Was it about the oven? It's working fine since the electrician came out. Turns out the circuit was overloaded."

"It wasn't the oven. It was the pretend baby in the cupboard: the reborn doll."

"Oh." The word gave nothing away.

"I wanted to ask you about the gown it was wearing."

She looked down at the pad.

"Only someone took it out of the drama department. That's locked up at night. And when there aren't lessons going on up there."

"That second-year kid." She shook her head, as though reproaching herself for her carelessness. "Olivia what's-her-name. She's got sharp eyes."

I said nothing.

"I only borrowed the clothes over a weekend." She sounded defensive now. "My sister's baby was christened a week last Sunday and she didn't have anything to put him in. I washed and ironed the gown and the cap when we'd finished. Even spray-starched them too."

"So you brought the clothes back in here?"

"So I could sneak — I mean take — them back to the drama department later on."

"But that didn't happen?"

She looked at me, eyes cold. "Someone nicked them from my bag while I was doing lunches."

"When?"

"The day before they found that doll in the cupboard. Must have been the Tuesday. I noticed that the clothes were missing. I just thought I'd forgotten to put them in my basket after all. Went home and checked. But they weren't there. So I knew they'd been taken from the kitchen. Thought it was one of the kids, mucking around."

"Did you see anyone come into the kitchen while you were working?"

She shook her head. "But you've seen what it's like in here when we're cooking and serving up. Crazy. The Queen could wander in here and help herself to a banana and I wouldn't notice her. Teachers come in to pinch bits of fruit or yoghurts. Kids, too." She walked to the sink. A dishcloth was soaking. She wrung it out and hung it over the taps, arranging it so that the ends were neatly lined up. Watching her tidy the kitchen was soothing. It made me remember being a small child again and sitting in the kitchen in our apartment with my mother, drawing on scraps of paper while she cooked supper. I ought to tell Tracey off for taking the clothes without asking first. I should ask more questions but I couldn't be bothered.

"You've had a bit of a time of it, haven't you?" she said.

It wasn't a question. For a second emotion threatened to overcome me. I swallowed hard. It was impossible to interpret Tracey's tone. She might have been expressing concern or even mild surprise.

"Yes," I muttered after a pause. "It hasn't been easy."

She fiddled with the detergent bottles for a moment, giving me time, perhaps. "I'm sorry about taking the robe and cap without asking. I just thought the drama department would say no. And the baby looked really sweet in them."

"I bet he did. Don't worry." What did it matter?

She looked down at the white plastic mules she wore in the kitchen. "It's not the same without her."

I didn't have to ask whom she meant. "No," I said. "It's not."

"Sometimes when I'm planning new menus I want to ask her what she thinks. Susan always encouraged me with my ideas." She gave me a little glance as she called my mother by her first name, as though afraid she'd overstepped the mark.

We stood there in the kitchen for a moment, saying nothing. Then I muttered a farewell and walked back through the main door, dodging the crowds of children heading to their second period, some dawdling, some bustling, all seeming far more purposeful and self-assured than I'd ever been at that age.

I'd never been a pupil here myself. Dad had thought it wiser for Clara and me to go to a girls' day school in Oxford when we'd finished at the village primary. When the other girls found out where our parents lived they were incredulous. "Your Dad's head of Letchford but you don't go to school there? Why not?" Sometimes I'd resented the fact that pupils my age would be lolling around on the sunny lawns or floating petals in the fountain at lunchtime while I'd been banished. But Dad had probably been right. School and home were best kept separate.

Letchford was starting to feel less like my home now, though. Something had been taken from me when my mother had died last August. I glanced up at the golden stones of the building, seeking reassurance; the reassurance that came from living and working around a house so many hundreds of years old, where people had received bad blows and carried on. How many times had messengers come to the door to pass on news of a soldier husband or son's death in battle? The family had taken the news, mourned quietly, and then carried on with life. But I didn't feel any strength emanating from the house this morning, though the sun had burst through the clouds, and the walls and remaining leaves on the trees around the grounds were gilded. Again I brushed against the rosemary and this time the scent mixed with something bitter in my stomach; longing for my husband, the anxiety I'd felt ever since he'd first gone off to fight. Iraq first and now Afghanistan. You marry a soldier, you know there's always a chance they'll be blown up, shot at, kidnapped, tortured. That they'll come back maimed and hurt. I'd known all that.

For the rest of the morning I stood in classrooms teaching like an automaton, feeling the attention of the children ebbing around me. From time to time I'd give myself a mental kick and manage to regain their attention. At lunch-time I slouched back towards my apartment, not wanting to face the others in the staffroom.

As I crossed the front lawn two boys dressed in cadet force uniforms walked past me. On their way to some drill session. The sight of them made my stomach curdle. Originally Dad hadn't been keen on the idea of a cadet corps at Letchford. It had taken some years of pressure from parents before he'd agreed. I watched the two fresh-faced lads as they strolled away.

It's bad when two of them come to the house. They don't ring, they come by car and they knock on the door. A man and a woman: a casualty notification officer, I think, and another officer of some kind, I forget the exact rank or title. But it's obvious why they've come even before they open their mouths. And even if you've prepared yourself a thousand times for the moment, told yourself it could happen, told yourself not to be complacent, you want to scream that they've made a mistake, got the wrong Hugh Cordingley. And yet you know that they haven't, that it's your Hugh Cordingley. This is real.

I was putting my marking and lesson plans into my bag and trying to find my bicycle padlock. I'd left the radio on in the kitchen and kept meaning to go and turn it off. In the meantime, I hummed along to some silly little song whose name I never knew but which I could never listen to again. Fate waits until you're not concentrating, until you've looked away. Sometimes, when it's really bad, I almost imagine that Hugh was blown up because I wasn't paying attention, wasn't keeping him safe in my mind.

After they've told you, they do the tea bit and ask if they can ring someone for you. They called Mum. She was with me in Wiltshire in just over an hour. But they waited there with us. I kept on thinking that I'd have to remember how kind they'd been so I could tell Hugh. He always liked to know these things. They kept explaining the arrangements. Everything was being done for my husband, I wasn't to worry on that score. They'd keep me posted. The team that had rescued him had been on an emergency course in an A & E department. They'd known what to do. He'd been stabilized at Camp Bastion. He'd be on a plane back to England within hours. Please be reassured, Mrs Cordingley — may we call you Meredith?

And then Mum arrived and I sank into her and there were more people in the room, kind women, wives of other servicemen in Afghanistan, and they were in the background just *doing* things: taking the dog for a walk, making calls to the head of my school, putting the kettle on again and again. It had happened enough times before by then, the bad news from Afghanistan.

I'd even been one of the comforters myself on a few occasions. I'd never belonged to the base in the same way as non-working wives. Each morning I'd cycled off to teach at a school in the town, so I hadn't attended all the coffee mornings, the charity functions, the mother and toddler sessions. But still I'd been a part of the community.

And Clara came down to the camp, too. God knows how she'd managed to get time off and find someone to look after the children for her at such short notice, but she came to be with me. While we waited for the arrangements to be made we sat in the little sitting room. All I could see was the threaded silk on the sofa cushion I held on my lap. I kept my eyes on those threads, knowing that if I lifted my eyes up the world would crash in on me and I'd be lost. Hugh was hurt. Hugh was damaged. Hugh had lost a leg. I repeated the words over and over, trying to make sense of them. Every now and then I'd jump up and pace the small sitting room. Samson would spring up from his usual station on one of the rugs Hugh had brought home on his last leave. Poor dog, he thought my pacings were the cue for a walk. Then I'd disappoint him by flopping down again and returning to my contemplation of the sofa cushions.

I did have to lift my eyes up eventually. Clara and I drove to Birmingham at the same time as the Globemaster plane from Kandahar airport was landing. At Selly Oak hospital I held Hugh's hand and looked at his face again. His eyes were closed, he wasn't conscious. I kept thinking he'd open them up and grin at me, but he didn't. I wanted to shake him, shout at him to wake up. Clara asked all the questions I wasn't able to articulate. She had lists of telephone numbers and emails. She booked me into a B. & B. nearby.

I would have stayed by his bed all round the clock but they wouldn't let me.

It took a week before he came back to us. "Stay back!" he'd shouted at me when I received the call that he'd regained consciousness and went to see him in the critical care unit. "It's not safe, get back." Then his eyes had registered horror. "Where are the rest of them? Where are they?"

I knew he was asking about his men, the men he'd loved. I didn't know how to tell him. I didn't know when he'd start to remember. Or whether to pray that he never did.

CHAPTER
TWELVE

Meredith

But I woke happy, those autumn mornings at Letchford. Or, if not happy, at least content. Sunlight dappled my wall. Birds sang. I couldn't recall why a heavy grey object hovered just beyond my consciousness. Then I'd remember. My husband was still in terrible pain. I couldn't help him. The space in the bed beside me would probably always be empty. My mother would never again wave to me across the staffroom or push a bowl of raspberries from the garden into my hand.

Today I told myself I'd block the return of memory. I'd feel light, full of energy. Here I was, not yet thirty, healthy, in good work, in pleasant accommodation, blessed with a supportive sister. And father, I made myself add. Though the relationship between my father and myself was shifting. More and more I found myself watching out for him in assembly, noticing that his hands sometimes shook as he read from the match reports, that sometimes his glasses had smears on them, or a button was loose on his jacket.

I tried springing out of bed to outpace sorrow. I dashed Samson round his morning walk as though grief were nipping my heels. The dog threw puzzled looks at me and quickened his pace to keep up, eyeing unsniffed blades of grass with regret. I ate a breakfast consisting of a roughly cut slice of bread and a glass of orange juice. No time to make coffee. I retuned the radio to the breeziest and most vapid local station I could find and turned up the volume. I showered and washed my hair rapidly, without care. I needed to be in the classroom, in front of the students. They wouldn't allow me a second for self-pity. *Come and get me if you want me*, I told the grey mass.

Last night I'd dreamed I was running down a corridor lined with doors. Classrooms, I thought, at first. It was my first day at a new school and I was running late. I'd thought I'd be teaching English but they told me I had to take physics, a subject I was not qualified to teach and had hated at school. I was given the number of a classroom and told to hurry, the children were waiting. As I ran along the corridor I realized the classroom doors were smooth grey metal, without windows, cold and hygienic in appearance.

I was in a morgue. There'd been a terrible mistake; Hugh wasn't dead, it was my mother who'd died, but the bodies had been switched. If I didn't find him in time they were going to bury my husband alive. Sweat beaded my brow. I wrenched open door after door to find Hugh. Each room was empty, except for the very last, where a young girl in a short purple tunic-style dress stood.

"He's not dead." I tried to explain how I knew this. "Please tell me where he is so I can save him."

She looked unconvinced. "If he's not dead, why aren't you at his bedside?"

I couldn't explain that my husband had sent me away, that I hadn't been any use to him.

"You let him go, didn't you?" She looked scornful.

"I didn't mean to."

"Why did you let them cover me up again?" she asked. "I liked people looking at me again."

I didn't know what she meant.

And I'd woken up, lying back against the pillows and listening to the birdsong, relieved.

I walked into the main hall on my way to lessons and saw Emily in front of the mural. She'd tied up her long hair today and it hung in a tight, low ponytail. Her face was free of any kind of make-up. Once again I admired her white porcelain skin. She was scrutinizing the plaster repainted during the restoration. One of her fingers traced the image of my mother as a young woman. My parents were proud of how my father had managed to restore her so that she looked exactly as she had done before she'd been scraped off, but Emily seemed to be looking for signs of what was underneath. "She's beautifully done, isn't she?" I felt the note of challenge in my tone.

She turned towards me very slowly. "It's only if you touch the paintwork that you get a sense there's something else there underneath her." To illustrate the point she ran her fingers over my mother's image. Her fingernails were bitten, I saw. "Did someone vandalize it, Meredith?"

I might have retorted that a polite notice on the wall beside the mural asked people not to touch; it was bad for the paint, but the expression in Emily's pale eyes stopped me.

"It had to be restored. Some of the surface was damaged." If it had been anyone else I might have said more. Very few people knew that the mural had been damaged twenty years ago and how it had happened. Dad had repaired it so quickly. Emily could not know what was underneath the paint. I said nothing. Some shame, decades old, kept me from admitting to Emily my role in the damaging of the painting.

"Your father was quite a talented painter, wasn't he?" she went on, her blue eyes on my face. "Art school in Prague, wasn't it? Then he stopped painting."

"School took up more and more of his time." I didn't say that I suspected he'd lost his passion for art even before then.

"He stopped," she repeated. Then her attention switched to me. "What about you? Do you paint, Meredith? Are you artistic?"

It seemed a strange conversation to be having so early in the school morning as around us pupils dawdled and chatted on their way to classes, but there was something about her intent expression that gripped me.

"I used to dabble with watercolours, but I haven't lifted a brush or a pencil since . . ." I gulped. Hugh and I. Hugh, asleep on the sofa after a mess night: mouth open. Me, drawing him in all his dishevelment in pencil on the back of an old envelope. His intake of breath the next morning when he found the unflattering sketch, the cushion he flung at me, the cushion I threw back, the laughter, the dog jumping round and barking at us both. I pulled a mental screen round the image. "My sister used to be quite keen," I continued. "She was supposed to be talented at sculpture, too." People had been excited by Clara's A level work. She'd won some kind of award for one of her pieces. I couldn't remember what it was now: not a sculpture but an embroidered work with appliqué tulips, blood-red against an electric-blue sky. Even I had been able to drop my usual sibling resentment to tell her that I liked it. Dad had taken the tulips to an expensive picture framer in Oxford.

"Is she an artist now?" Emily asked. From anyone else the question might have sounded like polite interest.

I smiled. "She works for a corporate law firm. She specializes in employment law." Clara regarded art as a hobby, something unworthy of studying any further after school because it didn't bring in a regular monthly income and a large annual partnership payout. Though her children's daubings were lovingly framed and displayed around the house in Clapham.

"Oh." Emily didn't smile. "I love textiles and design technology." I remembered seeing her in the art rooms helping some of the younger ones with screen-printing and batik. She'd certainly seemed in her element. "Some of the children are very talented indeed." She gave the impression that she wanted me to ask who they were. But the bell rang before I could put the question. "Better go," I said. "See you later, Emily."

She raised a hand in farewell, a formal and somehow final gesture, given that I'd probably see her in the staffroom at morning break, just hours later. As she did her face seemed graver than that of such a young woman. She was only about nineteen. Perhaps she'd had a hard life in New Zealand before coming out here and had acquired more maturity than most girls her age. I stepped into my classroom and promptly forgot all about Emily as the lesson started. I felt as though I was a ping-pong ball bouncing above waves of noise and movement, swept along, despite myself, by the energy of the children and the demands of the timetable.

At breaktime my father came into the staffroom as he sometimes did. He didn't like to appear too often, saying his appearance would stop people letting off steam if they needed to.

"Covering a German lesson for the upper sixth." He straightened his tie as he told me. He prided himself on still teaching German. I wondered how many of the sixth-formers even knew that he'd spoken German as a boy. "We always spoke Czech in public but my mother had been brought up speaking German and she spoke it to me," he'd told me. He never spoke German or Czech to us, though. Even Clara and I usually managed to take his perfect tweed jackets and Lobb shoes at face value. It came as a shock when he said something that reminded us that English wasn't his native language.

For these minor slips he would condemn himself to shakings of his head and apologies. He was so keen to be seen as entirely belonging to England. Perhaps it was no surprise that he'd become headmaster of a country boarding school. What could be more archetypically English? When occasionally he spoke German, or even more rarely, Czech, I caught a glimpse of another person, a man with a hinterland unknown to us, with thoughts perhaps untranslatable into English. For all his success in integrating, there must surely be a part of my father that belonged to a different culture.

"Have you ever thought of teaching art again?" I asked him when I found us both standing alone at the open window, everyone else clustered around a box of doughnuts a parent had brought in for the staff.

He gave me a sharp look. "We have excellent teachers. I'd just be in the way."

I nodded, unsurprised by the response but disappointed all the same. A tradesman's van was pulling up outside the front door. I craned my neck to see who it was.

"Ah, the glazier," my father said.

"Which window this time?"

"Gavin House. Ground floor."

"Football?"

"Yes."

"I hope you're going to make them pay towards the new pane." He was silent. "Dad?"

"It was just a small first-year. James Perry." He looked sheepish. "A misjudged kick. He'll never play by a window again."

"You're too soft."

"Everyone deserves a second chance."

After break I went into a third-year class and we talked about the first act of *Romeo and Juliet* and they all leant forward on their desks, thrusting their hands up to answer questions, desperate to read parts. I felt their energy fill me. I laughed and debated with them. Perhaps there would be more of these mornings when my job absorbed me totally, even though it was drizzling outside now, a fine grey English mizzle that soaked despite its tiny droplets. The pupils who passed me in the corridors smelled of damp uniform, but the bad dream of last night slipped from my memory. I didn't exactly whistle on my way to the dining room but my lips were almost remembering how to do it when my father came downstairs towards me, holding a sheet of paper in his hand.

"Meredith, a word in my office, please." His eyes failed to make more than a second's contact with me. My stomach contracted. Bad news. Please God, don't let it be Hugh. Some severe setback. Perhaps another infection in the stump of the injured leg. But Dad's rigid back seemed to speak more of anger than sorrow. What had I done? Someone must have complained about my teaching. Or about me. Or the dog. Samson must have jumped over the garden wall again and chased a visiting parent's car. Dogs were banned from school grounds.

"He'll always treat you more strictly than anyone else," Clara had warned when I'd first announced my intention of returning here. "You do know that, Merry, don't you? He'll take anyone's side against you, just to show he's being impartial. For all his talk about justice."

She'd been right. For a moment as I followed him I was that little girl who'd scrubbed at the precious mural, almost ruining it for ever.

It wasn't until we were in his office that he turned and waved the white sheet at me. "I'd like an explanation for this, please."

I took it from him. An order form from a company called Delicious Confections. My name and email address in the *From* field. It was an order: an order for a reborn doll, dated two weeks ago.

CHAPTER
THIRTEEN

"I didn't send this." I stared at the black print but the name of Meredith Cordingley and my email address were still there on the sheet. As was an order for an Alexander Reborn Doll for £195 plus delivery. A boy, I noted.

He said nothing.

"Why would I?"

Still nothing.

"Dad?"

"Shall we?" He nodded at the leather sofa. I was to be treated like a naughty fifth-year. But he didn't sit himself down at his desk. We perched on the sofa, slightly turned to each other, like interviewer and candidate. Except that I was not in the mood for an interrogation. The best form of defence was attack.

"Who gave you this?" I waved the sheet at him.

"I found it on my desk just now." He looked down at his folded hands. "Obviously if you tell me it's a forgery I will accept that completely."

But he'd needed me to tell him that I wasn't responsible for the order; he hadn't drawn the obvious conclusion himself. For God's sake, I was his daughter. He couldn't seriously think that I was so mucked-up that I needed to stick a paperknife into a toy doll to make some kind of point. I'd had one bad week, just one, when it had all become too much for me. It didn't mean I'd flipped and become some kind of nutcase. My father was supposed to be the great hater of injustice. At Letchford he'd set up a disciplinary system that presumed innocence above guilt, something he said he didn't believe was taken for granted in all schools. He never made accusations without solid proof. Unless it was me. Clara had been right to warn me off coming back here. It had always been like this, ever since I'd been a child.

But already my anger was passing, replaced by a burning need to work out who had done this. My brain was whirring, scanning an imaginary list of staff and students, trying to extract a name. Almost certainly a student. A *pupil*, we'd have called them once. We'd stopped doing that at some stage, turning them into our equals, removing the distance that had once existed between teacher and taught, transmitter and receiver, that allowed ideas to grow.

"You've no idea who put this on your desk?" I waved the sheet.

He shook his head.

"May I take it with me?" I stood up. "I'd like to check my email. Someone must have hacked into my account or something."

"I suppose they could have." His face seemed to brighten. I'd forgotten how clueless he was about technology. Most of the first year would have more understanding of what was possible on a computer than he would. Samantha, his secretary, sent his emails for him. Mum had built up the school databases, taking herself off to evening classes to master the programs. Samantha was learning how to do it now. He stood up too.

I waved the sheet. "I'll let you know what I find out about this."

He reached out and took my free hand. "Oh, Meredith. All we want is for you to be happy."

I stared at our joined hands. "You still think it's me, don't you? You still think I'm . . . disturbed?" I closed my eyes for a second. "You keep thinking I'm going to have another breakdown."

"I just want you to be happy," he repeated. "Ever since you were a little girl, that's what we wanted. And you were such a sunny little thing." On the fireplace still stood the silver-framed photograph of me on a tricycle out on the tennis courts, Clara standing behind me, an arm draped round my shoulders: the protective elder sister. We'd never have been allowed to ride our trikes on the courts in term time. The photograph must have been taken during the summer holidays when Letchford belonged to the family again. There was a big grin on my freckled face. Merry, they'd called me as a child. Still did on occasions. Not so often these days. I wondered if I could find my way back to this sunny person I'd once been.

My email folders showed no signs of an order placed for reborn dolls. I could find no confirmation messages, no delivery alerts. There was nothing in the deleted emails folder either. When I started to type the Internet address into the search engine it showed no signs of predicting the site. I checked the Internet history for sites I'd visited over the last month or so. Nothing matched the Delicious Confections address. Nor did any of the sites I'd actually visited have any connections with reborn dolls. So I hadn't actually ordered the doll in some kind of depressive trance as my father had implied.

He'd been thinking of that week after Mum's death. It had all fallen to bits then, my life. Dad had gone to Clara's for a change of scene. I'd stayed here, in this flat. I hadn't left it for five days, not even to walk Samson. I'd simply opened the door to let him out three times a day. If I'd moved from my bed it was only to sit on the sofa with the television turned on. Eventually I'd come down the stairs into the courtyard because Samson hadn't come in after one of his outings. I hadn't realized that Clara and Dad had returned to Letchford. Lucky for me that they had. Weak from not eating, I'd fainted out in the courtyard and banged my head. Lost consciousness briefly. They'd heard the dog barking and found me lying there on the ground beside the pot plants. I brushed this memory away.

Of course it would be possible for someone to use another computer and order the reborn baby in my name. The doll. I had to keep reminding myself that it really was just a doll, made of painted vinyl with metal filings in its head. But how lifelike it was, with its mottled newborn skin, expressionless eyes and curled-up wrist. My father still kept the thing out in his office. No wonder it was haunting him.

If anyone had accessed my account to print off the order confirmation they'd have needed my password. My password was Hugh's service number plus the first letter of his name. Nobody else would be able to guess the combination and it wasn't written down anywhere. I kept meaning to change the password as urged by the school IT department, but it seemed too final a step to take, as though I were accepting that my husband would never again be part of my life.

I tried to remember whether I'd ever used a laptop in a classroom to access my mail. If I'd left my email open or saved my password it might have been possible for someone to gain access to my account. The only other school computer I used was the old desktop in the staffroom: a huge old machine that my father kept promising to replace. Usually I just used it to access a timetable or a term calendar. But just in case, I was going to check.

The staffroom was full of people gulping down final shots of caffeine before afternoon lessons. A shaft of sunlight broke through the casement, illuminating dust motes and exposing the lines on the faces of those drinking up coffee and marking exercise books. Only Emily's young face could stand up to the brightness, the beam of light illuminating smooth skin like marble. She sat apart from the others, flicking through the pages of a magazine. Once again I noticed how, for all her youthful features, her expression had a watchfulness to it unusual for a gap-year student whose prime concern should surely be saving their small earnings for a night out in Oxford and hoping they'd have enough left at the end of the school year to go travelling in Thailand. She looked as though she was on guard.

The bell rang. With sighs and stretches people moved towards the door. Emily put down her magazine and watched them, her expression still blank.

"Don't forget the rehearsal this afternoon," called Jenny Hall, head of drama. "I'm relying on you to help, Meredith."

"I'll be there." I wondered how Emily was getting on with the repair to the doll's costume. Perhaps it could make an appearance in the play. I shuddered. Then I remembered what Tracey had said and what I'd seen for myself on the Delicious Confections website. The dolls were expensive: hundreds of pounds. Would a teenager have that much money or the credit card necessary to make the purchase? But I thought about the new and expensive hockey sticks and squash rackets, electronic gadgets and laptops that returned with the pupils at the beginning of term. A reborn doll would present no financial challenge to many of these kids.

Emily followed Jenny out of the staffroom. "Do you still want me to come and start measuring up for costumes?" she asked.

"Please," Jenny replied, as the door closed behind them. Good. Emily was throwing herself into school life. Perhaps involvement would make her seem less awkward.

Deidre was struggling with the computer, glancing at her watch. "Blast, I'm late already . . . Where did I see those French verb worksheets?" She sighed. Finally she found the fourth-year work she was looking for and managed to print it off. "Sorry, Meredith." She stood up to reach for the sheets on the printer. "I know I'm slow." She peered at them over her spectacles. "Damn, I'm two short." She scowled at the screen and stabbed at the keyboard. The printer emitted a couple of chuntering moans. "Come on, come on." She tapped the mouse again. The printer spewed out two more sheets, each rattle suggesting that its tired old heart was about to give up. "Your laptop broken?"

"Forgot to save something onto the memory stick." I gave what I hope was a casual smile and prayed she'd move off.

"Better dash." She gathered up her bag and glasses case. "I've got IB. They're little devils if I'm not in the classroom before them."

I only had about two minutes before my own second-year class would be waiting for me in the classroom. And if I wasn't there promptly, they too would be up to mischief.

I started typing in the Delicious Confections website address to see whether the Internet browser would predict it. It didn't. I checked the Internet history and found no references to the website. I typed in the address of my webmail account. The box for my password was empty. Nobody had used my account on this computer.

Mumbling a farewell to those teachers remaining in the staffroom I all but ran into the corridor. On the way I almost knocked over Olivia Fenton and Emily, each carrying a net of balls towards the netball courts. Emily looked startled when she saw me. I must have looked like a madwoman, rushing along at a speed forbidden to the pupils themselves. Olivia pulled down the sleeves of her saggy games sweatshirt. "So we'll both be doing the play together," Emily said. "Good."

Olivia mumbled something in reply. I wanted to stop, to exchange a few words with the girls, but I dared not leave my class unattended a moment longer.

Back in my own office again after my lessons I studied the sheet my father had passed me. It would be easy enough to set up a page like this using a word-processing or publishing program and make it look like the printout from a real email. I clicked on my email button to find a template I could compare with the printout. A row of neat folders opened up. One of them was simply entitled "Hugh". I felt a temptation I hadn't given in to for some months. I'd saved all the messages that Hugh had ever sent me from the time we were just boyfriend and girlfriend, through the run-up to our marriage, and up to the time he'd gone off to Afghanistan. Emails from him from then on had become much rarer but there were still a few, sent when he'd returned to one of the large bases where there were computers and Internet connections. *Can't wait to see you . . . Counting the hours . . .* I remembered some of them by heart.

I could feel the pulse beating in my neck. I could delete the messages, remove them from my life so I couldn't keep coming back to torment myself. But I couldn't do this. I longed to send him an email myself now, right this minute. I could button up my pride. I'd phrase it carefully so it didn't sound needy. A silly anecdote about the dog or something funny that a pupil had said or done in the classroom. Or perhaps a humorous slant on the discovery of the reborn doll. Those kind of stories used to go down well with Hugh. We'd spent evenings in the kitchen when he was on leave with him pressing me for my school stories. I tried to tell myself that those times were gone for good. It didn't work. I needed to know how he was, how he was getting on with the new leg. His mother had told me they'd had to alter the socket on the prosthesis as the stump was now less swollen.

"Your trouble is that you don't like to give up on anything or anyone," my sister had told me after they'd scraped me off the courtyard back in the summer. "I'm not sure if it's just stubbornness or a neurotic kink in your genes." She hadn't sounded judgemental, merely sad for me. "Sometimes it's a sign of strength, Meredith, just to let go, accept you have no control over people. Look at you. You're a wreck."

"You sound just like a self-help book," I'd snapped at her, clutching a handkerchief to the bleeding cut on my forehead. "He's my husband. He's badly injured. I can't let go." I'd made rabbits' ears round the last two words.

I started to draft an email to Hugh. *Great excitements here, we've had a "fake" stabbed baby found in a cupboard. Macabre or what? We're all playing Miss Marple. And would you believe I'm being framed for the "murdered" baby? The White Oak's still doing decent food and I've been down there a few times with some of the teachers . . .* The words seemed forced, over-cheerful. I could read the exclamation marks even if I hadn't inserted them. *How is rehab going? I hope the leg is feeling less . . .* Alien? Strange? Agonizing? My finger still hovered over the *Send* button. I looked at my watch. Time to go back over. I saved the message in *Drafts*.

An afternoon of teaching and then I was going to the rehearsal for *The Crucible*. It was almost a relief to have the decision taken from me. I'd simply ring Delicious Confections and ask them if they'd delivered the doll and who had paid for it. They'd probably be reluctant to give much away, citing data protection.

I dashed back to the main school for my afternoon lessons. When the bell went at four I made my way across the gardens to the gym, built at the same time as the boarding houses on the site of an old farm building. My father had chosen the architect with care and had made many suggestions himself. Although he'd always preferred paint to any other medium, he had an eye for structure and space. As I often did, I admired the building's clean lines. They'd used plenty of glass and wood in the construction, as well as local Oxford brick and Cotswold stone, and the effect was graceful; the structure blending into the trees around it and reflecting the pearlescent late-afternoon light. Even the teenage boys racing towards it for basketball practice or PE sometimes seemed to lift their heads briefly to admire the building's soaring beams. I remembered the strain that the building programme had placed on my father. He'd managed most of the project himself. Perhaps that was why he'd responded with such anger to my defacement of the mural.

I hadn't been to a full rehearsal before. When I opened the gym door a crowd of students from across the school was talking and laughing. A tall handsome sixth-former leaned against the gym wall, watching proceedings with a cool gaze.

"He's going to be John Proctor," I heard two girls whisper. "The hero. He gets hanged at the end." The awe in their tones was palpable. The sixth-former gave a brief grin, remembered that signs of enthusiasm were only for kids, and immediately resettled his features back into non-committal coolness. The girls nudged one another.

My knowledge of *The Crucible* was hazy — I'd read the play during the summer holidays when Jenny Hall had first asked me to help, but had never taught it in class. I'd rented a DVD of a recent film version and had watched some of it. John Proctor, fighting for truth and justice, seemed well cast.

Olivia Fenton hovered at the back of the hall by herself, clutching a script. She'd be too young for a major role, only a second-year. Good that she was taking part, though. Drama could be just the thing for shy teenagers, allowing them to be someone else for precious hours at a time.

Jenny Hall clapped her hands. "Stop talking now, please, everyone. And listen. We haven't got much time."

The gym door opened and Emily came in, carrying a sewing basket. She gave me a brief nod and went to stand beside Olivia, listening intently to Jenny as she explained what would be expected of the cast and backstage members over the weeks to come.

"Christmas concerts and other activities will inevitably interrupt us, so I want this play to be almost ready by the first week after half-term. Many of you had your parts before the summer holidays and you should know most of your lines. Those of you who have joined us since September have promised to throw themselves into learning their parts. The performances will be in the second week of December. There's a lot to get through in not much time." She described the schedule in more detail and my mind drifted.

"You look as though you're thinking deep thoughts."

I hadn't heard Emily glide across the floor towards me and I jumped. "Just daydreaming. End of a long day."

Her expression was unreadable. "Did you find out anything more about the reborn doll, Meredith?"

"Not really." Not quite the truth, but there was no way I was being lured into the subject of the forged order in my name, not with a group of teenagers standing round us. I wondered whether she knew about the forgery and hoped she wouldn't ask me anything else.

"The teachers here really care about the kids, don't they?" She was watching the group around Jenny.

"I hope so."

"There does seem to be a culture of staff supporting other staff too." She sounded curiously flat as she issued this praise, as though she were reading from a job specification or human resources website.

"That's what Dad has always worked for, yes."

"And yet sometimes there must be cases where your father has to let people go."

I looked at her in surprise. "It doesn't happen very often." Was she worried that she'd fail to live up to some imagined standard for a gappy?

"It must be awful to be sacked from a job at somewhere like Letchford. You'd feel so humiliated." She sat down on the bench beside me and opened the basket to extract a tape measure.

"I suppose you would." I tried to remember any teachers who'd been asked to leave and couldn't think of any. Dad and his heads of department generally chose well. Emily closed the sewing basket. On the top the initials *N.E.C.* were embroidered. Perhaps it had belonged to her mother. I was about to ask her if things were going well for her when one of the girls dropped a mobile phone on the ground. "Sorry." She gave an apologetic grin.

"Please put phones in bags at rehearsals. And turn them off." Jenny looked up from her notes, frowning. "We'll read through the first scenes. If you're in the first act you need to stay. Otherwise go over to Emily to be measured for your costumes." They shuffled into position.

"Tell us about your characters," Jenny said to those standing by the stage. "Sum them up in a few sentences before we start reading. Let's start with . . ." — she turned to Olivia first — "Mary Warren. Who is she?"

"She's a servant girl, working for the main protagonist. She's treated as a bit of a silly little girl who's even told what time to go to bed." Olivia raised her head, seeming to gain confidence as she spoke. "They push her around a bit. She's made to appear weak. But I think she's misunderstood."

"She gets me executed in the end." The sixth-former playing John Proctor crossed his arms. "Because she loses her nerve."

"She's a victim of the male-dominated society of Salem in the seventeenth century," Olivia went on, paying him no attention. "Why should she do anything to help them save themselves? She owes them nothing." She stuck her chin out. I cheered her silently.

"You've all been doing some research," Jenny said. "Well done, Olivia."

"It's interesting. I liked reading about it." She flushed.

"Women had their place back then," put in the sixth-form boy. Another boy nudged him and laughed.

"I suppose you think they should still just be slapped around." Olivia sounded more assertive than I could ever have imagined.

"What do you mean?" He folded his arms. "You think I agree with knocking women around?"

Jenny put up a hand. "Well, you've certainly all put some thought into your characters, well done." She raised her eyebrows at me in surprise.

After the rehearsal I stayed on to help Jenny and the fourth-years tidy away the stage blocks.

"Come and have a drink." Jenny pulled the curtains over the blocks and pulled down her sleeves. Like Simon, she lived in a cottage just outside the school grounds. "A few of us are absconding. Never mind the marking, let's go and have some fun."

"We're going to need it to get through all these play rehearsals."

She shook her head. "I always knew it was going to be tight to put on the play before Christmas. Even with rehearsals for the main parts over the holidays. I must have been deluded." She yawned. "Sorry, I'm shattered. Simon's definitely on for a trip to the White Oak. And Deidre. You're not on junior prep tonight, are you?"

"Nope. But I promised the dog a walk."

"Samson can come too. Nice stroll down the lane for him."

"I suppose so." One of the benefits of my newly single state: being able to decide what you want to do there and then, I thought sourly. Nobody who needed checking with. Though Hugh was often away on duty and I'd often had to fill months of evenings by myself. But that had been different because I'd known he *would* be coming back, eventually; that he was counting the days just as I was.

116

I felt it again: that sudden thump in the ribs. I wanted to go back to my apartment and curl up on the sofa, burying my head in the cushions, Samson lying beside me on the rug. I didn't want to gossip about the school or make plans for further excursions to Oxford for a curry. I wanted to ring my husband, talk to him, ask how he was.

"I'd love to come," I told Jenny Hall, forcing myself to sound enthusiastic. "Just let me go and get Samson."

"What about you, Emily?" Jenny was asking the girl. "Feel like a glass of wine?"

"I was going to start researching costumes." She wound the front of her long cardigan round her fingers. "There's lots to do. I was going to spend some time on the Internet."

"You can do that later. Why not come to the Oak with us?"

Emily was still making excuses as I headed off through the rose garden, reminding myself that I was going to be *normal* for an evening. I saw something in the dark. And stopped.

Standing on my doorstep was my father. With him stood Cathy Jordan, the school nurse.

I halted. "Is someone ill?" I felt suddenly sick. "Is it Clara? Or . . .?" I shook.

"May we come in?" My father spoke very gently. "It's not Hugh. Or your sister, don't worry."

Cathy put her arm around my shoulder. "We'd just like a quick chat, Meredith. Why don't you let us in and I'll put the kettle on."

117

I drew back. "I was going to the pub. With the others."

"I think you need to do that some other time, Merry." Dad's voice was still gentle but there was a headmasterly authority to it now. I unlocked the door and led them upstairs to my little sitting room. Cathy disappeared into the kitchen. I heard the chink of china mugs and the rattle of teaspoons.

"What is this?" Had I missed an anorexic girl in one of my tutor groups? Had a parent complained about me? I racked my brain for incidents where I'd disciplined a pupil. My blood ran cold. One of the second-years I'd sent to detention for scratching a desk with a compass point, perhaps? I ran my students' names through my mind.

"Is there anything else you'd like to tell me about the placing of that doll in Simon's cupboard?"

"No."

"You're sure?"

"Look, I've checked that order. It wasn't made from my laptop, I know that because I looked at the history of all the sites it had gone to over the last month."

He looked puzzled.

"It's easily done, Dad. I could show you. The IT department could check as well."

I remembered that he wouldn't necessarily know what was meant by Internet "history". "The Internet history is the list of all the websites opened during a period," I explained.

Cathy brought in a tray. She'd used an old china mug that had belonged to Hugh. I'd bought it for him

118

years ago when we'd first started going out. Nobody else ever drank from it. She gave me the mug and I stared at the cartoon dog on it. It had the loopy expression often also worn by Samson.

"You were seen, Meredith," Dad said.

"What?"

"You were seen going into that room with the doll." He spoke softly. "The person who saw you looked through the door just as you put the reborn doll into the cupboard. They sent me a note." His hand went towards his jacket pocket, where, presumably, the note rested.

I stared at him until his face broke up into indecipherable pigments and he didn't look like my father at all.

CHAPTER
FOURTEEN

I half expected Cathy and my father still to be in the apartment, waiting for me, when I returned from the pub. Simon walked me back up the lane and drive, despite my protestations. I thought I'd done a good job of putting on a breezy front while we sat inside the old inn by the fire, drinking and chatting. Emily had put aside her reservations about coming and sat in the Oak with us in near silence, nursing a glass of orange juice. Simon had been solicitous with her, trying to draw her out, asking questions about her education in New Zealand.

"It was a bit different from Letchford," was as much as she'd say. "There are very good schools out there but mine wasn't one of them. That's why I'll have to take some A levels if I want to go to a British university."

I hadn't realized this was one of her ambitions. "We'll help," I said. "Which subjects are you interested in?"

"Haven't really decided yet." Her eyes had stayed on her drink.

"If it's English, just let me know."

"Thanks." She acknowledged the offer with a nod of her head. The severe ponytail was gone this evening and her wave of hair was like a curtain over her pale eyes. I saw Simon watching her. He had a kind heart, always sensitive to his pupils and their ups and downs. He probably saw Emily in the same light.

When we reached the door he put out an arm to prevent me from unlocking my door. "I'm worried about you, Cordingley."

"Not you too." I folded my arms. "I'm fine. I'm not behaving oddly. I'm just trying to have a life again. Like everyone keeps urging me to do."

"I didn't say you were behaving oddly. You just seemed a little . . . brittle this evening, that's all." He screwed up his eyes at me. "What's up, Merry?"

I felt my shoulders slump. "I'm being framed." I sounded paranoid. Daft. This whole thing was a huge fuss about a doll.

"What?" He moved his arm.

"For the reborn doll stuff. My father thinks it was me who put the doll in your cupboard." I told him about the email. "And now he's had an anonymous note telling him someone saw me put the doll in your room."

"Why the hell would you do something like that?"

I shrugged. I didn't know if Simon had been aware of my mental and emotional crash back in the summer. He'd been abroad at the time. He examined me speechlessly.

"I'm surprised the men in white coats aren't here for me. Dad even brought in Cathy Jordan to talk to me."

"I thought you liked Cathy?"

I glowered at him. "I do. When she's putting cold packs on kids' strained muscles or talking to girls who won't eat because they want to look like twiglets. But not when she's making me cups of tea and murmuring soothingly." The wind was picking up now and it blew my hair into my eyes. I flicked it away.

"Your father can't seriously believe it was you." He spoke it as a statement. "It's all a prank. I can't believe Charles is taking it so seriously."

"I don't think he was, originally. But every time the thing dies down and people start to forget, something happens to remind him." I hadn't thought of this before, but it was true. First the email. Then the "sighting" of me.

"Your father's still mourning. He's vulnerable. That's probably why he's not observing his usual objectivity about the silly doll." He yawned. "How would you have unlocked the room anyway?"

"I suppose I might have stolen the key from your cottage one of those nights we were playing backgammon."

"Nah. Not you." But for an instant something passed over his face. Did he doubt me? But his voice was warm when he spoke again. "I'd better push off. I've got to plan tomorrow's lesson on the Plantagenets."

"Don't tell me that lesson's in the morning period?"

"First lesson." He grinned at my shocked face. "The heat is on."

"How can you leave your planning until the last minute like this? And go out to the pub?" I sounded like my sister.

"I dunno, feel the fear and all that." He grimaced. "You know what I'm like." But he sounded unrepentant.

"Hopeless. But a damn good friend." I kissed him on the cheek and unlocked the door before I could start to blub. "Thanks for the support," I muttered, going inside. As he moved off I heard footsteps from the other side of the garden and caught a glimpse of a slender figure. Emily. Had she been listening in to our conversation? I pushed the suspicion away.

Cathy and Dad had tidied away the tea mugs in my living room. There was no other sign that they'd been in the apartment. Perhaps they hadn't. Perhaps I'd dreamed them up. Perhaps I'd imagined that my father thought I was neurotic and attention-seeking. I sat on the sofa, staring at the plain white walls as though they could tell me whether I had in fact lost my mind. Just because I didn't remember doing those things mightn't necessarily mean that I hadn't done them. *Of course you didn't bloody do them, you idiot*, the phantom Hugh whispered in my ear. I told him to go away. It annoyed me that I could still hear his words although he'd made it so clear that he wanted nothing to do with me.

"If you were dead I'd probably like you popping back now and then," I told thin air. I blinked with the shock of what I'd just said. But it was true. It would almost have been easier for me had Hugh bled to death in the dust of Helmand Province. By now I might have been moving forward in life, instead of being stuck in limbo.

123

If I slept at all that night it was only to wake almost hourly to the sound of the wind blowing. I'd always hated the wind; even as a small child I'd stuffed my fingers into my ears and screwed up my face against its raspy stroke. But I forced myself out of bed when the alarm clock shrilled and tugged on tracksuit bottoms and an old jumper for my dog walk. Samson seemed to find the wind a stimulus, pretending he couldn't hear my calls and didn't understand the sound of the whistle. He ran in excitement after scurrying leaves, barking at them. His nose went down and he accelerated. He'd picked up a rabbit scent and was heading through the woods towards the fence marking the school's boundary with the road. As I sprinted after him I could hear the traffic humming along. Seven a.m. Commuters already making for the railway station, intent on making good time, not paying attention to the railings at the side of the road, railings a leggy dog could jump in the thrill of a chase.

"Samson!" Not as much as the twitching of an ear from the dog in response. He reached the fence and for a moment I thought he was going to leap over it into the traffic. I screamed at him again. But he slammed down his hind legs and lifted his front quarters to peer over the fence, tail wagging. As I reached him I saw that he was staring at a small red car parked in a field entrance on the other side of the road. A car in which Emily Fleming was sitting with the driver, whose back was turned to me. The car was similar enough in size and appearance for a dog to have mistaken it for Hugh's red Mini Cooper, now shut up in a garage.

124

Emily turned as I shouted and a flush of annoyance covered her face. She said something to her companion. The other figure turned towards her and away from me so I didn't get a close glimpse of whoever it was.

I snapped the lead onto Samson's collar and dragged him off the fence as the car's engine started up. We walked away as I muttered reprimands at him. No reason at all why Emily shouldn't be up and about and meeting a friend so early in the morning. But no reason for her to glare at me like that. Samson hadn't done anything more than show excitement at seeing her. Perhaps she disliked dogs, I reasoned with myself. Perhaps she hadn't recognized me in my sloppy outdoor clothes. I shouldn't be so touchy.

I dragged Samson home, showered and changed for school. Bad start to the morning. I gave myself a shake. This would be one of my together days. If I heard the voice of my absent husband I would deny it access to my thoughts. By now Dad would have had time to reflect on my vehement denial of involvement in the doll business. He must know I'd recovered. I provided evidence of my sanity every time I stood in front of the classroom. You can't fool a group of teenagers. The GCSE results of the class I'd taken over last spring had been good. Perhaps he'd also reflect on his own disproportionate response to this whole episode. Maybe Cathy needed to give *him* the tea and talk.

This was my busiest day of the week. No time for mulling. We had another rehearsal this afternoon. I was going to be a composed and focused teacher if it killed me.

I didn't see my father during the working day. It wasn't his day for taking assembly and I imagined him in his office: ringing parents, speaking to the heads of the feeder schools for Letchford and setting up open days, briefing the chair of governors. All those things he regarded as having nothing to do with the business of education. And he'd be doing all this without my mother. He couldn't really think I'd had a part in this silly doll stuff. He was distracted, grieving, as Simon had said.

I reached the gym for the afternoon's rehearsal a little ahead of time, in keeping with my new approach to life. My father's accusations had benefited me in one way: they'd given me a push forwards.

Two figures sat together on the stage blocks. Emily and Olivia. They looked up as I came in and something about the simultaneous raising of their heads made them look somehow in cahoots. "I'd love to see New Zealand," Olivia was saying. "Did you always live over there?"

"Well —" Emily checked herself as I approached. "We were just going over some of Olivia's scenes." She smiled, looking almost as though she wanted to put me at ease. There was something about the girl that always made me feel I was the one who was awkward and unsure, not her.

Olivia gave her habitual tug on the sleeves of her school jumper and stared at a spot on the gymnasium floor. The gym door swung open and a bunch of

126

fifth-years burst in, and there wasn't time to repeat the question.

"Let's get cracking." Jenny clapped her hands.

Olivia's part was not a large one, but as she stood up on the stage her face seemed to belong to a girl living outside the twenty-first century, someone from a time before electricity and reason. When she said that the devil was at work in Salem I almost wanted to look over my shoulder in case a dark shadow hovered in the corner of the hall.

Where had she acquired such fervour? I studied her hard but all I saw was a thin girl whose pale face glowed with an emotion too large for it. Emily was studying her, too, her expression unfathomable.

CHAPTER
FIFTEEN

"Meredith." My father's hand on my shoulder made me jump. I was standing at my usual station by the window seat in the staffroom looking out at the Downs. "Come for dinner tonight. Eight. If that suits."

"Er, OK." I blinked. He'd moved away before I could ask him whether he'd bring in Cathy Jordan to talk soothingly to me again about my state of mind and why I'd hidden the reborn in the cupboard. I wanted to call after Dad, say that I was busy this evening. But it wasn't true. I'd already done most of my marking. No way of getting out of it now. If only I could be eating my dinner with my husband. Eating a meal he'd cook because my own culinary skills were so lacking. But perhaps his maimed left hand precluded cooking now.

This meal together was possibly Dad's way of offering an olive branch. Mum would have wanted me to go, to make things up with him. I'd have supper with him. For her sake.

I half expected Cathy to be sitting on the sofa in Dad's drawing room, but he was alone. We made half-hearted conversation about school business while we finished our sea bass. He fussed about having overcooked the fillets, but he'd gone to some trouble with herbs and lemon juice and they were good. He asked questions about my classes and proffered a few observations about some of my pupils, noting that several had been in to receive commendations in the last week for good pieces of English work.

All the time I waited, trying not to show impatience. It felt strange, being alone in this dining room with my father, both of us single, reliant on one another for company, a latter-day Emma Woodhouse and her father. Through my mind flashed the image of us both still sitting here together in ten or twenty years' time, encouraging one another to have just a little more soup or another piece of shepherd's pie while worrying that the heating was turned up too high. My shoulders drooped. *My life wasn't meant to be like this.* Memories of family suppers were all around me. At the far side of the table stood the chair where my mother used to sit. She'd be urging us to eat up, offering seconds, laughing, talking. A happy marriage, most people would have said. I'd have said just that, too. But how could I really know?

He nodded at the fish. "Every time I think I'm making some progress with my cooking I realize how much I have to learn."

"It's fine." I carved a piece off and ate it. It was actually tasty, despite the black bits on the outside.

"Somehow I missed the domestic revolution that meant men started doing these things. Like Hugh." He grimaced. "Sorry."

"I don't mind you talking about him."

"Have you heard anything recently?"

"No."

He made no comment and I was grateful. "Your mother was too kind to me," he went on. "She did everything."

Too kind, indeed. She'd left him almost incapable of doing things for himself. But he was a practically minded man, I reminded myself. Good with his hands. He'd learn how to cook. "I don't suppose you ever saw your father doing much in the kitchen when you were growing up?"

He smiled. "I don't think Papa ever went into the kitchen. But then my mother wasn't much of a cook either. She'd had servants as a girl. Even during the war there was usually someone who'd cook whatever they could find to eat. Communism brought big changes. I remember her cooking us some good hearty middle-European soups and stews when she could find the ingredients."

Stories from his childhood were rare. The family printing works had been taken by the state, I knew. The big house in the centre of Prague had gone. Only the house out in the country towards the German border had remained. The authorities had filled it with incomers from further east, people considered ideologically sound, who'd keep an eye on a bourgeois family with German connections.

"You must look at some of these children and think that they're very spoiled," I said.

"I didn't know any other way of life," he went on. "So it wasn't so bad for me as a young child. It was only as I got older that I realized that my life would always be constrained."

It had been made clear to him that he was unlikely to go to university. The state regarded his parents as too unreliable politically.

"Then in 1968 we thought we were leaving the restraints behind." His eyes took on a faraway look. "We thought it would all be so different, that we'd be able to do what we wanted, be what we wanted." It was so rare to get him to talk like this about his past. I leant forward.

"I'll just fetch the pudding." He stood up. Probably said more than he'd attended.

"I'd like to hear more about your childhood," I said to his retreating back. "It's so interesting." No answer came.

A door opened and closed in the hallway outside the apartment. Someone was walking across the landing. I thought I heard someone say something. I wondered who it was at this time of the night. Dad was coming back into the dining room, carrying bowls of stewed apple he must have defrosted from the freezer, topped with scoops of vanilla ice cream. The apples would have been last year's. We hadn't bothered picking any of the Bramleys this year. It had been one of my mother's favourite tasks. This year the wasps would have them. The ice cream accompanying the apples had ice crystals on it: Dad must have had the tub in the freezer for a long time, probably since the week of Mum's death. The weather had been good those last few days. She'd served dinner for the two of them out on the terrace. Even then she'd had a slight headache, but a few paracetamol had kept it at bay. Once or twice she'd felt dizzy but we'd put that down to the warm weather. She'd probably bought the ice cream to go with the raspberries she'd picked from her garden.

"Let me." I took the bowls from my father and placed them on the mats in front of each of us. "Tell me about 1968. Your life must finally have seemed to be on a different course that year."

"We thought we were going to be like other young people elsewhere in the world." A hood had fallen over his eyes. I knew he wasn't going to talk any more about it. But there was still another subject we needed to discuss. I needed to wait for him to bring it up.

"This doll," my father said at last. "I think I took it all to heart too much, obsessed about it."

I waited. Watched him struggling with himself.

"The letter sounded convincing."

"Do you still have it?"

He shook his head.

"Shame. I might have recognized the writing."

"I should have thought of that." He made a gesture with his hands that suggested contrition. "It was the way it followed on from the email . . ."

"Well, if you're going to stitch someone up you need to make it convincing, don't you?"

"I suppose so."

Still I waited, breaking up the crystals in my ice cream with my spoon. "I'm sorry, Merry," he said at last. "I should have trusted you."

I nodded.

"I don't think I'm functioning properly. Still. Even though it's been months now."

Since my mother had died. "It's not long, Dad."

"Perhaps not." He laid down his spoon, his ice cream untouched. "What do you think we should do about it?"

"Sell the doll on eBay and give the money to charity. Or spend it on booze for the staff Christmas party."

"You can sell such things on the Internet?" He looked amused. At times the sceptical, amused, middle-European persona rose to the surface.

"Where is the damn thing now?" I hoped he'd put it away. I wished we could return to the subject of Czechoslovakia in 1968. To the artistic career he'd started on with such expectations.

"Still on my desk."

I made a note to myself to put it back in its cardboard box and hide it in a cupboard until I had time to sell it. Which I would do in half-term week.

"Meredith . . ." He pushed his bowl away. "I want to tell you again how sorry I am that I didn't believe you. It's as though the object possessed me somehow."

I thought of a voodoo doll. Perhaps someone had pricked the reborn's vinyl skin with pins to set us all on edge. Either that, or the paperknife plunged into its innards had worked some weirdness on us.

"I know what you mean. It's spooky."

"You forgive me?"

I reached out and squeezed his hand. "You know I do."

We continued our meal, though neither of us seemed to have much of an appetite this evening.

"Strange," he said, "how at a time of . . . change one's thoughts go back right to the beginning of one's life."

I tried not to show my intense interest. If I asked too many questions he'd find an excuse for leaving the room. I'd let the conversation drift and hope it took us where I wanted.

"I always told your mother I'd take her there one day."

"She always wanted to go to Bohemia." There'd always been some reason why it hadn't been convenient for them to make the trip, even though they could have booked cheap flights to Prague, hired a car and spent just a weekend touring around. It wasn't a large country, the Czech Republic. But something had always come up. I'd been to Prague myself once, with Hugh, in the early days of our courtship. We'd found the street where the family's town house had once stood. It had been converted into apartments. I'd taken photographs and brought them back. Dad had studied them in near silence.

"That was my bedroom," he'd said at last, pointing at a shuttered window. "When I was very young. But I always preferred the house in the country. As my studies progressed I had to spend more time in Prague so I slept on a camp bed in a distant cousin's house. It wasn't very comfortable so I took to staying at friends' places when I started at the Academy of Fine Arts."

134

I thought of the girl underneath my mother's image. Had she been one of these friends?

I was about to ask when someone knocked on the apartment door. My father raised an eyebrow. "Who's on duty tonight?"

"Simon," I said, rising to open the door. It was very rare for Simon to disturb us on a weekday evening, especially since my mother's death.

Emily Fleming stood outside the door, face apparently even more drained of blood than it normally was. "You'd better get your father," she said, without a preamble. "And call nine nine nine. We need an ambulance."

"What is it?" My father was already behind me. "What's happened, Emily?" We followed her out of the door.

Emily pointed to the staircase. "She fell down there."

As one we rushed towards the stairs. At the bottom, on the marble tiles in front of the mural, lay a motionless slight figure, arms out, head down. Emily ran down ahead. "I didn't have my mobile with me to ring for help. The office was locked." She bent over the body on the marble, fingers moving over the neck. "I'm not sure I can feel a pulse." Now I was close enough to see who it was lying on the ground. "Oh God, suppose she's dead?" Emily wailed.

And now I could see that it was Olivia Fenton lying there.

CHAPTER
SIXTEEN

I ran down the stairs two at a time and pulled Emily away from the girl's body.

"Let me get to her." ABC, I remembered from the first-aid course I'd taken a year back. Airways, breathing, circulation. Olivia's head and neck seemed unharmed; it was probably safe to move her head. I tilted it back gently so the jaw opened and ran my fingers round her mouth. Clear. I placed my open palm against her mouth and nose and felt her warm breath. My fingers searched her right wrist. "There's a pulse."

"The ambulance is on the way," my father called. "I told them you were a trained first-aider. They want to speak to you." I held out my left hand for the telephone.

"You seem to have done everything just right, well done," the operator told me. I felt like a first-year who'd scored a winning goal. "Try and keep her still and warm."

I hung up and placed my hand on Olivia's arm. "Bring a blanket or a coat," I told Emily. "She's getting cold lying on the marble." Olivia seemed to blink. "Can you hear me, Olivia?" I thought I saw her blink again. "Help's on the way." She moved a hand slightly. "Take it gently." She moved her head from side to side and vomited onto the marble. I was worried she'd choke and propped her sideways. "I'm going to keep talking to you."

She coughed and gave a low moan.

It was my father, not Emily, who handed me a coat. I recognized it as his own thick black Crombie and placed it over the girl. Dad normally wore the coat on the touchline at rugby matches; he'd had it for decades. Another of his typically English pieces of clothing. After the warmth of the panelled dining room upstairs the marble floor made my skin prickle with goose-pimples. Once, as a child, I'd tripped over my shoelaces and fallen flat on my face on almost this exact spot. I remembered the cold stinging slap of the slabs against my face, the shock, and I shuddered. How must it feel to have fallen from a height?

"Did she fall all the way down the stairs?" my father asked. "What happened, Emily?" His voice trembled. He placed a hand on Olivia's. "She's so cold." His accent had taken on the slightly guttural central-European edge.

Emily shrugged. "I was just walking through the hall when I heard her fall."

Why? I wondered. What had brought Emily into the main house? She'd been given rooms in Gavin House. Perhaps she'd left something in one of the classrooms. And Olivia certainly shouldn't have been in here; the house was out of bounds to pupils outside school hours.

"I'd left some books upstairs in the staffroom," Emily went on.

Olivia moaned and her muscles tensed up beneath the overcoat. I hadn't realized that I still had my arms over her.

"Lie still," I told her. "Wait for the ambulance men to check you over. Stay awake, Olivia."

"Arm," she said. "Arm hurts. That's all. Want to sit up . . ." She struggled slightly under my arm. Good. She was very much conscious now. I sat back.

"Very slowly. Tell me if anything else hurts, especially your head and neck." I helped inch her up. She shivered and I pulled the coat around so that it covered her shoulders, taking care to avoid touching her dangling right arm. "Put your head between your legs if you feel dizzy." I noticed a bruise on her right temple, already swollen, and a cut on the back of her left wrist. She must have caught it on the banisters as she tumbled.

"Could we have an ice pack?" I called to my father.

"I'll go and get one and fetch Cathy over, too," he said. Even at this moment I felt myself stiffen at the mention of Cathy's name. I told myself to be sensible; Cathy certainly wouldn't be accusing me of more pranks while a pupil lay badly hurt beside me on the cold marble.

"The ambulance will be here soon," I told Olivia. The station was only in the next town. It would take less than ten minutes.

"I don't need one."

"You were unconscious. You need checking over and that wrist needs treatment."

"Her wrist?" Emily was crouching next to us now, talking to Olivia in a low tone I hadn't heard before. She sounded more anxious about the arm than the possible head injury.

"Hospitals scare me." Olivia was weeping now. Huddled in my father's coat she looked much younger than she was, a pale waif, her eyes wide and scared, reminding me for just a moment of my father's own expression at my mother's funeral, when he'd clung to Clara's arm for a second as the coffin was being lowered into the ground. Reminding me, too, of Hugh's face when he'd woken up in the hospital in Birmingham and started screaming at me to run away from the dangers he still saw around him.

"I'll go with you." Emily squeezed in beside us and stroked her hair.

"Will you?" Olivia swallowed.

Normally it would have been my mother or Cathy who accompanied casualties to hospital, not a gap-year student. I heard Cathy's high heels click over the marble and stood up. She held the blue ice pack, wrapped in a dry tea towel. I moved back to let her apply it gently to the bruise. Blue lights bounced off the windows and I heard the crumple of ambulance wheels over the gravel.

Cathy was talking to Emily. "How long was she out for?"

"I don't know." Emily's voice shook.

My father was opening the front door to the crew, ushering them in. I took another step back, feeling suddenly awkward, in the way. Cathy put a hand on my arm. "You did well with the first aid, Meredith."

"Never thought I'd have to use it." To date my ministrations had been limited to applying an ice pack to swollen ankles or knees following soccer mishaps. I thought of Hugh, bleeding on the dusty road, his brother soldiers trying to stop the flow, radioing for help, knowing every second brought him closer to death. I realized I was shaking and started pacing the hall in an attempt to disguise this from the others.

"Meredith . . ." I swallowed. "I hope you haven't found this all too disturbing." Cathy's voice was low, confiding.

I blinked. "No."

"You've had quite a time of it, haven't you, dear? Don't push yourself too hard."

What did she think my options had been this evening? Leaving Olivia on the ground where she'd fallen?

I made a muffled noise of dissent. "Excuse me." I moved away.

One of the ambulance crew was talking to Olivia now while the other one stood with Emily and discussed what she'd seen of the fall. "Can I go with her?" Emily asked.

"I'm the member of staff who accompanies pupils," Cathy said. "I'll follow in my car."

"But —" Emily pinkened. "I'd just quite like to stay with her."

"It won't be necessary, thank you, dear." Cathy gave her brisk smile. "You could go and fetch my bag from

140

my desk. And my mobile. Just in case we have a long wait at A & E."

Emily's flush seemed to deepen to the colour of one of the dark-pink dahlias in the vase beside her, but she did as she was asked.

The crew were helping Olivia to her feet. They'd already strapped her broken arm. "Nothing else broken, as far as we can see, but they'll check you over properly at A & E," one of them told her. "You've been lucky. Falling onto this hard floor . . ." he shook his head. I wondered whether we'd be forced to carpet the marble.

Emily's shoulders drooped as she walked away. "Emily," I called after her, wanting to say something to comfort her, to reassure her, but she didn't respond to her name. I watched her trudge slowly back towards the accommodation block where her rooms were; a slight figure, bundled into an oversized cardigan.

My father was sitting on the stairs, a faraway expression on his face. He looked simultaneously older and also like a young boy, gazing down at the grown-ups below. I'd never seen him sit on the stairs like this. "She looked so young lying there. So still."

"She is young," I said briskly. "Just thirteen."

"No, she's —" For a moment it seemed as though he might contradict me. "Sorry, yes, of course she's thirteen." He put a hand to his throat, as though to dislodge something stuck there. "I must have been confusing her with someone else."

CHAPTER
SEVENTEEN

Charles

Confusion. Collins the disgraced bursar. The defaced mural. At the time it seemed just one of life's ironies that the two events should occur together.

At first it was easy enough to imagine that it was simply Charles's ineptitude with figures that was making him worry where no worry was necessary. Reserves, depreciation, writings-off; all these conspired to draw a veil over what was really happening. And there always seemed to be perfectly good reasons for everything: an amount earmarked for one thing — music scholarships, for instance — might dip a little, but at the same time another — special-need bursaries, say — would apparently increase.

"Fewer musical children this year, Charles, and more good all-rounders whose parents are going through tough times." Collins's eyes would be fixed on Charles's as he said this and Charles could feel his concern for the children and their parents.

Collins cared about these families, that was certain. He wasn't just a bean counter. He'd sat with the widowed mother of a thirteen-year-old for an hour, reassuring her that her son's future at the school was certain, that financial help would be provided, that she shouldn't worry about it. The woman left the bursar's office with a smile on her tired face. And all the while the new buildings — the gymnasium and swimming pool — were taking shape in the grounds and they were saving every pound they could on unnecessary expenditure. For a time it really did seem as though Collins was a financial wizard.

The governors back then lacked any real financial acumen, too. Afterwards Charles could appreciate that Collins was moving money around so quickly for a reason: he wanted to make it hard for them to keep tabs on how much there actually was. And the sums he withdrew himself were small: two or three hundred pounds here or there, occasionally a thousand, easily explicable as cash in hand to pay for materials needed for the building work. "The builders can get a better deal on the tiles if they pay cash," he told Charles once.

The tenders received for the building work: how many of them were inflated to provide Collins with a payback? It would be hard to prove either way. And it wasn't in the builders' interests to admit to any kind of bribery.

At three most mornings Charles would wake and listen to the steady breathing of Susan beside him in the bed. Around him the old house sighed and relaxed. Letchford at night was a soothing place. But not any more. Something wasn't right. Someone needed to take a closer look. The governors were the first people to whom he should report his misgivings. But suppose he were mistaken?

He rolled over in bed and tried to will himself to sleep. But still the anxieties chased around his mind. Then he thought of an answer. John Andrews. He'd retired by now but was still doing a bit of maths coaching for common entrance or GCSE. John had always been a figures man, not just one of those mathematicians who see numbers as beautifully theoretical. John had run a black-market business with Charles's father from a prisoner-of-war camp in northern Bohemia. They'd managed it with ruthless efficiency; mistakes could have meant a bullet through the head. John Andrews had kept books, encoded so the Germans couldn't understand them, and every last cigarette, every stale crust had been recorded. John was the man Charles needed here at Letchford. And it would help him, too. His retirement was not a prosperous one.

"There'd be some maths teaching," Charles told him when he went to visit him in Abingdon. "Fairly straightforward stuff: just the younger children, first- and second-years." Even now he couldn't bring himself to admit to suspicions.

John nodded.

"They're generally interesting and bright children," Charles went on. "We try and give out as many places as we can to boys and girls from poorer backgrounds, and fortunately the fund has stood up well."

"But?" He sat back in his shabby armchair, his eyes sharp. "Maths teachers are two a penny. You don't need me for your teaching staff. What's up?"

144

"Something's not right," he blurted out.

John gave him that shrewd look of his. "Tell me, Charlie."

"It's the building work."

"I thought that was going well."

"It is. To plan."

"But not to budget?"

"The books seem in order."

John nodded. He moved forward in the armchair. "Tell me about your bursar."

"The bursar came with excellent references."

"Family?"

"Wife's just had their second child." A boy. Susan had lent them an old linen christening robe.

"Is he having an affair?"

Charles shrugged. "I'd be surprised. He seems quite the devoted father."

"Big fancy house? BMW or something similar in the drive?"

"A smallish semi, as far as I know. And an old Ford."

John had promised to ring soon and let him know when he could come to Letchford.

John Andrews was ill for much of the early part of the New Year; that damp cottage on the Thames played havoc with his bronchitis, and so it wasn't until February that he joined the Letchford staff.

During the day John taught a few lessons and at night Charles sat with him in his office with the books. It was almost like the old days, John said: he and Charles's father sitting in the dark, whispering about their black-market transactions, an ear open for the guard. He'd sounded nostalgic. Perhaps he'd been lonely in that house by the Thames. He had no family, Charles knew. Just a much younger sister, a brother-in-law and small nephew he rarely saw.

In those days the bursary was in what became Simon's history room. Collins had his desk beside the big oak cupboard on the wall. Charles and John would unlock the oak cupboard and take out the lever arch files housed above the pile of old papers and books referring to Letchford house that lived, for want of anywhere better, in the bottom of the cupboard. Charles would try not to look at Collins's neat desk, with the blotter and silver paperknife and calculator lined up ready for the next day's work. Whenever John removed anything from the oak cupboard he put it back exactly as he had found it. Files were replaced to the exact millimetre. John read their contents without comment.

A few mornings later a letter arrived from the bank, an apologetic note informing Charles that the school overdraft limit had been extended for the last time. If the school wanted to borrow any more money it would have to be in the form of a loan guaranteed by a mortgage or some other kind of security. The bank manager looked forward to discussing the matter with Charles at his convenience and sent his best wishes to Susan and the girls.

He'd known nothing about the overdraft. He passed the letter to John and his sharp eyes scanned it in a few seconds. He didn't look surprised. "Noel is on the fiddle."

146

Charles winced. This was Collins, after all; Collins who was good with grieving widows.

"We have to confront him," John said. It was unseasonably warm and the casement window was open. A group of youngsters was meandering across the lawn. One of them said something and the others responded with guffaws. "No time like the present," John added.

Noel looked up from his desk as they walked in. The quick smile that spread across his face fell away. "I'm so sorry," Charles started.

He stood. "It's all right." He looked at John and his expression darkened. "Come to look at the books again?"

Charles felt his cheeks redden.

"I know you've been looking." He put the lid on his fountain pen. "You're right, of course, Charles. I've been taking money."

Charles willed him to take back the words, to say it hadn't been him, that it was all a mistake.

"I'll pay you back," he said. "Obviously if you don't press charges I can do it more speedily, as I'll be able to get another job. But that would mean you'd have to give me a reference." He spread his fingers out in front of him on the desk and gave a short laugh. "I'm not being realistic, am I? You'll probably need to call in the police." The fingers curled and he gripped the edge of his desk.

"Why?" Charles asked. "You, of all people . . ." Noel Collins, with his open face and his sympathy for the unfortunate.

He shrugged. "I could try and explain but there's no point in trying to excuse myself."

"I wish you would explain."

"What's the point?" He pulled his jacket off the back of his chair. "It probably sounds strange to say this, but everything else is in perfect order." Charles held out the bank letter. "Ah, yes. Well, cash flow will start to become positive again almost immediately, now that I've . . ." He shook his head and bent down to pick up his briefcase. He scooped up the possessions on his desk, the photograph of his baby son dressed in the linen gown and cap, and the little daughter whose name Charles had probably been told but had forgotten. A shaft of sunlight glinted on his silver paperknife as he placed it in the case.

"Why?" he asked again.

Collins shook his head. "Family business. It doesn't matter now." He looked down. "Not if you don't remember. No excuse, though. I'm so sorry, Charles."

He watched him leave the office. John Andrews hadn't said a word while Collins was in the room. As soon as he'd shut the door carefully behind him, he turned to Charles.

"You'll have to get the police involved."

"I don't know if I can do that."

"You have a responsibility to the governors."

Charles shook his head, coldness settling on his stomach. Family business. He thought about the conversations he'd had with Collins over the last month or so. He couldn't remember mention of financial woes. Collins's wife was working now, too, wasn't she? He thought of the photo of the little girl and boy. There had been something, something about the baby. He wasn't well. That was all he was able to remember. Damn the minutiae of detail about bricks and double-glazing that had saturated his memory.

One of the daughter's paintings had been pinned on the wall for a while. A Christmas tree, with presents around the base. Collins had been good with Charles's own girls, too. Once or twice he'd come into the room to find them eating chocolate digestives and drawing on sheets from Collins's notepad.

"I'm not sure I'll be able to do that."

But a day or so later John had worn him down with arguments as to what he owed to the school and to the board of governors, and to the pupils themselves, who'd been robbed of funds that would buy them textbooks and equipment. Charles had agreed to call the police. By then it was too late; Collins and his wife and children had left the country.

"He must have been ready for this," John told him. "Possibly planned his escape some time ago. Guessed you'd wait a bit before you did anything." His face was inscrutable. "You should feel angrier than you do, Charlie."

"I feel disappointed more than anything. I missed something important."

"You're still thinking of him as your friend."

"He was my friend."

The police corroborated John's guess when they telephoned the school one Saturday morning. They told

Charles that Collins couldn't be traced beyond Amsterdam.

That was the same morning Meredith and Clara stripped the paint from the mural. It didn't seem coincidental. The smooth, managed surface of the life they'd built at Letchford was being cut open: exposed for all the world to see.

"Who was that woman underneath the painting of me?" Of course Susan wanted to know. "Why was she on the wall?"

"She was just someone I used to know."

"Someone you used to know very well, it would seem, if you remembered her in such detail."

"Someone I haven't seen for twelve years. Someone I have never even had a letter from."

"But someone so dangerous you had to cover her up."

They came down harshly on Merry. She'd been the scapegoat. Clara seemed to escape with less blame because it was hard to believe that she would have been the instigator of this mischief. Things were said to Merry that were too harsh. Even for Merry, who seemed to bob serenely through life. Her small face had been white after he'd finished telling her off. "I'm really sorry, Daddy," she'd whispered. His heart had throbbed. She'd only been doing what any inquisitive ten-year-old would do.

But he was busy. Busy and shocked at what had happened with Collins, mourning him, really. And full of annoyance with himself. Some of the anger that should have applied itself to Collins, and to himself for

150

his lack of care with the school's finances, had fallen on Merry's slender shoulders.

He should have spent more time with his younger daughter. Just as he ought to have spent more time with Collins. Asking about the sick infant. Now he thought about it, Collins had mentioned some operation for the little boy. But he'd been too busy to take in the details.

First Collins and now Merry. For all her lack of interest in art, Merry was always the child of his heart.

She still was.

CHAPTER
EIGHTEEN

Meredith

Olivia and Cathy returned at around midnight.
Fortunately, my father told me when I bumped into
him on the way to lessons, A & E had been quiet on a
weekday night.

"We now have a difficult situation," Dad went on.
"Olivia should really be sent home for a few days. She
banged her head quite badly. Cathy spent the night in
her room, waking her up every three hours to make
sure she wasn't slipping into unconsciousness, but
Cathy doesn't work full time."

I silently thanked my lucky stars.

"And Olivia's housemistress can't really be responsible
for her in this condition." My father paused. "There
was something else. That cut on her wrist. Cathy says
it's probably not accidental. They asked questions at
the hospital."

"Someone cut her?"

"Or she cut herself."

Our eyes met. We knew about self-harming; how
could we not, with a schoolful of teenagers? I couldn't
remember a case here since I'd arrived. But youngsters

this age were notoriously secretive. All the same, I reminded myself, they had to get changed for swimming lessons or PE. Usually someone would notice cuts. Unless the girls were exercising their monthly right to have time off games. I knew my father was thinking the same thing as I was: that this was an area that would have previously been part of my mother's ambit, that we were lost without her calm, quiet ability to sort out these situations.

"So she'll have to go home for a few days." I spoke automatically, then realized that it wouldn't be as simple as that, not for Olivia Fenton.

"I think that's best. I'm going to try and ring her family now. There's lots to discuss." I found myself following him upstairs and into the apartment, as though I were a little girl again and the first-floor rooms were still my home. I had a few minutes before my first class started. 3b were on assembly duty this week, putting away chairs and benches, which meant it would take them longer to make their way to their first lesson. Dad logged on to the laptop and entered a password to get into the pupil database. "Samantha's taken on the management of the database but she's on a training course this morning. I don't really know how it works." He frowned as he read the screen. "Olivia doesn't really seem to have a settled home. Her aunt is her guardian and she lives at her place of work. There's a mobile number."

He dialled it on the office telephone. He shook his head. "Voicemail," he whispered. "This is Charles Statton calling from Letchford School. I'd be grateful if you could call me back as soon as possible." He explained what had happened.

He hung up and turned back to the computer screen. "Usually pupils have an emergency contact number for someone else but it's blank on Olivia's record."

"Isn't there anyone else?"

"There's only an email address." I let my eyes move towards the screen. Normally I was very careful not to let myself see anything I shouldn't when I was with my father in his office. Teachers at my level didn't have access to the full database. I caught sight of the address and noted that it was a village near Wokingham. The boxes for other emergency contacts were blank.

The waif Olivia, who had nobody else but the absent aunt.

"I expect we can organize some kind of rota for Olivia. She's in her house at the moment; Tracey's sending over some breakfast." He stood up. "Let's go down, shall we?"

As we reached the ground floor Emily appeared from the kitchen carrying a tray. "I said I'd take it over to Olivia." She paused. "Tracey's really busy. I don't have much on this morning. I could sit with Olivia if it helped." She watched my father as she suggested this.

"Where are you supposed to be?" my father asked.

"Putting out cones for Jeremy for fourth-year hockey. It's not exactly essential work." Something in her tone made me look closely at her. "I'd like to look after Olivia."

154

My father contemplated her. "There may be other things you could be doing that are more useful for you than sitting with Olivia." It was said gently but firmly. "This year is supposed to be about expanding your knowledge of teaching in a school."

"I don't mind."

"You need to spend your time with the teachers," he went on. "Even if it is just putting out cones. It gives you an opportunity to observe. Take the tray over but come straight back."

Emily seemed about to debate the point. The bell rang. A crowd of teenagers moved across the hall, drifting round us as though we were rocks in a fast-moving stream. One or two turned curious eyes towards us. "You'll need to hurry, Emily," my father told her. "Jeremy will be expecting you at the hockey pitch."

There was something approaching a glint of dislike in her eyes now but she nodded.

"I don't get it," I said as she disappeared with the tray of breakfast. "What's this obsession with Olivia?"

My father turned to watch Emily as she walked away. "Perhaps she just feels concerned because she was the first one on the scene last night," he said, sounding so confident that I could almost believe this was all there was to the case, until I remembered the cut on Olivia's arm.

"Do you think Emily knows about the self-harming?"

He gave me a sharp look. "If she does, she needs to speak to Cathy Jordan immediately."

"There's something about her I can't make out." I'd watched her walk along a corridor, encountering a group of sixth-form girls, standing against the wall to let them pass when they ought to have stood aside, according to the Letchford unwritten code on good manners.

"Thanks," one of them had said, over her shoulder. The others didn't appear even to have noticed Emily. I'd wanted to remonstrate with the girls. But something in Emily's cool gaze prevented me. I sensed she'd hold it against me if I said anything. And yet I felt the resentment in her. And understood it. Some of the pupils here had a sense of entitlement that sometimes made me yearn for the less poised pupils at the state school I'd left.

My father was still staring at me intently. "Sometimes you look at a pupil and something about them perplexes you. Then you realize they remind you of someone you once knew, years and years ago." He blinked, looking surprised at what he'd just said.

The bell rang before I could ask him which pupil's features had been preying on his mind. I looked at my watch. I needed to sprint; if running inside any part of Letchford hadn't been forbidden. Another of the rules Dad had had to bring in as the school grew larger. "I used to think that people ought to be allowed to move around at any pace they felt fit, as long as they didn't endanger anyone else," he'd told me once. "But these days we're told nobody must run." And his face had become set and I'd known he was thinking of the principles so dear to him: of freedom of choice and anti-authoritarianism, all ideas rejected by the state in his home country. He'd wanted this school to be so different, but little by little it had absorbed values he'd originally rejected: conformity, conservatism, risk-aversion.

"I'll take Olivia's tray over at lunchtime and check up on her," I called to him over my shoulder.

"Would you?" He sounded grateful. "I've asked Cathy to have a word with her about that . . . other business."

When I reached the house at 12.30p.m. Olivia was sitting in the lounge at Gavin watching an Australian soap. "I brought your lunch over." The smell of the lasagne made me feel hungry. Which was good. Hunger and I hadn't seen much of one another in recent months.

"Thanks, Mrs Cordingley." She gave a little smile. "I'll come through to the kitchen, we're not allowed to eat in here." She led me through to the kitchen, appearing steady on her feet. A slight tint of colour had returned to her cheeks. The housemistress wasn't in the kitchen so I put the plate of lasagne into the microwave myself to heat it, wondering whether some health-and-safety directive prohibited untrained personnel using a school microwave.

She ate the meal with a good appetite. "They have gluten-free pasta for me." She sounded proud of this. As she forked her lasagne her sleeve fell back. The cut on her arm looked less red today.

"So you're feeling better?" I asked.

She nodded, mouth full of pasta. "Should be back in class tomorrow," she said when she'd swallowed.

"We've called your aunt."

Her eyes narrowed. "Yes."

"Really, you should be at home."

"She's working."

"You must miss her."

She shrugged. "She usually manages to take some time off when it's the holidays. Then we go away. Or else she arranges activity camps for me. Tennis or crafts or something. That's probably what will happen at half-term." She sounded resigned but unenthusiastic.

Poor kid: weeks away at boarding school and then shoved into a camp during the holidays. I couldn't imagine Olivia enjoying holiday camps: she looked more like the kind of girl who'd prefer to curl up with a good book. I hoped my pity didn't show on my face. "She lives near Wokingham, doesn't she?"

Olivia nodded. "A small village."

"Is it nice?"

Something passed over her face. "It's all right." She forked a piece of frisee lettuce. "Not like this, though." She stared through the kitchen window and across the lawn, over which long shadows fell from the oaks. Sunlight bounced back onto the stone of the old house, making it look as though someone had painted it with liquid gold. "They said this place was wonderful but I had no idea before I came here." She spoke with quiet intensity. I'd never heard a pupil in raptures about the beauty of Letchford before. In fact it had been one of the things I'd found most irritating about them in my younger days, their blindness to what was all around them. Once, aged seventeen, I'd come across a boy of about thirteen digging the point of a compass into the low limestone wall on the terrace.

"What the hell do you think you're doing?" I'd felt the sparks in my own eyes. "Leave that alone." He'd jumped away, panic in his eyes. How dare he deface the wall, *our* wall! Clara had once caught some fourth-years carving initials into one of the oaks and had given them a tongue-lashing so sharp they'd visibly quivered every time they'd spotted her. But Olivia, strange, pale, awkward Olivia, was almost vibrating in sympathy with the glowing October light and I didn't mind at all. I didn't resent her being here. I wanted to hug her, and the suddenness of the emotion startled me.

"I'll take the tray back," was all I said.

She was still staring out of the window. "Why don't you have holiday camps here?" The wistfulness in her voice was clear.

I carried the tray back across the lawn to the main kitchen, hearing the shouts of boys kicking a ball around on a field. A huddle of girls sat on a bench underneath one of the oaks and their heads were bathed in golden light. They looked as though they belonged in a painting. Soon it would be winter and the lawn and terrace would be painted frosty white. Another year would almost have passed. I felt a knot of panic in my throat that life was passing me by, my injured husband was still apart from me. At the same time I felt an urge just to let go, to let myself float along

159

to the rhythm of the school year. My father needed me here. I was useful.

Tracey was in the dining room, serving lunch, so I stacked the dishes in the dishwasher, paying close attention to getting the task exactly right, since Tracey was so particular about how the kitchen was run. Something Olivia had said back in Gavin replayed itself in my mind. "They said it was wonderful . . ." Who were "they"? Her aunt and who else? They must have come to an open day like the one we'd held here the afternoon the reborn doll was found. Such enthusiasm for the school seemed out of character for the aunt who never seemed to visit her niece.

It wasn't until the bell rang for the end of afternoon lessons that I was able to escape to my apartment with my mobile and the Delicious Confections email. Samson greeted me with ears back, tail waving. I hadn't walked him yet. "In a moment," I promised as I dialled the number.

The phone answered on the second ring. When I spun my line about having received a present with no tag the woman sounded doubtful. "I'm not sure I can give you information about our customers."

"I'd love to thank my friend," I said, trying to sound sincere. "It's a gorgeous present."

"We put a gift tag on it," she said.

"My dog tore it off," I lied. "I don't want to cause offence by thanking the wrong person. I had so many lovely gifts for my thirtieth." I hoped I didn't sound as near to vomiting as I felt.

I could hear her rustling through papers. "There was a doll sent out a few weeks back." She sounded cautious. "Whereabouts are you?"

"Oxfordshire."

"We didn't send anything there."

"But my friend doesn't live in the same county as I do." I crossed my fingers that she wouldn't ask me which county the friend did live in. Was Wokingham in Berkshire? Or was it Buckinghamshire?

"What kind of doll was it?"

I reached for the email. "A Sebastian."

"Oh, that's one of my favourites. Very popular."

"I can see why. He's adorable." My teeth wanted to crack as I told the lie. Thank God the shop assistant couldn't see the grimace on my face.

"We sold a Sebastian in September."

"Oh! I wonder if that was mine?" I held my breath.

"To a customer in a village near Wokingham."

I sat up straight. "Now I know which friend it was. Oh, how lovely of her. She knew I really wanted a Sebastian."

"They are one of our most popular reborns. And our ability to paint a real child's features onto the face makes them doubly popular." I heard the rustle of papers. "I see that's what your friend did for your reborn." Her voice had dropped to a confiding whisper.

"She's gone to so much trouble for me." I hoped that the astonishment I felt wasn't palpable in my voice. Olivia was responsible for bringing the doll into the school. "I must write and thank her," I went on. "Thing

161

is, that's a new address and she hasn't told me her postcode yet. I usually just text or Facebook her." I tried to inject sincerity into my voice. "But for something as extraordinary as this, well, I really think I should write a proper thank-you card."

"Would you like me to give you the postcode?"

"Oh, would you? It would save me having to ring her."

"RG40 9QS," she said. "Anyway, I'm glad you found out who she was. If you need any accessories for Sebastian, clothes, perhaps, or a baby carrier, just ring." She sounded so sincere in her offer that I had to gulp.

I thanked her and hung up. The question I'd been burning to ask her remained on my lips. Had there been a photograph for the artist, or however they styled themselves, to work from? If this baby had a real child's features, to whom did they belong?

I pulled up the map program on the Internet and tapped in the postcode. The satellite image of a small village, Bellingham, appeared. I zoomed in on it. There were few houses and most of them were large commuter-type places. I asked for directions from Letchford and the computer duly produced a route and told me it would take about an hour to get there. It would have to be on Saturday, when most of the pupils had gone home for half-term. My father would be expecting me to be around, I'd promised to go through some more of Mum's things with him. I'd make this trip first thing so that there was plenty of time to do that.

162

It wasn't hard to find the village of Bellingham, just a few miles north of the M4. As I'd seen from the satellite image on the Internet, it was largely comprised of big houses, none of them as old as they appeared to be at first glance. A few smaller and older-looking cottages huddled round a duck pond at one end of the green. The pub looked like a yuppified village inn, promising an extensive menu, fine wines and designer beers. I parked the car and made for the first of the three large houses opposite the pub. As I reached the door I saw two small children playing in the front garden, each of them with dark skin. Their mother was raking leaves and was as dark as the boy and girl. It didn't seem likely that this could be the pale Olivia's aunt, so I decided to save time and go to the other two houses first.

Nobody was at home in the next-door hacienda-style house. When I peeped through the letter box I could see through to the kitchen. A zimmer frame stood next to the table and next to it two pairs of slippers. Busy Lizzies spilled out of pots with butterfly patterns engraved on them. Beside the teapot sat two flowery mugs and a sugar bowl, with a plate of rich tea biscuits. I walked on.

The third house seemed more promising. Outside on the drive sat a new silver convertible. When I rang the door a suntanned woman with expensive-looking highlights in her hair answered. "Yes?"

"I've got a parcel for an Olivia Fenton. Does she live here?"

"Olivia Fenton?"

"I think that's what the address says."

"No Olivia Fenton here." She spoke with a trace of an accent, Russian perhaps. A noise behind her made her turn her head. She frowned.

"Careful, Sofia!" She added something else in a different language. It sounded Slavic.

"Sorry." Over her cashmere shoulder I saw another woman who looked as though she were in her thirties, thin and worried-looking, stoop to pick up a wastepaper basket she'd dropped on the hardwood floor.

"I must have the wrong address. Sorry to have bothered you." I smiled and walked away.

Behind the house ran a little lane, used to bring the dustbins and wheelbarrows out, I imagined. I walked along it, hoping I was safe from prying eyes. As I'd hoped, I found myself peering into the back of the house, into the large kitchen with its oak cupboards and granite worktop. Exactly the kind of house you'd expect a Letchford family to possess. Except that I didn't think the woman I'd spoken to was anything to do with Olivia. I stood still and watched. Eventually the back door opened and Sofia came out, carrying a dustpan. She emptied the contents into a black bin and put down the dustpan. After a quick glance over her shoulder she pulled a packet of cigarettes and a box of matches out of her pocket. She lit up and her face relaxed as the nicotine hit her bloodstream. Her features were pretty, I noticed, but lines and shadows had aged them. Sofia exhaled the smoke slowly and closed her eyes briefly.

"Sofia," the woman called from the house. "I'm going out now. You make a start on dinner while I'm gone? The lamb's on the kitchen table, it's nearly defrosted now. And make that soup you did last week."

"OK, Mrs Smirnova," Sofia called back, whisking the cigarette behind her back. "You have the apricots for the lamb, yes?"

"On the table with the almonds. And don't forget to polish the wine glasses." She said something else in Russian.

Sofia closed her eyes again, as though attempting to block out the sound of her employer's voice.

I waited for the sound of the Mazda to pull off the drive before I walked back to the front door and knocked again. "Hello," I said when she answered. Her pursed lips told me she was annoyed at having to stub out her cigarette. "May I come in? It's about Olivia."

Her eyes widened. "She is ill?"

"She's fine. I just want to talk."

A look of relief crossed her face and she looked past me as though to reassure herself that her employer had really left. "Just ten minutes. She doesn't like me to have visitors."

And no doubt Mrs Smirnova wouldn't welcome a niece staying with Sofia during school holidays. I entered the neat hall. Sofia nodded at me. "Yes?"

"I work at Letchford School."

She looked down at her white trainers.

"Your niece Olivia is a pupil." She said nothing. "Did you receive the message about her injury?" Still she was silent, but a muscle twitched at one side of her mouth. "It's just that it's almost half-term now and Olivia is much better. Perhaps you'd like to see her? There are some nice walks around school and Olivia could show you round. If you're working during the days I'm sure we could arrange for you to come along one evening."

"I can't see her," she muttered. "I have to work, days and evenings." The dark shadows under her eyes told the story of late nights. "But Olivia's well, that's good." She folded her arms around her body as though she were trying to defend herself. "I send her some more money last week. So she could go shopping. Buy new clothes. She grows so fast. She likes new things."

"You must work hard to keep her at Letchford." How many jobs did she have? I wondered. This one and several others. Perhaps bar work in the pub on the evenings Mrs Smirnova didn't need her for her dinner parties. The boarding fees for Letchford were £28,000 a year. Most of the parents who paid them worked in the City or ran their own successful businesses. There were bursaries, but not many because the school hadn't had the centuries of rich endowers to build up a large fund.

"I don't mind hard work." She met my gaze with a firm stare. "I do whatever is necessary. For Olivia."

"You ordered a reborn doll, didn't you?" At the cost of £195 pounds. Something passed over her face.

"And you asked them to paint a real child's features onto the doll, didn't you?"

166

She shook her head, eyes wide, scared, pointing at the door. "I don't know what you talking about."

"But the doll came to this address."

I thought I saw a glint of understanding flash across her face but it was gone as quickly as it appeared.

"You should go now, she'll be back soon. I pay the fees, Olivia is a good girl, always has good reports. She works hard at school, they say."

"The head is my father."

And now all the colour seemed to drain from her face so that she really did look like her niece. "You're his daughter?" She stared at me. "Mr Charles Statton is your father?"

I nodded. She seemed to fall into a trance. Then she blinked. "You go now." She opened the door and waved at me to leave. "Please don't come here again, Mrs Smirnova would be very angry. If you need to speak use the mobile. Or email me. I always phone back. I always pay on time. Olivia is a good girl, she work hard. We know nothing about this doll."

The door slammed behind my back.

CHAPTER
NINETEEN

"I don't understand any of it." My father sounded weary. "Why would Olivia be hiding dolls in a cupboard? She doesn't seem to be the kind of girl who'd indulge in practical jokes."

The reborn episode had been downgraded to a practical joke now. What a contrast with his paranoia last week. Dad certainly could perform a neat mental three-point turn.

"Why did you go there, Merry?" He gave me a sharp look. "I didn't ask you to do this. We have to be very careful about abusing parental privacy."

We were sitting in his office.

"Perhaps I was a bit over-impulsive," I admitted. Between us sat a pile of application letters. He was reviewing the reports on the children sitting entrance exams here at the school this week. Some were marked with letters, A, B and C. I knew it was his own personal way of categorizing the children he was really interested in, regardless of their academic talent. The governors would push him to take the brightest batch, just as they did every year. But Dad would be drawn to the interesting loner who hadn't done well in the exams, or the talented eccentric.

"One of these days he's going to choose a kid who'll bring a gun in and shoot you all," Clara had declared to me over the weekend. I'd defended him.

"They blossom here, even the loners, because we've got more time for them. Some of them go on to great things."

"Some of them," she'd said.

Olivia herself could be categorized as one of these children who bloomed in the golden-stoned environment. She was still shy but now that half-term was almost upon us her teachers were talking about new confidence. "No, Olivia doesn't seem the type for silly pranks," I agreed. "But the address was definitely hers. Or her aunt's."

"I haven't met the aunt. She doesn't often come to the school. The one time she did make an appearance at a parent-teacher evening was the night I was caught up with parents who were disappointed that we hadn't yet discovered their son's genius." He looked briefly amused. "It's unusual to have so little contact with home, though. She did actually ring me this morning to check up on Olivia but the child is so much better now that I couldn't really insist that she came and took her home. So Olivia will stay here for half-term." He examined his watch. "I should go over and check up on her in a moment."

"Let me."

Doubt covered my father's face.

"I'm not going to give her a hard time, Dad."

"You shouldn't say anything to her at all unless you've got someone else with you." He'd switched back into headmaster mode. "If it's a disciplinary matter we need to do everything in the correct manner. Especially if she is self-harming as well. This is a job for Cathy, Meredith. You need to be careful not to over-involve yourself." It was the accusation I myself had mentally made of Emily: getting too close to a pupil.

"I'm not going to bring up the subject. And I won't mention the cut on her arm."

As I left the office my father was still sitting at his desk, staring at the computer screen as though there might be something written on it which would change the facts. But I couldn't see that there was anything doubtful about what had happened. Olivia was implicated.

But when I reached the house, Olivia's housemistress told me that she'd insisted on going to play rehearsals. "I found this on the table while I was organizing the laundry."

"Gone to rehearsal," the note said. "Just for my scene." The housemistress looked anxious. "What should we do?"

"She's under supervision there," I said. "If there's a problem there are people on hand. But I'll go over and bring her back when she's finished her scene."

The sixth-former playing Judge Hathorne in *The Crucible* was so stern I found myself clenching my fists as I watched them in the scene. Jenny nodded approvingly. "I'm getting more of a sense of the passion behind this play," she told the cast when they stopped for a break. "But some of you still need to work your way into it. Have a think about it. The terror, the hysteria. The sheer insanity breaking out. Then remember that events similar to Salem were happening all across Europe and in Russia too, well within living memory. They could arrest you on phoney charges and try you without any need to prove your guilt. And then punish you severely. And of course in Miller's America there was this fear of Communism spreading, of reds under the bed."

Olivia Fenton listened with serious eyes, her face set and expressionless. She looked completely recovered now. Only the arm in a sling and a mark on her head told of her accident.

"Another thing to consider is this," Jenny went on. "It only takes one or two people to refuse to play the game, to refuse to implicate their neighbours, and the whole thing collapses. Judge Hathorne knows this: it's the one weakness in his strategy. I'd like to see more of a reaction from those of you watching the trial. As though you're changing your mind as you hear the different characters. Let's see emotion: doubt, anger, fear."

Olivia walked off the stage. She saw me and flushed. "I just wanted to do my scene."

"You were supposed to be resting. You've had a serious head injury. Go back over to the house now."

"I'll keep an eye on Olivia." I hadn't noticed Emily before. Now she was standing beside Olivia.

"As soon as it's over you go back." I ignored Emily. "And Olivia . . ."

She nodded. "I know. I should have asked first before I came over here. I'm sorry, Mrs Cordingley."

Emily was watching our interaction intently. She'd continued to attend rehearsals, though her role was that of wardrobe mistress. Apparently she was working late on the costumes each night.

Half-term was in a few days' time. I wondered if Emily would take the opportunity to go off to London or somewhere else with more diversions than Letchford. I asked what her plans were for the coming week.

"I haven't planned anything yet." Her hands knotted together in her lap. "I thought I'd just stay here. Perhaps go up to London for a day or two."

"You should. There's plenty to see. Shame for you to spend all your time in the country."

"But it's so beautiful."

"London's worth spending time in. Or you could visit Bath. Or even Edinburgh."

"Perhaps."

I had to admit that the prospect of a few days without Emily hanging around Letchford was inviting. I couldn't understand why I disliked her so much. *Disliked.* I was able to admit to that word now. But why? She was efficient and helpful around the school. The younger children seemed to like her and she was good at getting on with the older pupils. She took on tasks teachers were glad to hand over: tidying classrooms, hunting for lost memory sticks and exercise books, stepping in to take over breaktime duties. The objection to putting out the hockey cones had been the only one of its kind. And then there were the costumes. Apparently she'd been meticulously researching and

172

designing and sewing them, with the help of a group of sixth-formers.

"I'd say she'd make a good teacher," Deidre had said in the White Oak that evening while Emily was in the Ladies. "There's something very intense about the way she works. And she has real maturity. Some of the gappies we get need almost as much attention as the children."

"Perhaps." Simon had poured himself another glass of wine.

"She said her father'd worked in a school," Deidre went on.

"The teaching gene can run in families. My dad was a teacher, so was his father." Simon had nodded at me. "And look at Mrs Meredith Cordingley here. When she's standing at the front of the classroom you can see her father in her, can't you?"

Deidre had smiled. "I've noticed that, too. It's that gleam in the eye when they talk about their favourite subjects."

Me, like my father? I'd always thought that Clara was the one of us who'd inherited Dad's force and drive. I'd imagined myself more like my mother, happy to drift along in life. But perhaps they were right, perhaps there was something of Dad in me. I felt like a bit of a child, suddenly pleased that they thought I resembled my father.

But now my mind went back to Emily. Something about her made me nervous. She seemed to be watching us carefully, looking out for something. But I was being silly: Emily was young, away from home, a long way from home, for the first time. She was bound to be feeling uncertain among strangers and it would be this that would be making her seem awkward. I should be more tolerant.

I looked again at Emily now. For all the warmth of the gym the girl shivered in her expensive-looking petrol-blue jumper and the long, very casual but equally costly hooded grey cardigan that had replaced the silk one she'd worn earlier in the term. She must have saved up for this trip to England. Or come from a well-off family. I wondered whether she'd thought some more about studying for A levels. Strange situation for her, helping the teachers, being on their side, but really not being any more qualified than some of the sixth-formers here in this rehearsal.

Jenny clapped her hands to hush everyone and the rehearsal resumed. Olivia was in the next scene and stood ready to take to the stage, script in hand, moving her lips as she memorized her lines. She still wore her school pullover, sleeves dangling over her wrists. I wondered whether she'd harmed herself again and hoped that Cathy Jordan's interventions would be enough to stop the girl from taking another knife to herself. The thought of her deliberately cutting her pale skin made my stomach turn cold. All the blood flowing in Helmand Province and yet people could still choose to inflict wounds on themselves. I reminded myself what it was like to be a teenage girl: the academic and social pressures, the insecurities, and told myself not to be so judgemental. Olivia was pretty: I noticed the boys watching her as she stood on the stage. Beneath her shapeless jumper a slim but slightly curved figure could be made out. Her hair was thick and brown and although her face was pale its features were delicate and perfectly proportioned, with high cheekbones and those grey eyes. Emily was watching her, too, brow slightly furrowed.

I found myself wishing it was already half-term. Whatever was unfolding in this gymnasium was winding itself around me. I didn't understand it but I didn't like it. The remaining forty-eight hours could not go quickly enough for me.

CHAPTER
TWENTY

First morning of half-term. I lay back in bed and let the shadows from the curtains blow backwards and forwards over my face. Peace. Samson snoozed beside me in his basket. Soon he'd want to be let out; it was nearly eight. But I could enjoy just another five minutes before . . .

My mobile made a sound I hadn't heard for a long time. I reached out and grabbed it from the bedside table, almost uncertain what the two-tone ring meant. Incoming text. I didn't have much call to send or receive them here, as everyone I needed to speak to was on hand. I opened the message and the sender's name made me sit bolt upright in bed. Hugh. *Just wondering how you were. Sorry, really none of my biz. now.*

I switched off the mobile with a shaking hand. This was not how I had imagined starting the first day of half-term. I'd promised myself tranquillity: a long walk with the dog without the need to keep peering at my watch in case we were running short of time. Lunch in the pub with Simon and then sorting out Mum's clothes. With a possible early evening cinema outing afterwards, if the previous exertions hadn't worn me out. Communication with my husband hadn't been on my list. I got up and carried out my morning tasks, the mood spoiled even though I forced myself to have a long, hot shower instead of the usual working-day quick one. I needed to respond to the text message. I needed to untangle the twisted emotions that stopped this from being a straightforward task. But first I'd check on Dad, see if he needed help with arrangements for the entrance examinations.

Today I'd expected to feel the relief I'd felt as a child when term had ended, the pupils had gone home and we'd had Letchford to ourselves again. For a week or four or eight Clara and I could slide down banisters and make a noise at any time of the day anywhere we wanted. But as I approached the lawns in front of the house they seemed lonely and abandoned. I took the dog home and then walked over to the big house. The quietness pressed itself into my head. As I entered through the oak doors I almost longed to hear the roar of an approaching classful of pupils returning from a games lesson out on the fields, the low laughter of sixth-form girls gliding along the terrace on the way to the art studio.

The pupils' absence had dissolved the protective membrane between us and the memories layered in the house. I realized how much I'd let myself be distracted away from the reality of my mother's death. I'm sorry, I told her silently. Instead of going into Oxford perhaps I'd spend the afternoon in her garden, doing all the things the school gardener wouldn't have had time to do: deadheading the remaining roses and sweeping leaves. I'd pick the last of the asters and put them on her grave.

Her grave. It seemed bizarre that she lay in the churchyard. Surely she must really be upstairs in the apartment, helping with preparations for the entrance exams?

A footstep behind me made me jump. I turned to see Olivia Fenton standing by the door.

"Sorry, Mrs Cordingley, I just wanted to get some bread from the kitchen. There isn't any over at the house."

I wondered whether her aunt had told her about my visit to her workplace yet. The workplace that had been given as Olivia's home.

"Help yourself." I hoped I looked relaxed, teacher-out-of-term-ish. "What have you got planned for today, Olivia?"

"Emily's going to take me shopping later."

"That's nice." I wished I meant it. Olivia gave a half-shrug, looking unsure. I wondered if she had much money to spend on clothes and accessories. That aunt worked hard, no doubt about it, but she must be living on air if she was paying all the fees by herself. "Have you heard from . . . home?" I went on. "Presumably they know you're better now?"

She concentrated on an invisible spot on the marble floor. "Yes."

"Olivia . . ."

She looked up at me, her shoulders tense again.

"Did your aunt tell you I'd spoken to her? That I'd been out to the house where she . . . lives a few days ago?"

Her eyes widened. "She hasn't said anything," she mumbled. Without another word she spun round on her heel and headed towards the kitchen.

"Olivia!" I called after her. She stopped. "I haven't finished talking to you."

"I'm sorry, Mrs Cordingley." She hung her head.

"Oh, off you go."

I'd handled that well, hadn't I? I found myself walking upstairs to my father's apartment. I couldn't get used to the change in terminology. Not my parents' home any longer; just my father's. I knocked on the door and he called for me to come in. He was in his office, the files open in front of him. Beside him was a scrap of paper. He'd been drawing on it: a figure emerging from or vanishing into trees. I tried not to show my surprise. I thought he'd push it aside or hide it under one of the files, but he didn't.

"I find myself doing it more and more in the last few days," he said. "At first I felt almost ashamed of it, as though it were a bad habit. What you said to me about teaching art made me think. I don't want to teach it. But I want to let myself sketch."

Let himself. An interesting way of putting it.

"As a boy I sketched all the time."

"Were you still out in the country then?" In the wooden-shuttered house in the Bohemian forest. I was trying to look at the sketch more closely but its small

179

size and the fact that the pad was upside down made it hard to make out whose likeness it was.

"That's right. The people who'd moved into the house with us were not . . . sympathetic. As a lad I used to take my drawing things into the forest."

I glanced down at what he was sketching. Trees, dark and foreboding. A slight figure, sex unknown, peering from behind a pine. "Who's that?" I asked.

"A ghost," he said, smiling and sitting back in his chair. "What did you want to see me about, Meredith?"

"Nothing in particular. Just checking that everything was in order for the entrance exams."

"Samantha has it all organized." He patted the pile of files. "She'll be in tomorrow." He looked at me as though giving me permission to leave him and get on with enjoying my day off.

"I just saw Olivia. I'm still worried about her."

"She seemed fine when I saw her earlier on. Emily is looking after her." He raised an eyebrow. "Though perhaps that's one of the things that's worrying you?"

"Yes."

"There's not much we can do. Olivia's aunt can't have her for the holiday and nobody else has invited her to stay with them." I felt a pang for Olivia. "So we should be grateful that Emily is taking an interest."

"The cutting, self-harming . . ."

"Appears to have stopped." He peered at me. "Cathy Jordan has been monitoring Olivia. She is good at counselling, you know."

I had to push my prejudice aside and agree. Cathy seemed to have nipped a few cases of anorexia in the

180

bud last term, I remembered. And had insisted on referring a more seriously affected girl to a specialist in Oxford, despite her parents' assertions that their daughter was just suffering from exam nerves.

But what about Emily, I thought. Cathy had no jurisdiction over her.

He was frowning at me. "Why are you so anxious, Merry? Why now?"

"Why are you drawing again?" I looked at him directly. Take the fight to him. "Or rather, why did you stop for so many years? I know you're busy but there have been those long summer holidays."

"Perhaps we both need our own displacement activities at the moment." I had to lean forward to hear him. "I don't know what's making me want to draw again. Perhaps it's normal, when you've lost someone, to look back to the earlier part of your life, to be the person you were then, before adult life swept you up."

He'd given up his childhood as soon as he'd reached England, obtaining a scholarship to study German at university before going on to teacher training college. "Britain took me in," he had always told me. "This was a generous country."

But his painting had been discarded. Was he regretting this now? Perhaps every time he passed the mural in the entrance hall he asked himself why he'd let it go. Perhaps he was asking himself whether the sacrifice had been a worthwhile one.

I sensed that the revived interest in drawing was a delicate flower. If I commented too much on it he'd

181

give up. "I'd better go," I said. "I'm having lunch with Simon. I'll be back to sort out Mum's things later."

"You've earned it," he said. "Seriously, Merry, I don't think I've told you how grateful I am to you for all you've done for me and the school since your mother died."

"It's nothing." I sounded gruff. Anything else would have finished me off.

CHAPTER
TWENTY-ONE

"You might as well spit it out." Simon was on to his second glass of Merlot and let out the long breath of a teacher who wouldn't be seeing any of his pupils for a week.

I started to apologize again for being late for our lunch-time meeting, but he held up his hand. "No need for that, just tell me what you've been up to these last few days." His eyes glinted with amusement. "I've hardly seen you and you've obviously got a guilty conscience, Meredith."

I blushed. "I don't know if you'll approve."

"Try me."

I told him about driving to Bellingham a few days earlier, tracking down Olivia's aunt at her employer's house. About Olivia's reaction outside the kitchen when I'd met her this morning. He frowned. "Not sure I do approve, actually. Does your father know you did this?"

I nodded. "He shares your opinion." My cheeks burned.

"And the aunt denied having had anything to do with it?"

"She looked flustered."

"Doesn't prove she or Olivia had anything to do with the doll, though. She was probably just worried sick you'd be caught with her and her unpleasant-sounding employer would be angry."

"But don't you think it's strange, the whole set-up, the aunt working her fingers off to keep Olivia here? I don't know how she can possibly pay the fees."

"But she obviously manages. Perhaps Olivia has a bursary?"

"I don't think so. Dad's never said."

"He's always very discreet, though, isn't he?" Simon finished his glass. "I must be getting on. I promised myself a trip to Burford. There's a second-hand bookshop I need to visit." He looked suddenly shy. I thought he was about to ask me to go with him. After all, we had talked about the outing. But the invitation didn't come. I noticed how a little smile was fixed to his face these days.

"Lovely drive." I gave up on my scallops, delicious as they were.

"I've been looking forward to it." He reached for his jacket. "Just one thing, Meredith. What exactly are you trying to find out here? Olivia Fenton's just a girl from a poor family who are trying to give her the best education possible. That may mean they can't see as much of her as you think they should, but that's their choice. Olivia's well looked after here. Emily seems to be taking an interest."

"That's what worries me." I spoke without thinking.

"Why?" He looked startled.

I shrugged. "Emily's strange. I'm just wondering . . ." I didn't finish the sentence. I didn't want to tell him what I'd started to suspect.

Simon put on his jacket but didn't make a move towards the pub door. "What about Hugh? You haven't mentioned him for ages. Have you heard anything?"

I told him about the text.

"You don't think that all this fascination with Emily and Olivia and the reborn doll is just a way of distracting yourself from the real issue in your life?"

He spoke so softly I couldn't be angry with him. "Perhaps," I said, feeling suddenly lonely, wishing he'd ask me to go with him to the second-hand bookshop.

But he didn't. "Go home and ring up your husband, Meredith. You know that's what needs doing."

I opened my mouth to dispute this, to tell him to mind his own business, but I closed it again.

CHAPTER
TWENTY-TWO

As I walked up the lane from the White Oak my mobile trilled. I yanked it out of my pocket without even glancing at the screen. "Hello?" I thought it might be Simon, calling to suggest a drink later on, keen to dispel any awkwardness following our meeting.

"Meredith."

My husband's voice made every muscle in my body contract. But he'd called me by my full name; I was no longer Merry.

"Is that you?" He sounded unsure of himself.

"Yes." The sound came out as a kind of squeak.

"I sent you a text this morning."

"I got it. Just haven't had a chance to reply yet." But why lie? "Actually, I didn't have a clue what to say. You caught me by surprise." I sounded more like myself.

"I know. After I sent it I was kicking myself for being such a damn coward. I should just have rung you."

"Like you're doing now." In the past months I'd played a hundred possible conversations with my husband, thought up clever arguments and ripostes. Now they'd all abandoned me and I couldn't think of anything to say. I couldn't even interpret my own reaction to hearing his voice after such a long time.

"Can I come and see you?"

No, I wanted to say. *Stay away, don't upset me any more.* "I'm not sure," I muttered. "I need to look at my diary. I'm away from my desk at the moment."

He didn't ask where exactly I was. "How are you, anyway?" I went on. "What's happening with the leg?"

"The new one's going to be fitted soon. It's a new design, designed for more active pursuits. I'm still aiming for the skiing at Christmas. I'm doing lots of rehab. Mum's been driving me around." I felt a cold pain: jealousy of his widowed mother who had no other children apart from Hugh and who'd been at least as desperate about him as I had. I felt ashamed of myself.

A pause. "The hand's much better, too. I can type a little and it's not much worse than it was before when I had all my fingers."

I couldn't help a laugh. "That's not saying much."

"And it's not just been my body that's been healing, it's my mind, too. I've had time to think." I had to hold the mobile right against my ear to hear the words, so soft had his voice become. "There are things that need saying, But in person, not over a phone."

"OK." I could feel part of my resistance crumbling. "How mobile are you?"

"I hope to be driving soon but in the meantime there's always the train."

"I could pick you up from the station. It's half-term this week."

"I know. I checked the website."

"Just don't come on Thursday because there are entrance exams here and it'll be heaving with kids and

187

parents. Friday would work for me." Specifying a day made me feel a little more in control.

"I'll ring you when I've checked the train times. It'll be good to see you . . ." He trailed off.

I thought of when I'd seen him after he'd come out of his coma, and found himself in a hospital ward in Selly Oak. He'd screamed at me to go away because he'd thought he was still in danger. I'd held his hand and talked to him until the black circles that were his pupils contracted back and he stopped shaking. Then he'd clutched my hand with his uninjured hand and I thought he'd crush my bones. "Look forward to it." My voice trembled. "Text me the time your train gets in." I ended the call before I could give myself away.

I was trembling. All the buttresses I'd built to prop me up: new job, new friends, new surroundings, had proved themselves to be as fragile as the late asters swaying in the flowerbeds.

I walked deliberately slowly over to the big house, making myself take in every detail of the October afternoon to distract myself. Sun already low so that it stroked the front of the building, bringing the shapes of the bushes into sharp relief. A pheasant coughing behind me in the woods. Again I found myself missing the pupils: their breath steaming in the cooling air as they ran in from rugby or hockey, boots pounding over the grass.

Neither my father nor I had been able to face Mum's clothes until now. I opened the heavy oak door. As I walked inside Dad was standing at the top of the stairs, holding something in his hand. At the same time as I

188

entered Olivia and Emily came into the hall from the back of the house, passing in front of the mural. Dad looked down at them. He made a low exclamation and dropped a photograph. It fluttered halfway down the steps.

"I'll get it for you, Mr Statton." Olivia ran up the stairs. As she stretched out her hand to pick up the photo I saw she was wearing a red elastic band around her wrist.

"Charles?" Samantha came out of the apartment behind my father, a frown on her face. "What is it? You look as though you've seen a ghost."

He took the photo from Olivia and blinked. "Thank you." He seemed to give himself a mental shake and switched on his headmasterly smile. "What brings you to the house?" Olivia looked at Emily, as though waiting for her to give the right answer.

"I left my laptop in the staffroom," Emily said. "We just came in to get it."

He stood back to let them pass him on the stairs, still gazing at Olivia. I followed them up to where my father was standing.

"Charles." Samantha sounded sharp. "Are you all right?"

He blinked. "Just a little weary suddenly. Excuse me. Here's the photograph. It came out fairly well, though you'll notice that my daughters didn't succeed in scraping off the top layer uniformly."

She took the photograph. I was close enough to look over her shoulder at it. Years fell away and I was ten again, staring at the forbidden woman on the wall. I felt my spine grow cold as the emotions of that day washed over me. Mum and Dad, so angry. My sister so anxious about the parental anger. Myself, half curious, half penitent.

Samantha turned to me. "I never knew that there was something underneath that mural before today, when your father told me."

"I hope he didn't tell you how it came to be uncovered."

She looked puzzled. Dad simply laughed. "Perhaps that story's for another time." I was surprised he'd shown her the photograph. I hadn't known he'd taken it. He'd been so keen to cover up the hidden woman.

After the big telling-off on the day, nothing more had been said about our terrible act of vandalism, as my father referred to it. I had kept expecting a punishment but it hadn't come. It was as though the shock caused by the paint-stripping had shaken everyone so much that nobody could act. I'd heard my father in his office making calls but because it was Saturday nobody seemed to be there to speak to him. Later in the evening the art teacher had been called in to advise on what we should do. ". . . Sand down the worst of it and simply repaint over it," I heard him say to my father.

Clara and I had lain in bed too miserable to talk. At least, I was miserable. It was hard to tell with Clara. Sometimes she went silent for reasons I couldn't understand. "She needs to be alone with her own thoughts," my mother would say. "Not like you, you chatterbox." Tonight I didn't feel like chattering. The woman on the wall was on my mind. I waited until

190

Clara's breathing became slow and even and slipped out of bed. My father only locked the apartment door when he and my mother went to bed, so it opened to my careful touch. I crept downstairs. The hall light was on and I could see the painted woman clearly. There hadn't been time to study her properly before. I'd thought of her as dangerous when I'd first seen her, but now, at night, she seemed to wear an expression more poignant than menacing. "You look sad," I told her. "They're going to paint over you, you know." The wind blew against the windows and the hall seemed suddenly lonely and at the same time filled with the presence of the past. And now the woman's eyes seemed to hint at something beyond my understanding, something I could feel but not describe.

I'd fled upstairs, creeping speedily in through the unlocked door and not breathing until I was back in my bed, covers pulled over my head as though whatever I'd sensed in the hall downstairs might take form and chase after me.

I could feel those same emotions in the hallway now. Not the shame, perhaps, but the other ones: the longing, the mixture of grief and joy. But I felt them from my father and they were directed at the two young women who had just passed him on their way to the staffroom. He saw me looking at him and dropped his eyes, his face shocked.

"What is it?" I asked. He shook his head.

"Sometimes I think I'm being haunted." He seemed to shake himself out of his trance. "Come on. Let's get cracking on your mother's things."

CHAPTER
TWENTY-THREE

I drove to meet Hugh at the station. Out of cowardice I loaded the dog into the car at the last moment. At least he'd provide a topic of conversation if things grew difficult. Samson's hot canine breath was reassuring on the side of my face. He gave a low contented sigh and settled into the passenger seat. Perhaps he thought we were off on an expedition culminating in a long walk. There was no knowing how he'd respond to seeing his master again. Hugh had been his first love. He loved me, too, but it had been Hugh who'd rescued Samson from a bombed house in Iraq when he'd been posted out there, who'd found someone to patch up his wounds and vaccinate him, who'd somehow managed to fly him home and put him into quarantine until he could come to live with us in Wiltshire.

"There's a bit of something smart in him," Hugh'd told me, showing off the dog in the kennels when we went to visit him. "Look at the shape of his head. He's probably descended from some aristocratic Babylonian dog. A palace dog, or something."

I'd tried hard to see this pedigree in the friendly mutt wagging his mottled grey-and-white tail at me. "If you say so."

I'd agreed to stay in the car in the pick-up area outside the station. I clutched the steering wheel, feeling the blood pulse around my body. I was still expecting Hugh to move like the man I'd seen months back: slowly, with obvious pain; but he'd reached the car and was opening the passenger door before I'd noticed him coming across the concourse. He wore jeans and a V-neck jumper rather than uniform or the tracksuits of the rehabilitation unit. I noted a couple of young women queuing for a bus glancing at him. I felt a prickle of possessiveness even though I wasn't sure I had any remaining rights to feel like that. "You made me jump," I said, to cover my awkwardness.

"Sorry." He was engaged with the dog, whose tail was flying around like a windmill. Hugh tried to push him onto the back seat so that he could get inside the car but Samson was having none of it.

"You'll have to have him on your lap," I said at last. I felt flat. The dog so obviously had eyes for nobody except Hugh and Hugh had hardly spoken a word to me yet. And I'd hardly greeted him with great warmth.

"That's OK." He bent to push his head down to the dog, crooning at him. The dog's tail was moving so quickly it could have sliced cheese. I noticed that the hair had grown back on the area of Hugh's skull the shrapnel had cut. I didn't dare glance down at his legs but he seemed to get into the car with only the slightest awkwardness. "Been practising," he said. "Getting up and down as often as I can. This car is lower than the one I'll be buying soon. I chose a small jeep because the seats are higher off the ground."

"It's great that you'll be driving again."

"I had to sell the Cooper."

I knew how much he'd loved that car.

"But it's great to have wheels again. Only short distances for now. In case I get migraines." He raised his fingers to the side of his head.

I had to bite my tongue to stop myself asking questions. Where he was living. What his plans for his future career were. Whether he intended to have a civilized talk with me about how we might bring the marriage to an end. But I kept my eyes on the road. We didn't speak. It would only take twenty minutes to get home when there was no rush-hour traffic but it already felt like the longest journey I'd ever made.

"It's been ages since I was last here," Hugh said at last, lifting his head from the dog. "Before Afghanistan."

Before Afghanistan. BA. Our new measurement of time. "Still pretty much the same as it was. Barring a few interesting developments." I told him how I'd tracked the reborn doll to a parent's address, but she'd denied any knowledge of it.

"Weird stuff," was all he commented.

I turned off the main road and pulled into the drive. "The place looks good," he said. And it did. The colour of the trees lining the drive was a few weeks past its best but enough of the golden and red leaves remained to be striking. "We missed this so much out in Helmand. The colours, the soft light. Sometimes, at dawn and dusk, you get the most wonderful light out there, though."

"Afghanistan looks monochrome when you see it on the TV news." Dun-coloured, arid, dusty. The kind of landscape humans weren't designed to inhabit.

"You still watch it?"

"Afghanistan?" I shook my head. "But I once looked on a Google map to see where you . . . where . . ."

"Where it had happened." His voice was neutral. Perhaps he'd gone past the stage of even feeling emotional when he discussed the explosive device.

"The landscape didn't look very inviting."

He laughed. "The mountains can be stunning, in its defence. And the irrigated fields can be picturesque: fertile and full of fruit. And there are wonderful mosques and forts in Herat. They produce good pottery and glass there, as well." He looked down at the small rucksack he'd brought with him. "But the part we were in didn't have much going for it."

I swung the car round into the stables. Once, I reflected, this courtyard would have been full of the sound of horses' hooves and grooms whistling and talking, the clink of tack, the sweeping of brushes in the stalls. Now it was quiet and neat with its planted urns of red geraniums. I wasn't sure why this somewhat lonely thought had struck me just now. Hugh was looking around in silence. "Do you remember these old stables? I'm in the grooms' apartment above."

"I remember your father converting it. Just as I first went out to Afghanistan."

We got out. I kept my eyes on the front door so that I didn't have to observe him negotiating the car door. The stairs up to the apartment were broad and shallow.

My mother had thought carefully when they'd had it converted, installing handrails on each side of the stairs so that they would be able to manage them in older age. She'd seen herself as older and frailer but still living here. Nobody could have believed that she'd be in her grave by her sixty-third birthday. Sixty-three was young.

"This is me." I unlocked the upper door. He gazed around at the bare walls. "Haven't had time to sort things out properly yet," I said.

"Me neither." He glanced at me.

"Coffee?"

"Great." He followed me out to the kitchen. Samson flopped into his bed underneath the worktop with a sigh of content. Both the people he loved most under the same roof again. I'd bought a new tin of the coffee Hugh had always preferred. The lid was impossible to unscrew. He held out a hand for it. I wondered how he'd manage with that maimed left hand of his but his strength was still there. "Just a fortnight ago that would have had me foxed," he admitted, handing the tin back. "Though I'm right-handed it's amazing how much you rely on the other hand for grip."

I handed him a mug. "We could sit, if —"

"No." A flash of something furious in his eyes. "I don't need to sit. I'm quite capable of standing like everyone else."

"I wouldn't mind sitting down." I felt weary. It was often like this at half-term. "I'll make the coffee first."

"I'm sorry." He gave a half-smile. "I'm like an explosive myself. This injury's left me paranoid. I think

196

everyone's out to get me. Or that they're implying I can't cope."

"That's understandable, that you should think like that, I mean." I was worried he might think I meant it was understandable people should imply he was paranoid.

"Other people aren't like this. Other survivors."

"Someone tried to kill you. That would make me feel uncertain about other humans."

He gave me a long look. "Yes, that's exactly how it feels. Someone tried to kill me. And they killed two of my men." His eyes narrowed. My heart felt like melted toffee, knowing how this must hurt. "It makes me furious, Meredith. But the anger seems to want to come out in the wrong places." I remembered the fury he'd shown in the rehabilitation unit and tried not to show this memory in my face. But it must have been there. "There's so much I need to say to you."

"You don't have to." I felt scared, even though I'd waited for such a moment for so long. Something bitter flooded my taste buds. I didn't think I'd be able to drink the coffee.

"I'd like to."

"I think you really will have to let me sit down, then."

He grinned. We sat opposite one another in the sitting room. I wondered if he'd noticed how sparsely I'd furnished it, as though I wasn't sure I'd be here for long. "I said awful things to you," he said. "I'm sorry. You were far and away the last person who deserved them." He didn't say he hadn't meant what he'd said, though. "When I heard you'd left the camp and given up your old job and come back here I felt . . . well, I was appalled that I'd had that effect on you. You liked that school. You were doing so well there."

"I don't mind this one."

"Of course not. But you wouldn't have come back here if what happened hadn't happened."

"I was probably due a change of school. And with Mum dying it was as well I was here."

"I still can't believe she's gone." And his face fell under a shadow. But we were skirting round the topic. I told myself not to make it too easy for him; something told me that wasn't what he wanted from this meeting. He needed to say what was on his mind without me pushing him off course.

"I've caused you grief and I'm truly sorry." He paused. "But I just don't know how we go forward. I don't know what you want to do. Or what I want to do either. I feel as if I'm not the person I was before the bomb. It's changed me. I want to spend some time getting to know myself again. It's selfish, I know. They've taken me off some of the drugs I was taking earlier on. That's made me feel calmer but I'm still not right."

"I wouldn't want to stop you doing anything you wanted to do." My voice sounded tight. "I'd want to help you."

"I've seen what happens to some wives of injured servicemen. It's like having a child to look after. Today's a good day. Not all of them are like this. My leg is still painful. Most nights I find it hard to sleep. During the day all my thoughts are concentrated on doing what is necessary to keep me on this." He raised his leg a little, with a grimace. "You don't know how many physio sessions and how many days' rest this trip has taken."

"Are you saying" — I took a breath — "that it's over?" Better to get this bit out in the open. No point letting it hang over us.

He hesitated. "I'm not saying that. But I can't go off again and leave you hanging on waiting for me. That's not fair. I think you should decide what you want to do, independent of what I may or may not decide I want." His voice softened. "You're only twenty-nine. Too young to be kept dangling."

"But do you" — I struggled to control my voice — "still love me?"

He took his time again. "When I was travelling here I kept telling myself I didn't. It was what I'd been telling myself at times in the unit."

I willed myself to keep my face impassive.

"But as soon as I saw you in the car waiting for me, with Samson, it took me back to all those times you were there waiting for me to come home, of how I'd look forward to seeing you. And of how I'd thought of you just before I'd passed out. And those feelings took me by surprise. The counsellor I've been seeing told me it might be like that but I didn't believe her."

A counsellor. Thank God someone had sorted that out for him. "I was surprised at how I felt when I saw you, too." I said the words carefully.

"You can't have been looking forward to seeing me." His blue eyes met mine.

"Not entirely." It was a relief to admit this. "But now I have seen you perhaps it's a bit the same for me. I can't see how we can go on like this. But on the other hand," — I struggled for composure — "I can't look at you and not have the old feelings for you. It's still there." I touched my throat as though whatever I felt for my husband was resident there. *Fool*, I scolded myself. *You shouldn't have admitted so much. You've left him with all the emotional cards.*

"So what do we do?"

I shrugged. "I don't know. I need to think."

He nodded. "Perhaps I shouldn't have come here today but I felt I had to apologize. And try and explain. Why I'm the way I am now, I mean."

"You don't need to explain."

"I thought I'd been out of it all the time since the bomb went off." He focused on a spot above my head. "But there is something I remember, or think I do. When they were loading me onto the Globemaster plane at Camp Bastion I think I regained consciousness briefly. I thought I was in the belly of a big grey whale. And the lines and tubes going into me were fishing lines. I thought I was a fish that a whale had eaten. Then a nurse stroked my hand and told me I was coming home. That I'd see you. And I felt a wave of, I don't know, bliss. Exultation because I knew you'd be waiting for me."

"Probably the drugs, inducing euphoria," I said. "Or adrenaline." I couldn't let myself accept what he was saying. It would mean letting down my defences.

"Perhaps. Perhaps not." He dropped his head towards the dog, now lying over his trainered feet. "Could we take him for a walk?"

Samson raised his ears and whined.

We headed out towards the woods. "We can start off here and then wind round back towards the house," I said. "Dogs aren't really allowed but you might like to have a quick look at the place."

"I'd like to say hello to your father." He looked awkward. "Can't get used to it just being your father. Your mother was great, Meredith, sending me cards regularly. And books."

I hadn't known that. "She missed you." Damn. Another weakness admitted to. To cover my annoyance I found myself moving faster. Then I remembered Hugh's new leg and slowed down.

"Don't worry about me. I need to speed up."

"You'll probably end up even faster than you were before." I remembered walks when his long strides had left me tearing along to keep up with him.

"At least I'll have one leg I don't have to worry about breaking when I go skiing."

Above us in the west I spotted a Globemaster plane curving round to land at RAF Lyneham, bringing home the dead rather than the wounded. I glanced away. But Hugh had spotted the plane. "Another poor sod coming home."

He kept his eyes on the plane until it curved out of sight behind the hills, and I could feel emotion coming off him. The autumn sun, fitful today, came out from behind a cloud and gilded him in its rays. He reminded me of a knight. His face was solemn: pensive, yet not broken. A small ripple of hope ran through me and I tried to smooth it over so that it wouldn't show on my face.

"When the bomb went off the blast wave didn't just cut off my leg and fingers. It shook my brain." He said it dispassionately but his hands were curled into fists. I remembered what the nurse had shown me with the orange but said nothing. "I feel better since they changed the drugs, calmer. But I don't know what damage's been done here." He tapped his head. "And nobody can tell me."

I put out a hand towards him but an invisible barrier seemed to prevent it from making contact with his arm. He didn't seem to notice the gesture.

"Shall we turn for the house?" was all he said.

As we reached the steps up from the terrace we met Cathy. I'd imagined she'd be away from school this week, as she wasn't involved in the entrance exams. "Ah, Meredith." The sight of Hugh beside me made her widen her eyes.

See, I wanted to tell her, *perhaps I'm not as mucked up as you think. My husband wants to see me, be with me. Don't count your chickens*, I reminded myself, immediately. Nothing he'd said had indicated a firm commitment to a future together. I nodded at her. "Just on the way to see Dad." I didn't introduce Hugh to her, even though he stopped to nod at her.

"Who was that?" he asked, when we'd moved on.

"School nurse," I said. For a moment I toyed with telling him how she probably still believed I'd put the

202

reborn into the history room cupboard. But I didn't want to talk about the wretched doll again. It seemed to insinuate itself into every situation.

My father was tidying up after the examinations: placing scripts in piles to post to teachers away for the holidays for marking. I hadn't told him Hugh was coming today. I'd felt superstitious that he might change his mind and not turn up. "Quite a good set of candidates," my father said as we walked in, without lifting his head. He turned when I didn't answer. "Oh, Hugh." A note of wonder in his voice. He stood up. "It's really you. At last." I'd forgotten or put out of my mind how fond of Hugh Dad had always been. The son he'd never had, perhaps. "Are you staying long?" He cast a hopeful look in my direction as he came towards us, arm out, looking as though he wanted to do more than shake hands, as though he wanted to embrace Hugh.

"Just a day trip." Hugh stepped forward and shook my father's hand. I noticed my father make the downward glance at his new leg beneath the new and expensive-looking jeans. "It's good to see you, too. I was so sorry about Susan."

"Thank you for your letter." Dad was still holding his hand. "I hope you got the card I sent back?"

Hugh nodded. I hadn't known that Hugh had written to Dad.

If she'd been here now my mother would have held out her arms and Hugh would have stepped into them, probably even keener to see her and Dad than he had been me, I thought. I couldn't remember whether he'd even given me a peck on the cheek when he'd got into the car at the station.

I felt rage, hot and sour, sweep over me. What a cosy little pair Dad and Hugh made. He seemed happy enough to see my father. And the dog. It was obviously just me, his wife, who was the problem. I stooped down to Samson and patted his head so that they wouldn't see the emotion on my face. *Pull yourself together,* I ordered myself. *You're like a jealous first-year. Or the envious little sister you were all those years ago when Clara seemed to have everything you didn't.*

"You look better than I expected," my father told him. "When Meredith described your injuries . . ." He shook his head.

"Been lucky with my treatment. The doctors and nurses and physios are great. Hard on me, you wouldn't believe how hard, but great."

"They've done a good job," Dad said.

"I'll probably pay for today tomorrow, if you see what I mean."

Someone knocked on the door. Olivia popped her head around. "Please, Mr Statton, can I help you with anything?"

"Emily not around?"

"She's gone into town. I didn't want to go." She was wearing a jumper with the arms rolled up. The red rubber band was still around her right wrist.

"There's nothing I can think of," Dad said. "Oh, hang on, why don't you help me sort out the filing. Mrs Evans would be grateful."

Samantha had long been complaining about Dad's filing. Hugh watched Olivia leave the room.

"What is it?" I asked him.

"Who's that?"

"A pupil. Olivia Fenton. She's staying at school over the half-term."

"I'd better go too," Dad said, holding out his hand again to Hugh. "Good seeing you."

"That girl Olivia's a bit of a mystery altogether," I told Hugh when we were alone again. I explained what I knew about Olivia's aunt in Bellingham and her job as a housekeeper, and the connection with the reborn doll. "I shouldn't be telling you all this, really. Dad doesn't approve of what I've been up to, all the sleuthing."

"She doesn't look the kind who'd do something daft like that," he said.

I knew what he meant. Olivia had a wide-eyed, honest look about her. And yet I still had the feeling of her hiding something away from us all. Secrets. Even if she'd had nothing to do with the reborn there was something Olivia was worried about.

"Shame about her arms though," he went on. "All those little scars. What happened?"

He always did have an eye for small details. "You noticed too. I think she's self-harming."

"What?"

I explained how teenagers sometimes responded to stress or unhappiness by cutting themselves.

He looked appalled. "Can't you do something?"

"The school nurse's been talking to her. It seems to have stopped now." I paused, thinking of Emily. "I think she might have had a kind of accomplice or partner."

He frowned.

"The gap-year student, Emily. I've started to suspect that she's doing the same thing."

"That's sick." He swallowed. "Have you spoken to this Emily?"

"Olivia just clams up if we ask her. And there's no proof that Emily had anything to do with it."

"I find the whole thing extraordinary." I imagined him thinking of all the blood and trauma in Afghanistan. And here were girls in the West, living in comfort and calm, subjecting their bodies to blades. "In Afghanistan the Taliban tried to stop girls going to school. Some of them would give anything to come to a place like this. If I told them that girls here stick knives into themselves they'd think they were mad."

"I know."

"I wish I could —" He stopped abruptly.

I waited.

"I wish I could tell them that none of the things they're worrying about matter. When you're in your teens everything worries you: friends, clothes, whether you're good enough at sport. And none of it really matters."

"Perhaps we could ask you to give a talk." I stopped myself. Assuming too much, assuming that he'd still be around. "It might help," I went on, because he was staring at me. "It might give them a sense of proportion."

He was silent. Hugh always liked to play it fair and he wouldn't want to raise my hopes by agreeing to another meeting if he wasn't sure we had a future together.

"Anyway, pop back sometime if you want," I said as casually as I could. "Samson would love to see you."

"I'd like to talk to them," he said. "About what we're doing out there, what we want to achieve. If you wouldn't . . .?"

"Oh, it wouldn't bother me." I hoped I sounded airy. I held the front door open. "Shall we go back to say goodbye to Samson in the stables? Your train leaves shortly." He paused on the doorstep.

"The history room, wasn't that where you said Simon found the doll?"

"That's right."

"Didn't that history room use to be something else? Not a teaching room. Some kind of office?"

"A bursar's office."

"That's right. Before I met you."

"What made you think of that?"

He shrugged. "I always thought it must be such a glorious classroom to teach in, with those windows and that big oak cupboard. It must have been great to sleep in that room when it was still a bedroom."

"Yes." I was still thinking about the history room as we drove to the station. Probably trying to keep my mind off the coming separation.

"It was good to see you," I said when we arrived. I gave him a kiss on the cheek and my senses flooded with longing. He smelled of the same shaving soap he always used. For a moment I kept my face close to his, hoping he'd want to kiss me again. But he stepped back. "No need to wait for the train," he said. "I'll be in touch."

And then he stepped away, moving swiftly through the crowded concourse. I stared at his back until my eyes filmed over. I switched on the engine and was just releasing the handbrake when a tapping on the window made my heart leap. Hugh. He opened the passenger door.

"Completely forgot I'd got this for you." He dropped a small parcel onto the seat. "Glass from Herat. They followed me back from Afghanistan when they packed up my things. But they'd gone to my mother's flat. Must dash."

And he was swallowed up into the crowds at the station.

I opened the parcel when I reached the stables. Layers of newspaper stripped away to reveal two tall and elegant bluey-green glasses with bases. A matching pair, I noted. I imagined Hugh on the trip to Herat, finding his way to some bazaar or glass-making factory and taking his time, finally choosing the glasses because he knew that they were exactly what I'd love.

I held them one in each hand for a long time, then I placed them on the mantel over the fireplace. At last my home had some personal possessions on display. I stared at the glasses in their new position for some minutes. Their soft blueness was just right for the muted neutral room. I jumped up from the sofa again and wrapped them up in their newspaper. Then I stowed them away in a kitchen cupboard. Best not to get my hopes up. I could manage alone. I'd shut up my hopes in a mental cupboard like the old oak cupboard in the history room until I knew they were reasonable ones.

The history room. Thinking about that cupboard had triggered a memory, but so fleetingly I couldn't retrieve it.

I thought about it for a moment but it didn't come to me.

CHAPTER
TWENTY-FOUR

"Tell me," my father said, peering at Olivia over his specs, "about your life before you came here, where you lived." We'd invited her over to the big house for an early supper on this last night of half-term. We'd asked Emily, too, but she'd been suffering from a virus all day and had retired to bed. We'd finished the shepherd's pie and chocolate mousse I'd brought over and now we were sitting in the drawing room. Olivia had chosen to sit by the fire in a low nursing chair. She looked curiously at home there. Clara and I had often sat in the chair as children.

"I grew up in Kent. I went to a village school for a while. Then we moved and I went to a secondary school in Reading. I didn't like that much."

"Have you always lived with your aunt?" I asked.

She nodded. "She's Czech. She had a permit to work here as an au pair, nothing more than that. Then she was allowed to do more work."

When the Czech Republic had joined the EU, I guessed. But would a woman be able to bring her niece over as a dependant? My father caught my eye. I knew he was thinking the same thing.

"I went to a nursery while she was cleaning. She married an Englishman and then she didn't need to work so hard."

So that was where Olivia had acquired her English-sounding surname.

"But her husband died."

And the aunt had taken on the housekeeper's job with Mrs Smirnova.

"Somehow she managed to save a bit of money for me to come here."

"Which part of the Czech Republic did your family come from?" my father asked, watching her closely.

"I don't know. My aunt doesn't talk about it." She pinged at the elastic band on her wrist. "She says our lives are in England now. I am an English schoolgirl." She sat straighter. "An English public schoolgirl." The pride was clear in her voice. "That's what matters."

"I'm glad," my father said. "I'm glad you're so attached to that idea. But don't you have a curiosity about your roots?"

Her hands wound in and out of one another on her lap. She shook her head.

"It's been interesting talking to you," he said. "You must come over again and eat with us. Perhaps next holidays."

She rose.

He gave her a smile. "Your teachers tell me you're working hard. Well done."

A blush covered her face and she almost sprinted from the room, muttering a thank-you over her shoulder.

"What's this about, Papa?" The old name for him fell from my lips. As a small child, that's what I'd called him. At some point around my early teens I'd replaced it with Dad.

"I can't tell you. Not yet." He stood. "I need to make a trip home."

"Home?"

"To the Czech Republic." The plates I'd been stacking rattled in my hands.

"What?"

He'd never once shown any interest in going there. "It was terrible, what happened to his family," my mother had once told me. "No wonder he wants to forget it."

But now this skinny thirteen-year-old pupil had apparently exorcized some of the memories.

He looked older, suddenly, standing there, fingers tapping the desktop, lips pursed, no doubt running through arrangements. "I wonder what the flights are like this weekend," he said, almost to himself, as though he'd forgotten I was still standing there.

I felt my jaw unhook itself and hit the floor. It was unheard of for him to leave the school during term time. He'd never taken any sick leave during term in all the years he'd worked at Letchford, sometimes collapsing at the beginning of the summer holidays with viruses that kept him to his bed for two or three days. It was technically still half-term this weekend, but even so.

"You want to go tomorrow?" My incredulity was clear in my voice.

He smiled. "I'd like a flight first thing."

"What's this about, Dad?"

"I can't tell you until I've been home."

Again, that word.

You're mad, I wanted to say. *Falling to bits. First you're in a flap about a doll and now you're suddenly feeling a pull to a place you were only too glad to leave years ago.*

Perhaps it was written all over my face. He smiled again. "I don't think it's premature senility, darling. Not yet."

"The school . . ."

"Will manage perfectly well this weekend. Your mother was always telling me I should get away more often."

I could go with him. But supposing I did and something happened to Hugh? Some setback with his treatment? Another infection. It had been known to happen, even this long after an amputation. "I'll drive you to the airport," I said. "Let's have a look on the Internet and see what's available." Then I felt a pang. To go home again after so long, alone, widowed. "I could come with you," I said. I blinked. "If someone can look after the dog at such short notice."

Simon blinked too when I asked him if he'd have Samson. "No trouble. The exercise will do me good. This seems very sudden, Meredith. Everything all right?"

"Yes. No." I scratched the side of my head. "I'm not sure."

"Well, if Charles thinks the trip is important, I think we can agree that it is."

"There's just one thing." I hesitated, not knowing how to phrase it. "We're trying to keep it quiet, about going to the Czech Republic. It's rather a private visit. You're the only person we've told." He looked pleased.

"Secret's safe with me."

And secret was the word. My father had insisted on us not telling a soul. I'd left the supper table to scan the Internet for cheap flights. There was nothing available that same night so I'd booked seats on a plane leaving Stansted at half past six the next morning. I'd managed to hire a car in Prague, too, and book us into an inn near the German border for Saturday night, and I'd pick up maps and guidebooks at the airport. And now I felt excited. For the first time since Hugh had flown home trussed up in tubes inside the giant grey plane, there was something propelling me forward through life. I realized I hadn't left the country for about a year and a half now. Leaving gloomy autumnal England behind couldn't be a bad idea.

CHAPTER
TWENTY-FIVE

Charles

"I think this is the hotel." Charles peered at the wooden sign over the door. He could make out the name now.

Meredith pulled up in front of the pension. It was actually more of a small hotel, he noticed with relief. He'd dragged the poor girl off here for the last days of half-term. She'd been startled by the proposal of the trip but had offered to go at once. He couldn't tell her what was on his mind, what was worrying him. He'd kept it secret for so many years, decades, in fact. But Susan was dead and he couldn't hurt her by letting himself remember. He could take out the memory and examine it and see what he thought. Decide whether he was culpable or not.

But it had to be done here, in Bohemia. The Czech Republic. Czechoslovakia. One place, so many names. Just as he'd taken on different names. Karel Stastny had become Charles Statton. But now Karel was demanding a chance to exert himself. The young artist was challenging the responsible, worthy headmaster, and he hadn't a clue who might win. Sometimes he felt as though the struggle within him must be manifesting itself externally. Perhaps Merry was noticing. There might be tremors in his face. His hand shook, that he did know.

He stepped out of the car. The cold wrapped itself around him like a freezing cape as he grabbed his bag and Meredith's. The warmth in the reception made him breathe out in pleasure. It was all wooden floorboards and glass. Good. Meredith would like this. She'd been sitting in that apartment in the stable block back at school unencumbered by objects. Minimalistic. She said it was what she liked but he wasn't so sure. When she'd first married she and Hugh had filled their married quarters with Persian rugs and pottery bought on their holidays or from Hugh's postings. There had been nothing minimalistic then about his younger daughter. He felt a pang for her.

The receptionist greeted him in English and for a second it would have been easier to respond in the same language but he forced himself to reply in Czech, saying they'd reserved rooms online the previous day. She gave a single blink of surprise at his reply and clicked away at her computer keyboard. He'd written letters to his mother in Czech but hadn't actually spoken a word in his mother tongue since he left the refugee camp in Munich. He wondered if he sounded old-fashioned and stilted. Probably. Languages evolved quickly these days.

The receptionist handed Karel the keys and pointed to the lift.

"Time for a shower before we eat?" Meredith was looking weary. It had been an early start this morning.

They agreed to meet in an hour. Instead of showering or unpacking he sat on the chair in the comfortable room and tried to corral the thoughts that had been darting around in his mind during the last twenty-four hours. First time back here since August 1968. He'd never seen his mother again after he'd left. There'd been occasional letters and Christmas cards, sent via friends in Switzerland, but these had dwindled. In 1976 had come the peremptory message via an official in the embassy in London that she'd died. When he had enquired about whether he could return for her funeral it was made clear that no visa would be provided. You were keen enough to take your leave, they meant. You made your choice and left your country and your widowed mother. Tough luck.

He'd always known it would be like that when he ran away, even though he was only eighteen years old. His mother had known it too as she waved him off from the front door of the house. He didn't dare look round at her as he pedalled away. And there was Hana beside him on her bicycle. As long as she was with him everything was possible. Art school somewhere else in Europe. Paris, perhaps. Why not? Others had gone that route. There was sympathy throughout western Europe for the invaded Czechs and help would be forthcoming.

Karel had some of his paintings and sketches with him, rolled up in a cardboard tube in his rucksack. Hana had taken some of the fabrics she'd designed and printed herself: vivid, coloured pieces. They didn't have much apart from that: a few clothes, some money, soap, toothpaste. You don't need much when you're young and you're running away with a girl who makes you feel you might dissolve into a puddle every time she looks at you.

"Should I bring warm things?" she'd asked when they were packing to leave Prague. "Or will we be back by winter?"

"Take them," he'd told her. Something had passed over her face then, just for an instant.

Eventually he forced himself out of the chair. The hot water in the shower seemed to rinse away some of his Englishness. He found himself thinking in Czech. *I am home. I grew up ten miles from here. We used to pick mushrooms in these woods, Hana and I.* The drive through country roads before the autumnal night fell showed them a quiet wooded countryside, even quieter than he remembered as a child. They'd thrown all the Germans out after the war and tried to resettle this area with incomers from elsewhere in Czechoslovakia, but the population never really recovered. Then the Communists had decided to keep the area under-peopled, a good cordon between East and West.

In the morning Merry and he were going to look for the old house. Karel wasn't hopeful.

And then they'd drive along that forest road he had taken with Hana. And that was the part that made him feel almost sick with nerves.

CHAPTER
TWENTY-SIX

Meredith

This little hotel in the woods was better than I'd feared it might be. I thought it would be darkly panelled, with antlers mounted on the walls; claustrophobic in that particularly middle-European way. I wanted distraction, other people eating and talking. I wanted not to be alone with my father. I flushed at this realization. Most people would consider my father good company. He was well read and thoughtful. He was a good listener but enjoyed debate. And yet as the plane had taken off this morning I felt something approaching dread. I shouldn't have come with him, I thought. Let Clara take time off work at some point and bring him here. Unreasonable, when my sister needed every hour of her precious spare time to ferry her children to their multitude of activities.

The water was hot and my weariness and the stress of the last day slipped away as I showered. I could do this. I could support my father through whatever revelations or self-revelations this trip uncovered. It wasn't my mother or the efficient Clara who'd come with him; it was me and we'd have to make the best of it, even if I couldn't be the emotional or practical support the other two would have offered.

I dressed in a new pair of straight-legged black wool trousers and jersey top I'd just had time to buy in the departure lounge before we left. My father gave me a nod of approval as I joined him in the dark, timbered cellar bar. He'd always appreciated new clothes, never begrudged my mother one of her shopping trips, thought it was important that the pair of them should dress the part of head and head's wife. He was drinking beer, I noticed.

"Local produce." He smiled. "There's wine, too, though, if you'd prefer." But I went to the bar and ordered myself a smaller version of what he was drinking, using a mixture of broken German and English, and wishing I'd had time to learn a few phrases of Czech from my father.

"It tastes as I remember it," he said.

"What are they likely to offer us for dinner?" I sipped the beer: cool and almost fruity. He described soups, meat dishes, pancakes, dumplings. I wondered how much he'd missed the food of his childhood. I couldn't imagine that the cuisine offered by Letchford back in the sixties and seventies would have been much of a replacement. Even my mother, fiercely loyal to the school, admitted to lumpy custard, stews the consistency of muddy fields, and steamed puddings that settled in the digestive system like concrete.

My meal of duck with red cabbage and dumplings was delicious. I found myself settling back in the comfortable chair, smiling, looking around, *enjoying* myself. How could this be? I was still bereaved, suffering a marital break-up, and this weekend in Bohemia was inconvenient and unplanned.

"I'm glad we came," I told my father. "Thanks for bringing me along." He'd insisted on paying for my airfare and hotel room. I'd argued the point but given in.

His eyes were soft. "You're so like my mother, Meredith. I look at you and it could be her. She was petite and dark like you."

"Tell me about her."

"She loved art. She was half German, or probably entirely, she was a bit vague, but she looked almost Italian. Fine-featured. Brown eyes."

"Was she as good as you at painting?"

He gave a modest shrug. "She was more interested in ceramics and sculpture. I see Clara in her, actually, in that respect."

"Not me?" I gave a grin to show that I didn't mind. He made a gesture with his palms turned up.

"Leaving her was hard. Selfishly, I assured myself she'd be all right, she was so confident, so resilient. It didn't bother her as much as it bothered me, the Russians coming, the restrictions reappearing. She lived in her own space. That was her strength. I was weaker. She knew I would only flourish in a place where there was freedom. We heard that a boy my age had been shot dead for painting an anti-Soviet slogan on a wall in Prague. She was scared by that."

"So you slipped over the border?"

"Not so far from here, actually."

I hadn't thought about this before, believing that he'd chosen to return here this weekend only because it was where he'd grown up. I supposed it would have made sense for him to have chosen his home ground to plan his escape from. He'd have known these forests and the border points.

"Did you cross at a checkpoint?"

He spent a moment adjusting the cutlery on his plate. "Someone said that the guards at the crossing near here were sympathetic. But the Russians were expected to clamp down any day soon."

His voice was neutral. He might have been describing someone else's adventure. I corrected myself. He might have been barely eighteen but this had been no adventure.

"Did they let you across?"

He looked up from the pancakes and cherries he was eating. "Yes." The silence was long.

I tried again. "Were lots of people trying to get out?"

"I crossed alone." He said it hurriedly. "Oh, you mean would-be refugees in general. Not everyone was as worried as I was. The Communists still remembered my father. He'd been sent to a labour camp and died there. And then there was my mother's German ancestry. The Soviets and their supporters thought we were just the kind of family who'd foment a bourgeois counter-revolution."

I couldn't help smile at the thought of my father, with his Lobb shoes and Crombie coat, as a fomenter of any kind of revolution.

222

"We might have got around that, but I'd written some things for a student publication. All about artistic integrity and freedom. Foolish teenage pronouncements on the meaning of freedom within a socialist system." He laughed drily. "The kind of thing our sixth-formers would write."

"So it seemed a good time to slip out of the country?"

He nodded. "Perhaps the Russians wouldn't stay long. The West would roar and tell them they wouldn't get away with it and they'd have to leave." He pushed his bowl away, suddenly looking tired. "But it didn't work like that. Nobody was going to risk war with the Soviet Union. Not with nuclear bombs on each side. Once I was across that border I could probably never come home again."

Home. He really did seem at home here, too. I was suddenly tired, for all the long and relaxing shower and the good meal in this womb-like cellar. Once again I sensed the presence of a family history I'd prefer not to learn about. I was going to suggest leaving the rest of the story for another time, but something told me that it had to come out now.

"What did you do when you reached Bavaria?" It sounded such a long way away, but Germany was so near: only ten or fifteen miles away from this little hotel, if you were a bird who could fly over forests and lakes.

CHAPTER
TWENTY-SEVEN

Karel, 1968

It might have been only days since the guard had let him through the control post but his face already wore the mark of the refugee: hope mixed with doubt. He'd looked away when he'd caught sight of himself in the mirror in the shower block this morning. It had taken him the three days to wake up to what had happened.

He'd written the letter in all the English he could muster, swapping his jumper for the help of a university professor who'd slipped over the border a few days after him. The professor had learned his English before the war and admitted it was probably rusty. "I don't know much of what the British call slang," he said. "But perhaps your friend in England will think that a good thing."

How do you write to someone you've never met? Karel ran through what he knew about John Andrews. His father had made this young British POW friend during the war when he'd been sent as a slave labourer to work near a POW camp. John Andrews now taught at a school in Abingdon some sixty-odd miles west of London. Papa had spoken of this friend with real affection. "He is the perfect English gentleman," Papa had said. John was still living in a village outside the town called Abingdon, because he'd written a postcard to Mama earlier in the summer, telling her that she and Karel should visit him now that things were easier in Czechoslovakia.

He'd taken John's address with him when he'd left home. Karel stuck the stamps onto the envelope and made sure that the sender's address was clearly written so that John could write back.

He knew it would be days, weeks even, before he heard anything. *If* he heard anything. He spent the rest of the afternoon walking slowly round the English Gardens, telling himself not to hope too much. She wasn't coming. She'd be here by now if she were. But even so, each time he saw a slender girl with auburn hair striding out through the falling leaves he held his breath.

In the evening he returned to the temporary holding centre they'd set up for the Czechs in an old barracks and sat in the tent. There was nothing to distract him now. Every time a new group arrived he scanned them intently. But not many were coming through the border any more. "You were just in time," a German official told him. "Were you looking for someone in particular?"

"No."

The official blinked. Karel must have sounded overvehement.

He scrutinized the clusters of people sitting around or standing and talking in low voices. *Sketch it,* something screamed inside him. *Sketch this tent and the people playing chess and cards. Record the emotions on their faces.* But he didn't want to reach for a pencil. He wondered if he'd ever want to draw or paint again.

Karel had taken to visiting the library and sitting with a *Times* and a dictionary, trying to force the synapses of his brain to accept the new language. He was going to learn to speak this language so well people would be surprised to know he hadn't spoken it from birth. He was going to stamp out everything linking him to the country he'd left.

At the refugee camp they interviewed him again and offered him the chance of staying in Munich permanently. He could study at the Royal Academy of Fine Arts. Munich was a comfortable city and not far from Bohemia. When things settled down perhaps he could even return home on visits. The woman with the horn-rimmed spectacles seemed to believe this was a possibility. But he waited for a letter from Abingdon in England. A little bit of him still waited for Hana, too, but only because he couldn't bear to tell himself to give up, let her go.

It grew chillier at nights and he wished he'd kept the jumper his mother had knitted for him. Each night he'd wrap himself up in his sleeping bag and drape his jacket over the top, but still the cold seeped in. He was glad. Feeling cold distracted him. Fighting it meant there was no energy left for his regrets. Or his hopes. *Forget her.* One night, his cold fingers twisted the buttons on his jacket. They were thick and padded, more so than he remembered. His mother had taken the jacket away on his last night.

"Just want to press it," she'd said. He'd laughed at her fussiness. The buttons hadn't been as chunky before that night. He'd never been able to do them up since. He pulled at one of them. She'd sewn them on tightly. It took several minutes before he could pull it off. He detached the fabric from the base. Inside the layers nestled an old gold coin with a middle-aged man's head on it. An Austrian crown from 1915. He pulled off the next button and the next. Three pieces of gold. They'd probably belonged to her father, from the period when their part of Czechoslovakia belonged to the Austrians. She must have hidden them all through the war and through the bad years when food was short. And she'd sent him off with this last treasure so that he wouldn't be penniless when he started his new life in the West.

Karel stared at the coins until his eyes ached.

A telegram came from England. *Dear boy, how soon can you come? Will wire you funds . . .*

He showed the horn-rimmed lady the letter and she took it away with Karel's identification papers for a few days to show to the British consulate. When she came back to see Karel she passed him a brown envelope of papers: tickets, visa, cash for food for the journey.

"I have these." He showed her the coins. "I was going to exchange them for sterling."

"Save your gold. Who knows when you might need it." She pushed the three coins back towards him. "You'll find the English food unhealthy," she told him.

"The vegetables are overboiled. My advice is to think again, but if you really want to do this, *Viel Glück*, Karel." And the note in her voice as she said this made it clear she believed he'd need luck to survive the kingdom of overcooked carrots.

But when the train reached Liverpool Street Station John Andrews was waiting for him. His thin face broke into a grin. "It had to be you." He patted Karel on the shoulder. Karel already knew that the English were a reserved people. "Here." He handed him a folded raincoat. "It's raining. I thought you might need this."

Karel put it on over his jacket.

"I imagine I probably ought to take you straight back home but I think we should make for the pub."

John knew one round the corner from the station. When they were inside its warm and fuggy interior he set a pint of warm ale in front of Karel. "So you slipped out of Czechoslovakia without any trouble?"

Karel made himself nod. The beer tasted different from what he'd drunk at home: heavy and oaky.

"Good." He sipped his own drink. "I was sorry to hear about your father. He deserved more. But that's all in the past. Question is, how we get your education back on track. I think," John Andrews said, "we'll work on your English first. Unless you still want to do the art?"

He made it sound like an interesting hobby.

"No," Karel said. "That's in the past." He said it with emphasis, just to be sure.

CHAPTER
TWENTY-EIGHT

Meredith

A bell was chiming in my memory as he told me about his arrival in England. "John Andrews taught at Letchford later on, didn't he?" I remembered the tall, lanky, elderly man with the sharp eyes.

Dad nodded. "He'd retired by then. He was sixty-eight, but his mind was that of a young man. His house had fallen into disrepair. He had to sell it because he couldn't afford to do the work. So there he was without a home and with not much of a pension. I needed someone who could cover maths for me." He laid his knife and fork together on his empty plate in the four o'clock position. At home he'd always positioned them at six in the English way. "And help with some bursary work."

The bursary role had probably been much more casual in what I viewed as the olden times of teaching, before computers. Bursars these days were usually professionally qualified people; accountants, often, who were whizzes at spreadsheets and cashflow projections and ran schools just as they would businesses.

John had lived in the main house, I remembered, as befitted someone who was really family rather than a member of the teaching staff. After Mr Collins had left he'd inherited the room with the large oak cupboard.

"You look weary, Meredith. Let's leave the rest of the story until tomorrow." Dad spoke softly to me, just as he had done when I was little. I'd been a high-spirited child, a girl who needed reining in. He'd been liberal in his tolerance of my liveliness, except for that occasion when I'd defaced the mural. Of late that softness had disappeared. While I'd been working at Letchford I'd felt a critical professional gaze on me. He didn't know whether he could rely on me after that week when I'd flipped. But now the gentler father I remembered was returning to me.

I thought the past would keep me awake, my brain trying to tie threads together. Something had happened at Letchford back in the eighties. I'd been there when it happened and it involved my father and John Andrews. I'd thought that it would be Czechoslovakia itself that would unsettle me but it seemed as though the old house we'd left behind was at the heart of the riddle.

My brain, incapable of forming the link, gave up the attempt. I slept long and deep, waking to the sounds of people talking softly in Czech in the courtyard below my window. Not understanding a word they said was strangely restful. No need to process the information or feel embarrassed at eavesdropping. We'd agreed to meet for breakfast at half eight. No reason to rush, no dog to feed and walk. I lingered over another hot shower before strolling down the wooden staircase to the sunny room where hot rolls and coffee were served. Dad looked bright-eyed this morning, his expression similar to that on a day when he was expecting to watch the Firsts play a victorious home match.

He had an open map on the table beside him. "I'd like to go here." He pointed at a village. "That's where the family house was. It may not still be around."

I spread cherry jam on a roll. "I'm surprised you didn't want to return before and find out."

"Time was always at a premium." He caught my eye and gave a rueful smile. "No, you're right. I could have come back before. But my parents were both dead."

"And there was nobody else to come back to?"

He stared at the broken bread roll on his plate.

"No." The waitress brought a fresh pot of coffee. She smiled at the map and asked him something.

"She wanted to know if I was looking for the lake," he said. "Apparently that's one of the main tourist attractions around here in summer."

I waited to see whether he'd return to the subject of the girl in the painting. He laid his napkin on the table. "Would you be ready to leave in about twenty minutes?"

As we drove away from the inn the forest continued, mile after mile. We hadn't seen many houses now for some time. The area still seemed as depopulated as it had been when my father had left.

I was looking at the map. "We're not far from Bavaria, are we?" We'd landed in Prague yesterday and driven the two hours to the hotel. I hadn't realized quite how close to Germany we were.

"Or Austria. We're right at the heart of Europe. Farther west than Vienna." Even as he said it he sounded more European himself, less the English gentleman headmaster, more the Continental.

"We had warmer weather than this."

"We?"

"I came here from Prague with . . . a friend." He was holding the wheel so tightly I could see the whites of his knuckles.

A friend. I said nothing and waited.

CHAPTER
TWENTY-NINE

Karel

He was always going to have to tell her. Of course he was. There'd have been no point in dragging her off on this pilgrimage otherwise. God knows, she'd got enough going on in her life with Hugh and losing her mother.

Her mother. His wife, to whom he'd never told all this, not entirely, though she had probably pieced some of it together.

"I was leaving with a friend. Hana, her name was."

Meredith said nothing but he was aware of her shoulders stiffening beside him in the car.

"Her name was Hana." He repeated the name because it felt right to be saying it aloud again and again after so long.

"And you ran away together?"

"I suppose we thought it would be romantic. Though, in fact, we didn't really need to run. We borrowed bicycles to take us to the border." There he was again, being a pedantic schoolmaster. "It wasn't a long or hard journey. We had food and money and we'd started from my mother's house, but Hana . . ." He swallowed the end of the sentence.

"Did she make it over the border, too?"

He shook his head.

"What happened, Dad?"

"She had a change of heart."

Merry said nothing for a while.

"That's where we're going now, the old house?" She sounded grateful to skirt off towards a different topic.

"If it's still there. Papa was dead by the time I left. My mother wept when I told her my plans but she gave me her blessing."

"So she sent you both off: you and Hana?"

"She kept asking Hana if she were sure that she was doing the right thing. Hana's parents were dead. She lived with a cousin in Prague. Nobody really minded what Hana did. Apart from me."

His voice was steady. He was worried about sounding like that young man — boy, really, not a headmaster in late middle age.

"Tell me about her."

"She was an art student. Very talented. Fascinated by colours and textures." The words were starting to come out now. "Everyone had noticed her from the first few weeks of starting at the academy."

"Was she pretty?"

Would it break Meredith's heart if he told her? Would she think he was somehow betraying her mother?

"She was vibrant. Fiery, almost, at times." He remembered her sharp tongue; the soft reconciliations.

234

"She was a typical Czech young woman: feminine, but strong and impatient. When she heard of my plans to come to the West she was scornful at first. She was an ardent Communist and she'd distrusted the Velvet Revolution. At first. Then she'd revelled in the freedom." They'd hatched plans about all the galleries they were going to visit in Paris and New York. Perhaps she'd imagined it would only be temporary; an adventure lasting no more than a couple of months, before things quietened down and she could return to Prague.

Even so, he was almost surprised that she agreed to come with him. He had never been so sure that she felt for him what he felt for her.

"On the train from Prague we fell in with another group of students who wanted to come west," he told Merry. "We shared their food. Sausage and ham. It tasted good enough at the time but it was warm on the train and I wondered how long they'd had the food. Later on, Hana started to feel sick. She vomited at my mother's house the morning we left on our bicycles for the border. My mother said it was just nerves and made her drink some camomile tea she made for her. We left my mother's house . . ." He had to stop. He could see it as clearly as if it were happening again now: his mother at the door waving to her only son. They'd got up early so that the other people in the house wouldn't notice what was happening. Mama didn't trust them.

They turned off the road, onto a lane seemingly leading into the gloom of a wood. "This was all cut back last time I was here," he said. "It's grown. And back after the war there were still houses along the road. Look, you can make out their outlines in the grass."

He showed her the rectangles of the long-gone houses. Then he turned the car again, up a rutted track which looked barely wide enough to take a vehicle. "Once it had a proper gatehouse," he said. They bumped along for about fifty metres. Then he stopped. "Oh." He got out. Merry followed.

Nothing. Not even bricks on the ground. The remnants of a garden still struggled to find a meaning for themselves. Apples and plums had fallen to the ground and rotted there. "I always thought they'd leave it alone. They had done after the war."

"When you wrote to your mother before she died she must have told you what had happened here?"

"Many of her letters never reached me. Perhaps the ones that were lost in transit were the ones describing . . . this."

He shook his head. "I should have done more research before we came out. Looked at . . . what's that place you have on the Internet, Meredith?"

"Google Maps?"

"That's the one. I knew we should do that but I was superstitious." Superstitious, he, the rational headmaster. He walked to a fallen tree and sat on the trunk. "I'm not surprised, not really."

She was looking at him, her expression tender. She reminded Karel again of his mother. She might have been Mama. He might have been the boy he'd been over forty years ago, not daring to look over his shoulder as he headed for the West. Young enough to be excited and accompanied by his girlfriend. That boy thought he'd only be away for a few years at most, until there was another revolution or until the western powers warned the Russians to back off. It was the sixties. Everything was changing, all over Europe, all around the world.

But that had never happened. Not for another forty years, anyway. And by that time he was the middle-aged headmaster with his own family and a life that had been completely redesigned and had gone smoothly and perfectly. Until this year.

"Can we look around a bit?"

As he walked around the rectangular outline on the grass he could make out where the rooms would all have been. This had been a large house. He walked his way through the ground floor: the dining room and the formal reception room they'd hardly ever used because dinner parties were not commonplace in the Czechoslovakia of the sixties; the kitchen, where the large stove had emitted its constant, comforting warmth. He couldn't remember what all the other rooms had been. His bedroom had been immediately above the kitchen, a good place to sleep in winter because the heat of the stove permeated the floorboards. Hana had shared it illicitly on that last night at home. She'd sweated as she lay beside him. He'd thought it was just the warmth of the room that had caused it but perhaps she'd been . . . he shrugged away the thought, unable to think these thoughts when his younger daughter paced the grass just metres away.

Free love wasn't widely accepted back then. Even Karel's art school friends were secretive about sex. But he'd needed Hana that last night. It would have been unbearable otherwise to wake in his old bedroom, see his books on the shelf, his early paintings and sketches, the few sports medals and trophies he had won as a child, and know he was looking at them for the last time.

He turned so that he was looking back up the track down which they'd driven. "Let's go," Merry said. "This is too sad." She sounded flat, as though she could feel the past seeping through the grass.

They bumped back down the track.

Meredith

I didn't ask him where we were going now. The signs to Germany, *Nemecko*, were clearly marked. Dad's face was set in an expression of concentration. We sat in silence for half an hour as we drove through the empty countryside.

We were only a kilometre or two away from the border when he pulled off the highway. There were more signs of life now. Big German Mercedes cars heading east from Bavaria on shopping trips. Food and clothes were cheaper here, the woman in the inn had told us. In the bigger villages and towns Vietnamese markets flogged tat to tourists and girls handed out cards for lap-dancing clubs.

Dad slowed the car. He pointed at the grassy verge beside the forest. "Somewhere round here is where

Hana started saying she couldn't go on any further, she felt too ill. We argued the point for about half an hour, even though she kept having to go off to be sick in the bushes. I told her she couldn't give up so close to the border, a new life was waiting for her. She said she didn't want to leave. I was being cruel to try and force her. I should leave her and go on with my dream of capitalism."

I stared at the roadside and saw them there, the young couple; he begging, imploring, she resting her head in her hands.

Karel

Hana put her head in her hands and started to weep. He'd never seen her cry before. He'd take her back to Prague, or at least back to Mama's for the night.

"We'll wait until you feel better. What's another day or so? The Russians aren't here yet."

She looked up and stared at him as though looking for something in him. It was a long stare. "What?" he said.

She placed a hand over her mouth. "I need to . . ." She got up slowly and shuffled into the darkness of the woods, leaving him with her bag and bike. When she'd walked about twenty metres in she turned. "Don't worry about me, Karel." And she sounded stronger. She gave him a smile that was almost her normal dazzling one. He watched her walk away into the gloom. Bushes rustled and he heard the snap of a branch. "Are you all right?" he called after her.

239

She said something in reply. He couldn't make all of it out but he heard her tell him just to wait. So he waited. For half an hour he waited. Then he grew panicky. She might have fainted, might be lying there unconscious in the undergrowth. He got up and followed her into the forest. There was no sign of her. He walked around for about an hour calling and calling. Once he thought he caught a glimpse of her in the trees but that might just have been imagination. Or perhaps a deer running through the undergrowth. Bushes rustled and he spun round, expecting to see her behind him. Then there was nothing.

CHAPTER
THIRTY

Meredith

She left you? I didn't speak the words; they stayed in my head.

"Was she the girl in the mural?" I asked instead.

He nodded.

I barely needed to ask the question. He'd tried to forget about her and most of the time he'd been successful but then she'd burst back into his consciousness and he'd painted her on the wall. Only to cover her up again. Nobody would have known she was there if I hadn't scraped the paint off all those years ago and exposed her. What had my mother said? Had she questioned Dad?

"But you looked for her?"

"Yes."

"And you never heard from her again?"

"No. Once I was in Abingdon, I tried writing to the last address she'd been living at before we left Prague. But I never had an answer. Perhaps the letter didn't get through to Hana, Perhaps she got it and replied but her letter didn't reach me. Or perhaps . . ." He switched on the engine.

Perhaps she simply hadn't wanted to reply. Perhaps her feelings for him simply hadn't been as powerful as his for her. Or her trepidation at the thought of crossing the border was too strong. I imagined him walking along the water meadows of the Thames around Abingdon, staring at the water, wondering what had happened to her. I felt the space between myself and my father shrink as my sympathy for him grew.

"We should start back for Prague now." He sounded like himself again, like his assured, headmasterly self.

"It all feels so rushed." I hadn't been able to persuade him to take any more time away from Letchford, not even just the Monday, the first day back after half-term. "Is there time to see your mother's grave?"

"She's not buried here. When she lost the house she moved north, to a job as an auxiliary nurse in an industrial town near the Polish border. She's buried up there. My father is buried near the work camp where he died."

I said nothing. This unknown Czech part of my family was starting to exert a pull on me. I longed to know more about my grandmother and grandfather.

"We will come back, Meredith. I promise you. We'll put flowers on your grandparents' graves. Now I've been back this time I want to return." There was a new firmness in his tone now.

"Could we just drive to the border quickly? Without crossing it, I mean? Just to look."

"I suppose so."

It gave us time to think. We pulled up about a hundred yards from the frontier. It was quiet, too early in the morning for traffic to have built up. As it was just a minor crossing there was none of the sleaze surrounding the more important crossings into Germany. As far as I could see the trees ahead looked just like the trees behind us. A black BMW with German plates drove past us, an elderly couple sitting in it, laughing. Visiting a childhood home, perhaps. Reminiscing. Their past all easily confrontable, innocent. We sat staring at the forest for a few minutes.

"There is just one thing we have time to do in Prague before we catch our plane."

I turned an enquiring eye towards him.

"It's hard to explain. But there's someone who might still be alive, someone I should see."

"Hana?"

He ran his fingers round the steering wheel. "I only have her cousin's address, though. And she may have died or moved away years ago."

I wondered whether he'd have married Hana if she'd continued the journey west with him. I thought of my mother and bit my lip. If Dad and Hana had continued their journey together I wouldn't be here. My life seemed to fracture as I considered this parallel history. No me. No Clara. No telephone ringing in that army house to tell me that my husband had been blown up. A girl changing her mind on the grassy side of a quiet Czech road had brought me into existence.

There was much to ask, but I found the questions stuck to my lips and wouldn't form themselves into words. I sat and watched the traffic on the roads leading us to the auto-route back to Prague. We drove in near silence, Dad briefly telling me something about the town of Pilsen as we bypassed it, stopping once for petrol and coffee. A frown came over Dad's face as we reached the south-western suburbs. "It looks so different with all these modern tower blocks. And there's so much more traffic."

"Had the tanks arrived by the time you left?" I was imagining the pounding of their tracks across the cobbles in the old part of the city, the people running out with handwritten signs pleading with the soldiers to turn back.

"Yes. Enough of them to make it clear the Soviets meant business. We didn't hang around to find out whether more troops were on their way. They'd already taken control of the airport by then." He was frowning at the roads and buildings. "I think I remember where I am now."

The hire car people had given us a map of Prague and its suburbs and I unfolded it.

After a mis-turn the wrong way round the ring road and a few other minor mistakes we pulled up outside a baroque church in a suburb to the west of the Vlatava; I'd given up trying to work out exactly which one it was. The streets were on the up, I thought. Signs of increased prosperity, even though there were still plenty of black-clothed elderly women and old cars.

244

Dad turned off the engine. "We'll walk the last quarter of a mile. I only ever went to the apartment by foot. The nearest tram stop was a block or so away. So I'm more likely to remember if we walk."

He'd told me before that cars had been fairly rare in his youth. I pictured him as a lanky young man, strolling out to meet his girlfriend after lectures. Or perhaps walking her home after a night out in the beer cellars. Or to one of the cinemas showing avant-garde films. I saw her long hair swinging in the moonlight, her bright tunic dress; I heard her laugh, this woman whose existence in my father's life had left its mark so strongly that he'd painted her on the wall at his wife's family home.

He stopped on a street corner, a frown on his face. "This feels about the right distance, but I probably walked more quickly when I was seventeen." He scanned the streets. "That *potraviny* might be a good place to ask." The *potraviny*, corner shop, looked promising: small enough for the shopkeeper to know his clientele and the neighbourhood.

The shopkeeper was Vietnamese and broke off from opening a box of Czech lager to greet us as we came in. He said something rapid and heavily accented in reply to my father's question. Dad shrugged and smiled. I assumed the answer had not been helpful. We walked towards the door. We'd reached the pavement outside when a woman called to us. A tiny Vietnamese woman came outside and pointed up a street. Dad thanked her. I noticed a look of excitement on his face. "She thinks

245

there's a family down here who might know something. They've lived in this area for years, she says."

He seemed to slow down as we crossed the road and approached the nineteenth-century apartment block. As he studied the list of names on the intercom I sensed that anything, a single word, a sigh, would be enough to divert him from this mission. He let out a breath. "I'll try this one." He pushed the intercom. No answer. He stepped back. "Oh well."

"Try another one."

"None of the names mean anything to me."

"Doesn't matter. They may still know something."

He pushed a second button. A man's deep tones answered. Dad said something in Czech and shook his head at the reply.

"This is hopeless," he said. "Let's go, Merry."

"No." I stood in front of him so that he couldn't move from the door. "Let me." I made a jab at the row of buttons and caught two at the same time. A young-sounding woman started shouting at me through the intercom.

"She's saying she'll call the police if we don't go away."

I held up a hand to stop him talking. "What was that?" A new voice, male, elderly, quavering, was saying something now. "What did he say?"

Dad approached the intercom and said something quickly. He shrugged. "He says to try the house two doors up the street."

I tried not to let him see me glancing at my watch as we walked along. Identical to the house we'd just left, this one also had a collection of names on plates. Dad scanned them.

"I don't recognize any of these. This is a fool's errand."

A woman appeared with a toddler in a buggy. We stepped aside to let them through. Dad asked the woman something. She shook her head and unlocked the front door. The door was almost closed when she thought of something and spoke.

"In hospital," Dad said. "She lives here but she went into hospital." He put out an arm to stop the door from closing and asked a question.

The answer came with some hesitation. He said something in reply, then turned to me. "We can't go any further with this."

"Which hospital?" I asked.

The young woman was answering when a door opened above. A voice, elderly, female, called down. The young woman blinked. Shook her head. Said something in obvious bemusement.

"She's back," Dad told me. "She wants this lady to buy her some bread."

The woman shook her head, turned round and went back through the door, laughing, seemingly unbothered by the request. She pointed up the stairs.

"I think we have to go up. She wants to see who we are."

We walked up an ancient staircase with a wrought-iron balustrade. "It might be the same place," my father said, his voice almost a whisper.

"You think this is it, this is the apartment itself?"

"It's hard to remember."

The old woman was standing on the landing. She was stooped over a stick but her eyes glittered. She rattled off a stream of Czech at my father and he answered. She looked uncertain. I looked for a translation but his attention was fixed on the old lady. She started to shout at him, waving the stick. He held out his hands, palms up, and seemed to plead with her.

"Dad —"

He held out a hand. "Wait, Meredith."

She lowered the stick but her eyes still flashed. He shook his head, muttered something in a low tone. She snapped a reply, brushing her spare hand over her eyes. He said something else to her. Then she was shouting again, pushing the stick against his shoulder as though she wanted to stab him.

I stepped forward. "Stop this." She had enough English to understand. "She's clearly not well. She's . . ." I didn't know how to label the fury. Perhaps the old lady was suffering from some kind of dementia.

"She has every right to be angry with me." He said something again in Czech, holding up his hands as though she were facing him with a pistol.

She studied him for a few seconds. Then she was brushing us towards the flat, ushering us into a stuffy room filled with bamboo furniture, a cage of canaries at one end, beside the balcony. "She says to sit," Dad whispered. He stared at the old-fashioned television set in the corner. "We used to watch cartoons. There was one about a mole, I remember."

248

"What was all that about?" I asked. "Is she demented?"

"Hana," he said, simply.

"It wasn't your fault she left you in the forest."

He made one of the central-European gestures with his shoulders.

I perched on a cushioned chair. The old lady asked him something.

"She doesn't really know who I am," he said.

"Did she say what happened to Hana after you left the country?"

He shook his head. But then the old woman spoke again.

"Karel?" she said slowly. "Karel Stastny?" As though she hadn't heard his name properly before.

He nodded. She asked something else rapidly. He answered, gesturing that we should leave. Her hand was on the apartment door, ready to show us out. She paused. I could almost see doubts, fears, questions passing through her mind. She nodded back in the direction of the sitting room. I returned to my chair. Dad said something else and she answered slowly, shaking her head, wiping her eyes. He blinked. Rested his forehead on his hand.

"Hana died," he said, letting out a long sigh. "Years ago. I didn't know and nobody knew how to tell me."

"I'm so sorry, Dad." I was surprised that I did feel sorrow for him. Before this morning I'd have classed this loss as very minor in comparison with the loss of my mother. Its scale might be smaller but a sorrow it was, all the same.

"Well, there we are." He started to get up. "At least I know." He managed a smile. "Better to know than to wonder."

The old woman brushed her hand over her eyes again. He put a hand on her shoulder. I saw her eyes soften. She looked as though she might take a chance on a pair of strangers from a faraway land. Though Dad wasn't a true stranger to her, of course. She'd have met him when he was Hana's boyfriend, in the happy days just before the Russians invaded the country.

"Stay there," she said, and I understood her perfectly now even though she was still speaking Czech. She went to a drawer where she rifled through papers and opened boxes. Whatever it was she was looking for didn't seem to be in its place. She hobbled off into another room.

I heard her sighing and muttering and the sound of drawers and cupboards opening. I hoped she was all right. She was only just home from a hospital stay. A smell of mustiness wafted through into the room where we waited. She brought in an old photo album and handed it to Dad, stabbing at the pictures with a wrinkled finger. He sat straighter and asked her a question. As she answered he was reaching into his inside pocket for his reading glasses. He studied what seemed to be a faded colour photo and nodded slowly. Then he lowered the album and met the gaze of the old woman and told her something. Some of the hostility I'd noticed in her seemed to soften. He asked her something urgently and she shook her head. He asked another question in a less urgent, softer tone, and she

250

answered, wiping her eyes. Then he lowered his eyes to the photograph and stared at it without speaking, a hand over his eyes so that his expression was hidden.

"Who is it?" I reached for the album and pulled it to me. A young schoolkid in seventies-style shorts, short brown hair, some kind of uniform with a knotted scarf, and a determined expression. He, or she, it was hard to be sure, reminded me of someone I knew very well.

He turned to me. "My eldest child."

CHAPTER
THIRTY-ONE

Meredith

"Clara?" I peered at the photo again. Then I saw it wasn't my sister. It was a boy in a uniform a bit like a scout's. The firm set of the jaw and the directness of the gaze were very like Clara's.

"Jan." My father spoke the name almost in a whisper. Realization was starting to sweep through me. I think the cells of my body began to comprehend before my brain had registered what this meant. My *brother*. Jan.

"Hana was pregnant, not ill, when you headed for the border." I spoke the words very slowly. Hana's sickness and fatigue had been nothing to do with the tainted sausage eaten on the train.

He nodded. "Mrs Novakova here doesn't know if Hana'd worked out what was happening when she ran away. Maria Novakova is Hana's cousin, by the way. She's lived here all her life."

I glanced at the old lady, who seemed to be softening by the second. She made some clucking noises at me and bustled off, calling something over her shoulder. "Coffee," Dad translated. I glanced at my watch.

"There'll always be another flight." I couldn't believe I was hearing my father say this. He smiled at my face. I couldn't remember my father ever accepting that a flight or a train should be missed, plans altered, the administration of his beloved school compromised. For the first time in many years Dad was going to let events flow instead of timetabling them into thirty-five minute slots.

"We'll have to pay extra," I warned him. "We don't have an open return." I sounded like my sister.

He made another of the gestures with his open palms, dismissing the added expense. "After Hana had our son she didn't finish her textiles course but managed to train as an art teacher. She was worried that the school authorities would remember her involvement with student politics but her father was a bigwig and the Russians approved of him. She worked in a school here until her death in 1980 from breast cancer."

"And she never thought to tell you that she'd had your child?"

"She died long before the Berlin Wall came down. She probably thought there was little chance that I'd ever get to see Jan, so what was the point?"

"Where's Jan now?"

He let out a deep breath. "He's no longer alive."

"Oh, Dad." The expression on his face was unbearable. He'd found his son. And lost his son. All within five minutes. Did all men, I wondered, have a yearning for a son? What could Clara and I, female creatures, offer in recompense? I stared at the blue-and-white porcelain coffee cups to give him a moment.

"Jan trained as a doctor." Dad had regained his poise. "He did well in life."

Naturally, I thought. He was your child.

"He settled down in his late twenties and married."

The old woman interjected, seeming to emphasize some point. He nodded. "They were both working at a paediatric hospital at the time their car was hit by a drunk driver fourteen years ago." He bit his lip. I reached over and squeezed his hand. "They both died."

I waited. There was more to emerge. When it wasn't spoken I voiced it. "Jan had a child, didn't he?"

He nodded. "I'm getting to that part." He always insisted on relating events in the right order. "I have to backtrack for a moment. Hana had married in her late twenties. Jan was a lad of about nine or ten by then. Some years after that she had a second child, a daughter, Sofia." My skin prickled. Dad turned the pages of the album. "Here we are: this is Hana with her two children." A slim auburn-haired woman with a boy in shorts, who must be Jan, and a baby. "Sofia, the baby in this picture, has been working abroad for some years. She'd be about your age now, Meredith." We looked at one another.

Mrs Novakova clattered in with a laden tray and I stood up to help her make a space on the low table in front of the sofa. "England," she said. "Sofia work in England."

As I already knew.

254

"But where is the child?" I asked Dad, feeling the urgency in my voice. "Where is Jan's girl, your granddaughter?" But even as I asked the question I already knew the answer. I turned to the old woman. "Do you have a photograph of Jan's little girl?"

For a moment I thought she hadn't understood the English. "Little girl?" Her eyes glazed. She said something and walked out of the room, opening another door at the far end of the corridor, and reappearing with a silver-framed photograph of a toddler sitting on a woman's lap. I peered and peered at the child's round features. "What's her name?" I asked.

"Irena," said Mrs Novakova, whose understanding of English seemed to come and go in waves, according to the emotional intensity of what was being asked. "She in England."

Irena. Not Olivia. Disappointment felt like cold water crashing over me.

I stared at Irena. But she just looked like any other little child of that age.

CHAPTER
THIRTY-TWO

Meredith

We made our plane — with an Olympic sprint to the gate. In his hand, along with his boarding card, my father clutched the photo of Jan; poor, dead Jan who'd never known his father or half-sisters, and whose own daughter had been orphaned so young.

When we had flopped into our seats and fastened our safety belts, I asked to see the photos again.

The old woman had let us take the picture of Hana with her two children: Jan and Sofia. She'd pointed at the framed photograph of the toddler Irena who was Dad's granddaughter and then pointed to her heart, looking anxious.

"No, no!" Dad had sounded shocked. "We wouldn't ask you for that picture."

Irena's photograph probably had pride of place next to her bed. How she must miss Sofia and Irena. The old lady must have understood some of what was going through my mind because she walked over to me and stroked my cheek and muttered something.

"She says you shouldn't be so sad for her," Dad told me. "She also says you're young and pretty and your husband must love you."

She'd obviously spotted the ring on my finger. Hugh's mangled body flashed into my mind and I had to blink hard. Perhaps the old woman wasn't as clear-sighted as she thought. She said something else, waving her hands.

"She wants us to find Irena and be her family. She's worried about the two of them: Sofia and Irena. She doesn't hear from them often. Sofia is vague about what she does. She's vague about Irena, too." Dad and I looked at one another. He must be suspecting what I was, that Irena was someone we knew, someone close to us at Letchford.

"Have you told her where you think Irena is?"

He looked away.

"Dad?"

"No. Not yet. It's too much to think about, that she's been, might have been, in the school all the time. Why?" His voice dropped to a whisper. "Why would they make it all so secret?"

"If she is Olivia."

As we were leaving the apartment I asked, "Does she have any other photos of Irena?" Dad and the woman exchanged words. She went back to the drawer in the sitting room and rifled through envelopes, tutting with her tongue. These strangers from England were causing disruption in more ways than one. She pulled out a photograph and handed it to Dad with a shrug.

"It's not as clear as the other photo," he said. "But she's older here."

I was looking at a girl of about four. Gone was the toddler's trusting grin. In its place was a watchful, serious expression.

I knew that expression well.

Olivia Fenton was my niece, as much my niece as Clara's two boys were my nephews. Was that why I'd felt protective of her? Some subliminal family system of recognition had operated when I'd encountered her. Perhaps I'd seen that resemblance to Clara, without being aware of it. Clara. We'd have to tell Clara about this as soon as we were back at Letchford; sooner. If we didn't pass on the information as soon as we touched down there'd be trouble from my sister. It would be as it had been when the reborn doll had been found in the cupboard and Clara had complained that nobody had told her and she'd had to find out from a text message. Remembering that doll again made me wonder whether there could possibly be a connection between it and these family discoveries. And yet Olivia's aunt, Sofia, had assured me that they'd had nothing to do with it. I'd believed her.

"What a revelation. I feel . . ." Dad shook his head. "I don't know how I feel. I keep wishing your mother was here."

So she'd tell him how to feel. That's the role that women have long performed and perfected in relationships: interpreting the dense and sometimes overwhelming world of emotions for their menfolk.

"I don't know what I should do about this, Merry."

I noted the use of my old childhood name.

"Your mother would have known how to go about managing Olivia's . . . situation. But then again, this might have been the one area she couldn't have advised me on." He shook his head. I couldn't imagine that Mum would have begrudged him a youthful romance with a consequence at once sad and wonderful. Though perhaps it would have been asking too much to expect her to feel easy about this. Or to give advice. Or to find it easy to have her husband's granddaughter living in the school. Even as I longed for her wisdom I found myself feeling relieved that all this had happened after her death.

"I really only knew Hana for a matter of six months," he went on. "And we were only . . . romantically entangled for three of them before we made that trip to the border." He broke off as the stewardess brought us a glass of wine apiece. I all but grabbed mine from her. Dad sipped his more slowly. "It was very intense at the time. But I left her like that. I ruined her life. Expecting my child. I can't forgive myself."

"You don't know that you ruined her life."

"Alone? Pregnant? With the Russians invading?"

"Perhaps having her child provided her with a lot of joy. She seems to have been well supported." I thought of the old lady in the apartment, of the well-thumbed photograph album, and imagined Hana's children, both of them, and her granddaughter toddling around the flat, perhaps asking to be lifted up to see the canaries in the cage. It might not have been Letchford with its acres of landscaped gardens and its lake; it might not

259

have been what Dad and Mum had provided for us, but there'd been love in that apartment. And Prague was beautiful. Even the oppressive state couldn't take away from the baroque buildings and the curve of the river, or from the hills and forests in the rest of the country. I pictured them going for walks in the winter, when snow reflected the light from the rivet, or spending Sunday afternoons in one of the parks.

"Will you talk to Olivia when you get back?" I asked.

"Only in the presence of her aunt. She's in a very vulnerable position and we must tread gently. I'm assuming she has no idea of her possible relationship to us?"

I rewound every conversation I'd had with Olivia through my memory and found no evidence. "God knows why the aunt decided to send her to Letchford in such secrecy, though." Changing her name from Irena to the more English-sounding Olivia must have been strange for the girl. I wondered what age she'd been when she was given the new identity. "Did they think we'd reject them if we knew who they really were?"

Dad was looking at the photo again. "I hope that was not the case."

Olivia's pale face haunted me. She'd found it hard to make friends at Letchford. Occasionally I'd see her drifting at the edge of a group. She had little interest in team sports, her housemistress had told me, though she wasn't a bad gymnast. "She's on a different wavelength to the others. She doesn't like social networking and she has little interest in clothes. She's always got her

260

head in a book. Thank God she's in the play. It's making a huge difference for her."

Now I longed to intervene, to encourage the flowering of confidence we'd seen this term. I'd bring her over to my apartment and cook her supper. I'd talk to her about the books she enjoyed. Perhaps I could take her round the bookshops in Oxford. I stopped myself, mid-thought. Doing anything like this would merely single her out as even more different from the rest of the children. I dreaded their response if they knew she was the head's granddaughter. A tough extrovert might muscle out the revelation. This girl hovering at the edge of the field at breaktime while the other girls chattered; well, her new self-confidence mightn't survive.

The plane was circling Stansted airport now. For a second I wished it would continue to circle so that we didn't have to confront what was waiting for us below. The image of the house I'd left at the army base came back to me. If only I could be back there now in that little square red-brick home, a day's work completed, Hugh home on leave, about to bounce through the door to say a quick hello to me before he went off to play tennis or squash with a friend. While he was doing this I'd be chopping vegetables or laying the table for the dinner he'd cook when he came back.

I gripped the arm of my seat. Dad looked at me. "Expecting a bumpy landing?"

CHAPTER
THIRTY-THREE

It was almost eleven when we reached Letchford. No chance to talk to anyone about what had been revealed in Bohemia; I'd decided I preferred the old name for that part of the Czech Republic. As we pulled up in the stable yard Dad muttered a few words of thanks to me for accompanying him. I could barely frame a response. I dragged my bag up the stairs to the apartment. Almost too late to reclaim Samson from Simon, but I longed for my dog, for the clean, earthy smell of his coat, his enthusiastic and uncomplicated greeting. Simon was a night owl. I'd ring him.

"Meredith?" He sounded flustered. Probably doing the next half-term's lesson planning. I asked if I could collect the dog. A pause. "That's fine. I'll have his things ready."

"It could wait until tomorrow morning if it's too late now?"

"Seriously, it's fine. See you shortly."

He greeted me at the door with a carrier bag full of the dog's food and bedding. "He's been good as gold." Samson shot out of the door, all damp nose and windmill tail. "Your spare key's in the bag, too."

I started to thank Simon for taking him on at such short notice but he interrupted. "Hey, Cordingley, you were the one doing me a favour. This boy and I've had some good long walks."

"I owe you." I handed him the bottle of Famous Grouse I'd picked up in the Prague airport duty-free, put the dog on the lead and waved a farewell. In the second before the door shut behind me I thought I heard him say something else but when I turned round, the door had already closed.

I'd probably annoyed my best friend here by asking him to look after the dog. Or by collecting Samson so late. I swore quietly under my breath and the dog pricked his ears and whined.

I woke the next morning ten minutes after the alarm. The rush to get to assembly meant there was no time for brooding over what had happened. As I watched my father stand at the lectern in the hall I scrutinized him for signs of strain. I don't think anyone else apart from me, or my mother if she'd still been alive, would have noticed the slight shake of the hand that held the results of the last hockey match before half-term had started. Perhaps nobody but us would have noticed the over-brightness in his eyes.

When it was over Olivia trailed out with her year, her eyes seemingly gazing at nothing. I examined my father's face as the girl who must surely be his granddaughter passed below him and saw a spasm threaten to overpower its headmaster's poise. He must be bursting to call out to her. I wondered when he'd call Sofia and ask her if they could meet. The old lady would have been in touch with her by now, surely, letting her know what had happened.

Into this train of thoughts broke Emily. The week's holiday seemed to have made little difference to her tenseness. "Can I have a word?"

I must have shown my surprise.

"It's urgent."

I looked over my shoulder. A group of long-eared sixth-formers was ambling by. "Let's go somewhere more private." Dad was heading towards the hall door and his office upstairs. Some protective emotion made me not want him to be burdened with this now. Perhaps I could deal with Emily for him. I was free first lesson. "The staffroom." But when we reached the room voices were chatting. I looked at Emily. "Simon's room."

Her eyes widened.

"He won't mind." I'd used the history room before to talk in private. I didn't have my own form room. Simon's first lesson was a free period. How long ago it seemed since I'd come up here to his aid after he'd found the reborn doll. I pulled two chairs away from desks and motioned to her to sit down. "What is it, Emily? What's wrong?"

"I can't go on working here." The girl looked almost ill, her normally pale skin now the shade of paper.

"I thought you loved Letchford?" I remembered her conversations about the gardens, how she loved the flowers, how hard she thought it would be to be banished from the place. She shrugged.

"I did. Still do."

"Then?"

"I don't fit in here." She tugged at the sleeves of her expensive-looking jumper. Over half-term she'd obviously bought some new and warmer clothes.

"It's still early in the school year. Often things don't settle down until after half-term. There's a lot going on later on. Parties and concerts." Although the school wasn't religious Dad had always encouraged Christmas celebrations. It had always been my favourite time of the school year. "And of course it's *The Crucible* at the end of term. You're helping with the costumes, aren't you?"

"I've done some designs. I've made some of them, too."

"Did you enjoy it?"

She nodded.

"You wouldn't want to leave Jenny in the lurch, would you?"

"Perhaps not."

"And if you've enjoyed it there'll be other plays. Once people know you're good at that kind of thing you'll be in demand."

"I'll think about it."

"We really want you to feel happy here." I laid my hand on her wrist. She gazed down at it. "You've made a good impression." She might not have enjoyed helping the PE staff on the games pitch but the work she'd done on the costumes had been invaluable.

Emily moved her wrist. "I think it was a mistake me coming to Letchford."

I thought of her awkwardness when asked to help put out the cones for sports lessons. "It can be a bit of a dogsbody job, being a gappy. But universities and training colleges really do rate the experience, they —"

"Another school might have been better for me."

"The kids here can come across as a bit spoiled and entitled. If they've been giving you a hard time we'll sort them out." Her eyes seemed to glaze over now. "Emily?" Funny. I'd felt suspicious of the strange relationship she had established with Olivia, protective of the younger girl even before I knew who she was. But now I felt sympathy for Emily. She was no ordinary bubbly gappy; there were depths to this girl we probably hadn't yet appreciated.

"Please don't be nice to me, please don't try and talk me out of going." She rubbed her sleeve over her face. "It's best for everyone. Really. You can't imagine . . ."

But I thought I could. "Emily, give it just another week. Until next Monday. If you still feel this strongly I'll do everything I can to find another placement for you."

"Another week?" She peered at me through her tears. "I suppose I could try and hold on for another week."

"Do." I reached across and touched her shoulder. "And try and spend more time with the teachers. Come out to the pub after school again. I'll let you know when Simon and I are planning another outing."

She stood up, knocking her chair over, eyes no longer filled with tears but filled with another emotion I couldn't exactly decipher. "Simon?"

"That's right." I had picked up something in her tone. "What's wrong?"

"Nothing." She flicked back her curtain of hair. "That would be lovely." Outside a group of girls chattered as they crossed the lawn towards their first lesson. I saw Emily's eyes narrow as she observed them. "Some of them find it all so easy, don't they? The friendships, the group stuff."

I knew what she meant. Some youngsters seemed to be born programmed to know how to operate in groups. School was a social doddle for them. Others, such as Olivia and probably Emily herself, were born without this innate knowledge. Living with other people constantly around them was hard work. "They seem to glide through life here," I said. "But sometimes when they leave they find the world a tougher place."

She seemed to swallow a retort.

I thought of myself, so happy and secure here at Letchford and at the school in the town. I'd done my A levels here but nothing else because my parents had wished to keep my education separate from my home life. I'd been one of those pupils who enjoyed the bustle of the classroom, the gossip of the sixth-form common room at break. Merry, I'd been, by name and nature. Yet life had still not spared me. Perhaps the pupils who'd been tried and tested at school had an additional toughness which helped them later on in life. "Don't worry," I told Emily, not even sure what it was I didn't want her to worry about. "Everything will be fine." I realized I was saying it to myself, as much as to her.

267

CHAPTER
THIRTY-FOUR

Emily

It confused the hell out of her when people were nice to her. Made her wonder if she should change her plans completely. Stay at the school. Be the person she might have been. Forget the rest of it.

Meredith had that seductive English ease about her. She hadn't met Meredith's deceased mother, but imagined someone similar, but older and even more appealing. Emily corrected herself. She *had* indeed met Susan Statton. When she'd been a toddler and had come to this school with her mother to borrow something. "I liked Letchford," Mum had said, years later. "It felt as though we were part of the family." And she'd laughed in that way that didn't sound as though she thought it was very funny at all.

Simon had been kind to Emily as well, taking her out for a drive through the countryside to the second-hand bookshop. He'd wanted to screw her, but that was OK. What wasn't OK was that he hadn't taken her seriously as a possible girlfriend. Either because he had thought of her as a guileless nineteen-year-old, or because he'd seen through her. Either way, he'd made it clear that it had just been a fling. To be honest, she didn't really want a relationship, either. But it bugged her that she wasn't considered worthy of the honour. So Simon Radcliffe, with his musty piles of old papers and photos of women in Edwardian costume promenading round Letchford's gardens, thought that he was too good, did he?

Anger hardened her. She wouldn't be sidetracked. Or it would all have been a waste of time. Remember what you set out to do, she told herself. Don't let Meredith or Simon or Olivia or anyone else sidetrack you. Remember Dad. Mum. Toby.

Toby. She barely remembered him at all. It was her mother's desperate scream when she found him dead that lived on in her memory. Emily's hand went to her left arm. She pulled up the woollen sleeve and examined her skin. Nearly healed over. She tried rolling the sleeve back down and forgetting about the cut. But now the impulse was in her mind she knew she'd be unable to push it away again. This was what happened when she thought about the past; she was drawn back to the blade. It did hurt when you cut yourself, she'd agreed with Olivia. Very much, at times. But that sense of the bad stuff flowing out of you with the blood, and the relief, numbed the pain.

Olivia had nodded. "You feel clean," she'd agreed. "That's why I do it, to feel pure afterwards." They'd done it together once, sitting out by the fountain at dusk. They'd let the drops of blood fall into the water. It had been beautiful. Emily had cut herself again after the interview with Meredith. The bleeding had calmed her, as it always did. Had made her resolute again.

Emily remembered the first time she'd taken a blade to her skin. It had been one of those mornings when Dad hadn't risen in time for work. He'd been drinking until the early hours. She'd gone into the bathroom to get ready for school, that dismal school that was so far from being Letchford it might have been on a different planet. Dad's razor sat on the shelf under the mirror, unused. On a good morning he hummed as he applied the blade to his soaped face. As a small child Emily had liked to sit on the edge of the bathtub and watch him shave, creating smooth lines through the white foam. She picked up the razor, a heavy steel instrument. He'd warned her about the blade before. *Never let me see you playing with this, Em* . . . She pressed her thumb on the blade. Nothing happened. Perhaps it wasn't as sharp as she'd thought. She pressed hard. A small bead of blood appeared, like a little berry. It stung. But there was another feeling too, a release, as though the hurting feeling was blotting out the pain inside Emily. A small hurt instead of a big one.

She'd done it again, not too often, but when the kids at school were being vile to her. Sometimes Dad dragged Emily off to church on Sunday and they sang hymns about the pure blood of the Saviour washing away sin. Perhaps that was what her own blood was doing, washing away all the badness. Keeping the three of them safe.

Finding someone else who understood about cutting had been a revelation. She recalled the first time she'd seen the marks on Olivia's arm and had asked her. "Yes," Olivia had whispered. "I am sorry, I have done that to myself. I know I shouldn't."

It had all come tumbling out: Olivia's homesickness, her aunt Sofia who worked so hard, her family abroad. She was reticent about her aunt. Probably screwed up by Sofia's absences. Emily knew most of it already, of course. "Will you tell the school?" Olivia had whispered. "Will they make me see the doctor or something?"

"No. I won't tell them." Emily had rolled up her sleeve and shown her own cuts. "I know about cutting. You don't need psychiatric liaison teams and all that stuff."

Olivia's eyes had widened.

"Sometimes it feels like the purest thing in my life." Emily touched the cut on her arm. "It gets me through hard times. Nobody else is harmed by it."

"That's what I think too. It stops me worrying people with my problems."

"But it's lonely," Emily had gone on. "I've heard of people cutting together." Olivia looked doubtful. "To keep an eye on one another. Making sure they don't hurt themselves badly."

"Keeping an eye out." Olivia looked thoughtful. "I can see that would work."

Emily had taken the plunge. "I feel like cutting now. But I don't want to be alone."

Olivia'd drawn back, eyes wide. Emily had sworn at herself silently. Too much too soon. "I have had a hard day," Olivia said slowly. "I know that cutting would make me feel better, but . . ."

"You shouldn't do it alone," Emily said quickly. "Look, just stay with me while I do it. See what happens." She'd had the razor blade wrapped up in a tissue in her trouser pocket. And a spare. "Never ever share your blades. These are new," she told Olivia. She'd unwrapped the first blade and drawn it over the skin on her upper left arm. A fine dark line appeared. Beautiful. Like an artist's brushstroke. Olivia was watching. "Thank you for staying with me," she told the girl.

And then Olivia had put out a hand for the second blade and drawn a similar line on the back of her own wrist. "We are like sisters now," she said. The crimson mark on her pale skin was like a silk thread. Then a drop of blood beaded at one end.

But not any longer. Olivia had stopped cutting. Perhaps the shock of tumbling down those stairs onto the marble floor had shaken up something in her brain. That had been regrettable. Emily hadn't meant to push her; it had just happened when Olivia had mouthed off about not wanting to snoop around the house when the rest of her boarding house were watching a DVD.

Now Olivia wore that stupid elastic band around her wrist. Said that pinging it was a form of acupressure or something, helped to relax her or distract her away from the compulsion to cut. And Olivia seemed busier these last weeks. The play, naturally, was absorbing her energies. And the pressure of work had gone up now that term was halfway through. They pushed them hard

272

here, for all the liberal wishy-washy stuff about allowing pupils to flourish in a supportive and encouraging environment. If Emily herself had been to a school like this who knows what she might have made of herself. Emily Fleming would have blossomed into her real, her fullest self.

But enough of this self-indulgence. Time was short. The play would be the obvious occasion at which to bring things to a head. Everyone would be there: parents, many of the staff, governors. There had to be a way of pulling it all together.

But first she needed to know what intelligence Meredith and Charles's trip to Prague had yielded. Emily had made calls, left messages on voicemails, but had had no replies yet.

Sometimes Charles looked at her in strange way. Did he know who she was? She could try to get into his apartment during the day when he was out and about snooping on the staff. But it was a high-risk option. People walked in and out of the main house all the time.

Which left the option of Meredith's flat. Meredith had left the spare key with Simon when she'd left the dog in his care. Emily had taken the key out of the carrier bag and placed it under a pile of bills and letters on Simon's kitchen table. If Meredith had missed it and asked Simon where the key was Simon would panic and root around in his debris. And simply think he'd forgotten to put it back in the bag. He was careless with keys, had left the history room cupboard key lying about in the staffroom.

Merry's spare key was still under the pile of papers. Emily would borrow it. Perhaps there'd be an email on Meredith's laptop that would spell out what they'd discovered in Prague.

CHAPTER
THIRTY-FIVE

Meredith

"Sofia said she'd be over at about half six, when she finishes work." My father sat up straight in his seat. "I'm fairly sure she knows what we want to talk about, though I didn't go into details on the phone." His eyes still looked over-bright. I wondered whether he'd had any sleep the previous night.

"You haven't said a word to Olivia?" I knew this must have been a temptation he'd find hard to resist.

He shook his head.

"Do you think Sofia would have said anything to her?"

"I don't think so."

"I still don't know why Sofia didn't say something back when Olivia started here."

He shrugged. "It makes no sense to me, either." His face brightened. "But it doesn't stop this from being a happy occasion."

"What will happen to Olivia, Dad?" I thought of all the gossip if it were discovered that this quiet girl was the head's granddaughter. "Will she be able to stay here?"

"I don't see why not." His expression became defensive. Having found this grandchild, his only granddaughter, there was no way on earth he was going to be separated from her.

I imagined how she'd hate people whispering about her. I knew myself how hard it was to work in a school where a parent was the head. How many times had I come into the staffroom to see people nudging one another in warning? I knew it was because they'd been moaning about my father. However hard he tried to maintain good relationships with his staff, there'd always be areas where people disagreed with him. For a vulnerable child it would be harder than for me. A teacher or housemaster would sometimes have to send a pupil to the head to remove a privilege or hand out a Friday evening detention. The pupil concerned might take out any resentment on Olivia.

I moved my eyes around the room to try and dislodge this uneasiness. The reborn doll in its cardboard box had moved from the top of my father's desk and now sat on the floor beside a bookcase. "I need to get rid of that thing." My father saw me looking at it. "I suppose the drama department might like it." He sounded weary.

I wished he'd removed it already. The box and its contents seemed to drag me back to the confusion of the early term.

A car drew up outside. I stood and looked out of the window. It was a small red Vauxhall, clearly not in its first youth. Something about it was familiar. I couldn't remember what. Sofia got out. She'd dressed very smartly

276

for this interview, in a black coat and cashmere-looking scarf. I stood back from the window in case she saw me watching her. "It's Sofia," I said, turning to Dad. "Is Olivia going to be here too? Shall I go and get her?"

"Not yet. I've warned her housemistress that I'll need time with Olivia later this evening."

"Shouldn't she be here with us as well?"

"Oh, I don't think we want to involve any other staff just now," he said, sounding vague. I wasn't so sure. A little voice inside me insisted that this had to be done properly. Cathy ought to be here. Or Olivia's housemistress.

"I'll go down to meet Sofia now." He stood up, straightening his tie and looking suddenly nervous as though he were the one about to meet the head, not the other way round. As he left the office he glanced over his shoulder. Looking for my absent mother, I guessed. Momentarily forgetting she wouldn't be here to help him through this potentially difficult meeting. I felt a double pang for her and for Hugh. I was still mentally recording everything that happened to me for playing back to him at some point. I switched off the mental tape recorder.

I'd only seen Sofia that once before when she'd been wearing jeans and a sweatshirt to carry out her housekeeping duties, her hair scraped up into a ponytail. This evening she was wearing a smart suit under her overcoat, with discreet make-up and heels. She looked glamorous and confident as she entered the room with Dad, every bit the Letchford type. I blinked.

She held out a hand to me. "We meet again, Mrs Cordingley."

I blushed in front of her stare. "Yes." I took her hand and shook it, realizing that this woman and I were relations of some kind by virtue of our relationship to Olivia.

Dad motioned to her to sit down. She took the small sofa at ninety degrees to his desk. I hoped he wasn't going to sit behind it in his headmaster's stance. He took the chair and moved it round so that he was sitting opposite her. Sofia sat with her smartly stockinged legs slanted, ankles crossed. She might have been a model. I perched on the edge of the desk feeling ungainly. "This has taken us by surprise," Dad said, his voice very gentle. "I didn't know that I'd left Hana, your mother, expecting my son."

"My brother, Jan." A softness filled her face at the mention of his name.

"If I'd had any idea . . ." He shook his head. "Were things hard for you and Jan as you grew up?"

"Jan was already nearly twelve when I am born. So we didn't play with one another. He liked my father. I remember the two of them playing football together when my father came home from work."

"Was it a happy childhood?" I asked. Her earliest years would have been spent in the old Communist regime. I couldn't imagine what that would have been like but it must surely have been in every way different from the childhood I'd had here.

"I remember it as happy."

"Was *she* happy?" Dad's voice held a slight quaver.

278

"It was hard for Mama" — she gave him an awkward glance — "being so young, by herself, with a baby. Back then you were expected to marry before you had children. And nobody else was interested in a woman with a son. It is still a bit like that at home. So she worked and her older cousin, Maria, the one you met in Prague, looked after Jan."

"Then Hana met your father?"

"He loved her and Jan. But he was a male, a Czech male. He expected my mother to do everything in the house after a day's work. There were arguments." She shrugged, suggesting that this wasn't surprising.

I wanted to ask Sofia how it was that she'd found her way to England in such a menial capacity. She was obviously intelligent. "I studied pharmacology," she told me, as though she knew what was on my mind. "But there weren't many jobs at home. A friend told me I would make money working in England as an au pair and I could send it home to Maria, my cousin. And then there was ..." She stopped and seemed to recollect herself.

"Tell us about Irena," Dad asked. "Olivia, I mean."

She moved her gaze away from his while she considered her answer. "She has nobody apart from me and Maria, our cousin. But I got married here in England and Olivia went to the village school where we were in Kent. But my husband died and I had to find another job."

She stopped, biting her tongue. Something about the story didn't seem to add up but I couldn't figure out which bit it was. I wondered when she'd found out about Letchford School and the family connection. And how? Hana was long dead and Sofia wouldn't necessarily have linked Karel Stastny with Charles Statton.

"When did you find out that I was Olivia's grandfather?" Dad asked.

She blinked at the words, as though the reality of who the girl was had suddenly hit her. "About a year ago. I knew that Mama's old boyfriend, Karel Stastny, had come to England as a young man in 1968 or '69. But it was only last year I found out that you were now Mr Charles Statton, the headmaster."

She took a breath. "A friend told me that bit. The children who went to this school had the world at their feet, she said. I thought then that Olivia belonged at this school where Mr Statton is head." Her eyes narrowed and took on an intensity of expression.

I wondered why she hadn't introduced herself and Olivia at that stage. I was about to ask her when she sat up, eyes fixed on something. "Are you all right?" I asked.

"Fine." But her eyes were still narrowed. I looked at what she was focused on and saw the box in which the reborn doll was lying. She saw me looking in the same direction and turned away, but not before I'd caught a glimpse of dismay in her expression. But this was not the time to question her about the doll.

"Was Olivia happy to come here?" Dad asked. He'd be desperate to know that this choice had not been forced on the girl. He prided himself on the idea that only children who were excited about coming to

Letchford should be admitted. "Do you remember who interviewed her?"

"Mr Simon Radcliffe. Olivia seemed happy enough. She thought she would miss me, though."

Until only a few years ago Dad had interviewed every pupil himself. Now he simply saw those applying for scholarships. Even if he had met Olivia alone it was doubtful he'd have worked out who she was.

"And she had no idea that she was related to me?" Dad asked.

"She would never have thought it, no."

"But why? Why this school?" I asked. "Why send her here if she wasn't even going to know what the connection was? You could have sent her to a day school in or around Wokingham, It would have been . . ." Cheaper, I was going to say. Then I thought of her job. Perhaps her employer didn't like having a child around.

"I knew it would be better for her to live at school during the term. My job is . . . Sometimes I have to work at nights." She sounded bitter. She had to serve food at Mrs Smirnova's dinner parties, I thought. Beneath her eyes, carefully made-up, there were shadows. Sofia worked hard. She'd have to, to pay the fees.

Her eyes moved back to the cardboard box. She raised a hand to her mouth and seemed about to chew her manicured fingernails before she realized what she was doing and removed the fingers from her mouth. She still hadn't really told us why Letchford had been her choice for Olivia.

"I have to say" — my father spoke with real warmth — "that the sacrifices you have made for Olivia fill me with deep admiration."

She gave a little nod and blinked hard.

"Perhaps we should discuss how we explain all this to her," Dad went on. "Obviously she needs to know that she's been living among family. But do we encourage her to keep a little quiet about it with her classmates? Or would that make her life even more complicated?"

"Even more?" Sofia looked puzzled. "What do you mean?"

"Olivia doesn't always find school life easy." I tried to make the words gentle. "She has struggled a little to make friends. The play has helped, though."

"Play?"

"She's got a part in *The Crucible*." She still seemed unclear. "A play by Arthur Miller. It's a small part but she's very good."

Sofia looked pleased. "I want her to be happy. That's what she told me, Olivia would be happy here."

"She?"

"The friend who told me about Letchford. She said it wasn't like other schools."

I wondered whether the friend had been a past pupil.

"How do you think she'll respond, Sofia?" Dad asked.

"She shouldn't know." Sofia folded her arms. "It's best she knows nothing." She looked distressed now.

But my heart told me Olivia needed to know she belonged in a deeper way than the other pupils. She

282

belonged to the gardens outside, now slipping quietly into their sombre white-and-grey winter colour, to the house itself with its old stone walls, to her grandmother's image under the mural. This house had proved itself my solace when I'd limped back here last summer. So it would be for my niece.

"Or else we perhaps take her away," Sofia continued.

"No." The objection launched itself so vehemently that they both turned to look at me. "Sorry. I just feel she's settling here at last. She should stay."

"So we not tell her then, not immediately?" Sofia's English had slipped. I saw that she was clutching her hands together in her lap.

"Will you at least think about it?" Dad sounded desperate.

The note of sadness in his voice seemed to shake her out of her trance. "Perhaps after the play, perhaps at Christmas-time." She spoke more softly now. "I need to speak to Maria first."

"Seems like a good plan," I agreed.

Dad nodded, looking disappointed.

She looked him directly in the eye and her expression was more open. "I was so sorry to hear about Mrs Statton."

"Thank you. I miss her terribly." Unlike Dad to admit to a near-stranger that he felt in any way vulnerable. But then Sofia was almost a member of the extended family. The telephone rang. "That will probably be Clara." He looked guilty. I was amazed that my big sister hadn't steamed down the M4 to be present at this meeting.

"My elder sister," I explained.

"I must get back." Sofia rose.

"I can call her back." Dad was peering at the caller identification on the receiver.

"No, you take the call."

"I'll show you out," I said. She nodded a goodbye at Dad and indicated that he should pick up the ringing phone.

As we walked across the hall the door below opened and Emily came inside with a handful of files. No reason why she shouldn't: a teacher had probably asked her to bring over something to the office, but her presence made me feel like Samson when he spotted a cat.

Sofia, too, hung back for a second. Emily had looked up at the sound of the door to Dad's apartment opening. Her face when she saw Sofia was stony. She put down the files on the console table beside the front door and left.

I wondered about asking Sofia if she knew Emily. But then it all fell into place. Of course she did. I'd seen the two of them together in this red Vauxhall that early morning before half-term. It would be interesting to hear Sofia explain the relationship.

"I've got to go now." She pre-empted further discussion. "Mrs Smirnova expects me back to prepare supper." She pulled an ancient-looking car key out of her bag. I wanted to ask her about Emily but the look in her eyes told me the subject was closed.

"You work very hard, Sofia." I wondered whether she ever had a day or an evening off. And all the money she earned, or most of it, was coming here in the form of Olivia's fees. I glanced guiltily round the polished entrance hall.

She narrowed her eyes at me. "So?"

"I didn't mean any offence." I felt my cheeks burn. "Please don't think that."

"Perhaps you think it is a menial job, no?"

I couldn't meet her eyes.

"You're right," she said quietly. "It is not what I was educated to do. Naturally I'd prefer to work in a lab or a hospital instead of worrying that there are stains on the steel range or that the champagne isn't chilled for the party." She shook her head. "You think I don't hate smiling at people I despise and pretending I find them fascinating?"

I must have looked puzzled at the last remark.

She let out a breath. "I'm sorry, excuse me, I know you weren't saying anything bad about me. It's just so . . . hard."

I noticed the dark shadows under the foundation now.

"Is there more we can do to help?" I asked. "A bursary . . .? You could still apply. This revelation doesn't affect that."

"I think it does." She sounded flat. "It would look like special treatment."

"What will happen to Olivia at Christmas?" I asked. "Perhaps that would be a good time to tell her who we are."

285

"Perhaps. She may be in Prague with Maria for Christmas." She smiled briefly before the sadness returned to her eyes. "They'll be so happy."

"Christmas in Prague must be magical." I pictured markets and candles, snow glistening on baroque buildings. "Can you go back yourself then?"

"Mrs Smirnova wants a big Christmas Eve dinner party."

I touched her arm. "You're entitled to time off, Sofia. Don't let her treat you badly." I thought of Olivia, of her cut arms. Should I talk to Sofia about this? Dad might well have mentioned it to her privately, when he'd phoned to ask her to come over. Or Cathy might have been in touch at the time of Olivia's fall. I was treading on dangerous ground. "You need time with Olivia," I said in the end.

"She needed me and I failed her." She swallowed. "Her arms . . . When I saw them . . ." She looked away.

"The cutting seems to have stopped now."

"She promises she won't do it again. She wears the band." She made a pinging action against her left wrist.

"I'm keeping an eye on her," I said. "So is my father. And her housemistress. And the school nurse. Don't worry." I felt surer of myself and touched her arm again.

Her eyes welled. "You're a kind lady, Mrs Cordingley."

"Meredith."

"Meredith." She spoke it slowly. "I wish I hadn't . . ."

I waited for her to finish, but she shook her head. "I must go now. Tell Olivia I ring her on her mobile. Send her my love, please. And I will ring you and your father at end of term. To discuss how we tell her."

CHAPTER
THIRTY-SIX

"So we can't tell Olivia who she is and things stay in limbo?" Clara summed it up. She'd rung my mobile almost as soon as she'd finished talking to Dad.

"We have to do what Sofia says. She is Olivia's legal guardian."

"Suppose so." I could hear her doubt crackling across the miles between us. "Something doesn't add up, Merry."

"I know." I hadn't been able to admit it to myself before but I knew Clara was right. She usually was. I wondered whether I should tell her about having seen Sofia with Emily earlier in the term. But could I be absolutely sure? The woman sitting with Emily had had her back to me.

"There's no doubt that Olivia is who they say she is?"

"We saw the photographs."

"Photos mean nothing. You need a birth certificate to be sure."

"What do you mean?"

"Think about it, Merry. Eventually Dad is going to leave us a fairly substantial inheritance. Even if the school belongs to the trust. They'd have to pay something for the land and house to stay at Letchford. Dad's heirs are going to benefit quite nicely. Until a few weeks ago we assumed that would be me and my family and you and . . . well, just you."

I waited.

"Merry, I've got to tell you that we need money badly. Marcus's job, it's looking rocky. There's the mortgage. And school fees. And my partnership won't pay out as much this year."

"That's why you wanted Dad to sell up." I tried to keep the accusation from my tone.

"I admit it crossed my mind." She sounded so quiet, so unlike her normal self. "But perhaps Marcus and I will simply have to sell the house." She seemed to regain her balance. "If Olivia is who we think she is then she deserves her fair share of anything Dad might leave us. There's a moral responsibility on us to look after her. But we need to know more about her."

She made it all sound matter-of-fact. Clara might be bossy and keen on her rights but she was always fair. As a little girl she'd counted all the Smarties out of the tube to divide between the two of us. When we'd shared a bed on holidays she'd measured out the mattress carefully and allocated us each the same amount.

"You don't think Olivia is who she is supposed to be, do you?"

I could see her shrug all those miles away in Clapham. "Nobody's ever talked to her about her childhood. She could be anyone. Dad says she looks like Hana but that doesn't mean she's necessarily Dad's granddaughter."

It sounded blunt but it was true.

"Just don't let him get too carried away with this," she went on. "Don't let him go changing his will or anything like that. In fact, he should probably take advice from the family solicitor. He's vulnerable, Merry."

I supposed he was. Widowed. Lonely. Drawn to a girl who seemed as lost as he probably felt at times.

"Keep an eye on him. I'll be down at the weekend. There's a governors' meeting with the bursar on Friday night to look at the latest figures, so perhaps I could stay with you?"

"Of course!" I couldn't wait to see her. After we'd hung up I found myself staring at the silent mobile. It was dark now and I drew the blinds to hide the gloom outside. My sister's mention of the bursar reminded me of what Dad had told me about his journey to England in the sixties, about John Andrews, who'd given him a home. That same John Andrews had become the bursar here years later because he had been such a good friend to Dad.

I tried to work out why John Andrews was on my mind now. There'd been a bit of trouble with the previous bursar, Dad had told me. He'd needed someone he could trust absolutely. I dialled Clara's number.

"Merry?" She sounded weary.

"What do you remember about John Andrews?"

"John Andrews?" I could hear the sigh in her voice. She'd be trying to get the children to bed, cook a late supper, talk to Marcus about his looming redundancy.

"Sorry. It's late."

"No, it's all right. Funnily enough I'd been thinking about him quite recently. It could never happen these days. What had gone on before he took over, I mean."

"Some kind of embezzlement?"

"That's right. The previous bursar, can't remember his name, had been operating a fiddle while they were building the new boarding houses and the gym. Getting kickbacks from contractors. Taking out money supposedly to pay suppliers in cash." She broke off to shout a reprimand at one of the boys. "It was quite sad. The bursar had a baby with a serious illness or disability of some kind in special care. He wanted the money to pay for treatment in a hospital in America."

"And Dad found out?"

"He was gutted. Obviously he had to sack the bursar. But he didn't prosecute."

"Was the money paid back?"

"Don't think so."

"Where did the family go?"

"Australia or somewhere like that. God knows how they managed with the baby." Something crashed to the floor. "I told you not to stack those plates so high, Sam! Got to go, Merry, speak soon."

The connection between what had happened in the school all those years ago and recent events was there deep inside my subconscious but I couldn't pull it out to examine it logically. I needed to talk through what I knew. I needed my husband's completely rational outlook. His brain was good at this kind of puzzle. I still

291

had my mobile in my hand. My thumb pushed his number before my head could stop it.

"Merry?" Did he sound put out or merely surprised? I wondered.

"Do you have ten minutes?"

"Fire away." He still sounded guarded.

"Something's bugging me. I need a fresh outlook." I started to tell him, coming to a halt when I'd finished relating what Clara had told me about the bursar. "That's it, really. I don't know if it means anything."

"I don't see how that can have anything to do with what's been happening here. And the stabbed baby in the cupboard was just a doll, Merry."

"It had a paperknife through its chest."

"Nasty, but a bit like something a teenager might have picked up from watching horror movies."

"I suppose so."

"And the doll was sent to Olivia's address."

"Her aunt denies ordering the doll. I think I believe her."

"Olivia's not related to the old bursar, is she?"

"No. I don't think any of the children here can be. They're far too young." I did some calculations. It must have all happened about twenty years ago now. "Unless he had more children after he left here."

"Let me think about it." There was curiosity in his voice now. "I've got some time and I could do some Internet research. What was the bursar's name, do you know?"

"Noel Collins." That was it. I remembered Mr Collins as a sad-faced man. But kind. He'd given Clara

292

and me chocolate biscuits on a few occasions when we'd scampered into his office.

"You all right?" Hugh sounded concerned.

"Fine. Just grappling with other old family stuff." I didn't know whether or not to tell him about Olivia yet. But he was still my husband. "I think I might have a new niece."

"Clara and Marcus? They're having a third? Wonderful. How'll she fit another baby in with being a law partner?"

"Not Clara." I explained about Olivia and my father's secret love affair in Czechoslovakia all those years ago.

"Holy Moley, Charles was a dark horse," he said. "Poor chap. This must have come as a shock."

"He seems delighted."

"You said the child's actually in the school?"

"And knows nothing about the relationship. If she is in fact who we think she is."

He said nothing for a second. "I might come up and see you again, if that's OK? Will it be frantic between now and the end of term?" He obviously remembered the usual frenzy at school this time of year.

"It's not too bad for the next week."

"Why don't we say tomorrow evening. What time do you finish?"

"I can be free by five."

"Don't get me from the station, I'll grab a cab. I've had some compensation come through and I haven't exactly had the chance to spend much in the last few months. I'll take you out for supper, too."

"I'd like to cook." He said nothing. "I've been practising. Before she died Mum gave me some tips."

"I'll bring the wine." He cleared his throat. "Give Samson a pat from me."

CHAPTER
THIRTY-SEVEN

Emily

An occasional word of praise or a pat on the head, as though she was a pet dog. Well, let them patronize her. It wasn't long now until the play was performed. End of term was approaching. Already the cast members were holding their scripts in their hands and murmuring their words as they made last efforts to learn them. Extra rehearsals took place in the lunch hour. Emily was still working on the costumes, probably being over-fussy, worrying about finishing touches and making sure seams were straight and buttons secure. But those were the things that made the difference between a professional and an amateur appearance. And Emily was a professional. No matter what else she was, she took this work seriously.

"You've quite a talent," Jenny had told her, watching her finish a tuck on one of the maidservants' dresses. She sounded mildly surprised. Emily thought of the years she'd spent learning how to design and sew things. She'd sewn her dolls' clothes and made most of her own outfits as a teenager. The only way to find fashionable things in the dump where they'd lived.

"It's just a shame these costumes are so plain." Drab old things.

"That was seventeenth-century New England for you," Jenny said. "All Puritanism and primness."

Why did they have to choose a gloomy play like *The Crucible*? All about guilt and blame and responsibility. Emily herself knew a thing or two about those themes. Perhaps it did no harm, she conceded, to show what happened when rumours started flying in a small community and the innocent suffered along with the guilty. That part of *The Crucible* was interesting enough. All the same, it would be more enjoyable to be creating something sumptuous, for a Shakespearean play, say.

Designing clothes was what Emily was born to do. In her dreams she was studying fashion or textiles in London. Becoming a costume designer for the Royal Shakespeare Company. Or perhaps working for a fashion designer in Paris or New York. In a way she'd have preferred to have created her own gown for the reborn doll. But the linen robe and cap had been what the real child, the one the doll had been modelled on, had worn to his christening.

Taking the robe and cap from Tracey's basket in the kitchen back in September had been almost too easy. It had saved her walking over to the drama department and helping herself from the racks. The ivory fabric had looked so right on the doll. She'd had to keep touching its cold skin to reassure herself it wasn't the real infant.

"Shall I send in Olivia for her fitting?" Jenny asked.

"Yes, please." She didn't look up as she cut the last thread and hoped her burning cheeks weren't apparent. Olivia. The reason this whole business was simultaneously harder and more enjoyable than she'd thought it would be.

When the grey gown was pulled over Olivia's shoulders and the white apron and cap added to the costume, Emily couldn't prevent a smile from escaping her. Olivia might have stepped out of the seventeenth century. The dress was that awful dark grey but Emily had put some thought into how it was tailored, and it showed off Olivia's slender waist and delicate collarbones and hid the marks on her arms. The drab colour wasn't so bad with the girl's complexion. In her school uniform Olivia looked gawky and uncomfortable. Not now.

"She's transformed." Jenny stood back beaming, astounded. "You're so clever." Emily wished Jenny would leave the two of them alone. Something was happening deep inside her. Olivia had been something to use at first, a convenient way of hurting the family. It had taken so long to find the chink and it had been so satisfying to find it. She recalled how she'd sat back in amazement when Sofia had told her about her family. It had been just another ordinary slow night in the club in Reading. They'd found themselves talking over Diet Coke while waiting for more men to turn up. It had taken a while to get Sofia talking about Olivia but Emily was good at extracting confidences.

"I always wanted to come to England," Sofia had said. "My mother nearly came here in sixty-eight, when the Russians moved in. But she stayed. Her boyfriend got away, though."

"Did he ever go back to Prague?"

Sofia shook her head. "Not that we know. Mama always thought she'd read something about him. Or that he'd return one day to give an exhibition of his work. He was a wonderful painter as a boy. But he never seemed to become famous in England."

"What was his name?" Emily collected people's names the way some collected badges. You never knew when a name would come in handy.

"Karel Stastny. He left my mother pregnant." Sofia's lip had curled.

Karel Stastny. Emily's mouth opened and she had to work hard to hide her surprise. Well, well, well. Emily knew from her father that, far from developing his artistic brilliance, Karel had become Charles Statton, head of Letchford. A person in whom Emily had a deep interest. It had seemed remarkable. So remarkable Emily had been almost unable to continue the conversation with Sofia. But she'd recovered herself, made an excuse and gone to sit in the toilet to think it over. So Sofia was Hana's daughter. Charles and Hana had had a kid, an older brother of Sofia's. Sofia sometimes talked about a young niece she was bringing up. And Sofia had no other sisters or brothers. Ergo, Sofia's niece, Olivia, must be Charles Statton's granddaughter. Emily had sat on the cracked plastic lavatory seat until the manager had rattled the door and ordered her out.

Up until then Emily's plan to take a gap-year position at the school had been vague. She hadn't really known how she could leverage her presence to cause trouble for the Statton family. But if she had an accomplice . . . All it took was for Sofia to agree to send Olivia to Letchford. "You said you were saving a lot of money by living in for the housekeeping job," she reminded the Czech woman. "No rent. And there's as much work here for you as you need." Sofia had looked across to the bar. A pair of sales reps in ill-fitting suits and loud ties had eased in and were eyeing the women over their beer.

"I don't make much by getting them to buy champagne."

"There are much more lucrative areas."

Sofia had frowned. "What do you mean?"

Emily nodded at a door to the right of the bar. "Private dances."

Sofia sat straighter. "I would never ever do that. It's . . ." She shook her head. "What they do in there, it's awful."

"Well, there are other possibilities," Emily went on. "Outside this club. I suppose it depends how much you value education. Some people earn a lot by going out with men on a professional basis."

"You mean escorts?" Sofia said the word with disdain. "I'm not like that. I have an education. A degree."

Emily shrugged. "Plenty of students and graduates feel it's worth while. To help their families. Get some money behind them."

"Just because I'm a woman from eastern Europe I must be a sex worker, is that what you think?"

Emily leant closer. "I've done it myself," she whispered. "There are some respectable agencies. You don't have to sleep with the men. Sometimes they just want to hire an attractive girlfriend for a work do. You go along and make conversation and look pretty. Sometimes they take you to really good restaurants for dinner."

She swallowed the last of her Diet Coke and raised her eyebrows at the sales reps. "And the men are often more interesting than those. Bankers. Lawyers. Internet millionaires."

A few months later Emily and Olivia had started at the school.

Olivia had been the medium of her revenge. But now? Now Charles and Meredith had probably found out for themselves who Olivia was when they'd visited Prague. Emily had rung Sofia and interrogated her about whom they'd seen and what they'd found out. Sofia had claimed ignorance. Said she'd been called into school to discuss Olivia's grades and ways of maintaining her improvement. Prague hadn't been mentioned. Nor had family secrets. For this lie she, too, would pay. This damn play had kept Emily too busy to get into Meredith's apartment yet, to discover what she'd nosed out.

Best to face the worst case. The possibility of using Olivia as collateral had gone. And anyway, despite everything, despite the coolness shown to her by the girl, Emily felt increasingly warm towards her. She wanted to hold Olivia in her arms, untie the hair from its severe bun and run her fingers through it. Perhaps this unexpectedly deep emotion for another person was reward enough for her time at Letchford.

But Emily had made her promise. She owed it to her parents and to Toby, innocent little Toby. She should never for one instant forget the discovery of his cold little body that morning and her mother's long, desperate howl.

Olivia was shuffling in front of her. "Have you finished?"

Olivia didn't like her any more. Viewed her with distaste. Was far less easy to manage. Time was running out.

Jenny was saying something. ". . . time to look at John Proctor's waistcoat?" She was staring at her with a strange look on her face that told Emily that some of her emotion had shown itself. She had to be very careful.

She clenched her fingers round the scissors in front of her on the desk and wanted to throw them at Jenny's silly face. "Fine," she said. "I've nothing else planned tonight."

"We were going to the White Oak after rehearsals. Why don't you do it tomorrow?" Jenny suggested.

"I wouldn't mind a night in." Maybe she'd let herself into Meredith's apartment tonight and look at her laptop. Emily threaded a needle and pondered talking to the newspapers. The *Daily Mail*, perhaps.

Idyllic school whose upright head isn't what he seems.

Charismatic head left pregnant girlfriend to Russian invaders.

Teacher at top private school abandons injured soldier husband.

She felt resolution pour through her veins with each invented headline. Charles Statton hadn't seen her mother start hoarding her sleeping tablets. Or been with Emily when she'd come home from school to find Mum lying on her bed, her mouth open, a thread of vomit on her pillow. He hadn't seen her father, his former colleague, sitting with the whisky bottle in the evenings, offering to help her with her maths homework when he could hardly sit upright.

The pupils here would draw their own conclusions when she explained it all. And the head himself and his precious Merry would start to learn a bit more about the nature of suffering. She pulled the thread hard through the eye of the needle.

CHAPTER
THIRTY-EIGHT

"Can't I come to the play?" Hugh asked as he topped up my wine glass.

I blinked. Usually only the cast's parents and grandparents wanted to sit through school plays. "I suppose so."

"Don't do me any favours. I could always stay in and watch a boxed set." He sounded amused.

"I'm simply stunned that you'd want to."

"I know it'll be excellent. And I like *The Crucible*. Saw the film with Winona Ryder and Daniel Day Lewis in it."

Not with me, he hadn't. Must have been while he was on tour. Or in hospital. "I'm not sure we're quite up to that standard."

"I'd like to see Olivia again. Does she know yet?"

About her headmaster actually being her grandfather? "We're keeping the revelation until after the holidays." I hadn't dare ask him his own plans for Christmas. "How's it going with the new leg?" I ventured.

A long silence.

"Let's just say that my brain hasn't yet accepted that I don't still have a shattered left leg," he said at last, quietly. "Some nights are . . . interesting." I'd read up on the pain of phantom limbs in an attempt to understand what he was going through and winced. "Some evenings I just give up trying to sleep and drive around."

"Where do you go?" He hadn't brought the new car tonight for dinner, saying that he didn't dare risk a single drink when he was in it. Obviously an evening with me was only bearable with an alcoholic crutch.

"I just drive around aimlessly." He fiddled with the garlic press I'd taken out of the drawer.

I only hoped he'd ask for all the help he could get. I cooked the pork strips and vegetables in a wok with chillies and sherry and some other bits and pieces the recipe book assured me would do well together. Some of the onion stuck to the wok and the pork was a bit overdone but Hugh ate with apparent relish. "You're a good cook these days, Merry." We ate in companionable silence.

"May I use your laptop?" he asked when we'd finished.

I waved him towards the living room. "On the sofa." Perhaps sitting with me in the kitchen wasn't as cosy and familiar as I thought it was. But he brought the laptop back to the kitchen.

"I'm just going to search on a few names." He put it on the table. "I haven't any hopes of finding much about the Czech side but I have a few other ideas."

I stood behind him to clear the plates. His body felt very warm beside mine. It would have been easy to let myself slip back. Every cell of my flesh longed for

304

contact. But something told me to let him make the first move.

After we'd finished the chocolate mousse I'd prepared before school Hugh returned to his Internet search. I made coffee and watched him. "Tell me more about the bursary fraud," he asked. I related what Clara had told me about it.

"A sad story."

"What are you looking for?"

"Just seeing if there is any archive newspaper coverage of the story."

"Dad didn't go to the police."

"Thought as much."

"What do you mean?"

He gave a shrug. "He doesn't like to think badly of people." He got up, moving so fluidly that I forgot he was wearing his prosthetic leg. "I'll do some more on this at home. I suppose I should ring for a cab now."

"You don't need to do that." I stopped and wondered where the words had come from. It certainly had not been my intention to invite my husband to sleep over tonight. To my annoyance I realized that I was blushing like a third-year girl when one of the pin-ups from the sixth form strolled past.

He looked at me and then downwards towards his leg. "I don't know." He touched it. "It's too quick for me, Merry. This . . ."

"There's the sofa-bed," I said wildly. "It's quite comfortable, I've . . ." I'd spent a night on it in that lost week. I'd drunk my way through a bottle of wine and fallen asleep on it, Samson curled up beside me on the floor. "It would be a start," I said. "Just being in the same building overnight. It would be the first time in —"

"Nine months," he said. "I know. The first time in nine months we've spent the night together." Samson padded in and flopped down by his master with a relaxed sigh.

"Have a think," I said, brightly, falsely. "I'll just put a few things away in the kitchen. I can drive you to the station if you still want to go. I didn't drink much." My hands shook as I stacked plates and glasses in the dishwasher. I told myself that tonight's decisions meant nothing. He hadn't been expecting to stay, hadn't brought a washbag with him. Hugh never liked plans to change at the last minute; he always liked to be prepared.

I heard him talking to the dog in a low voice, heard the *swoosh swoosh* of the dog's tail against the wooden floor. He came into the kitchen. "I'd like to stay," he said. "But not on the sofa, so not this time, Merry. When I spend the night with you again I want to do it properly." The blaze of blue in his eyes made me take a breath. He put a hand out to push my hair off my shoulders. "You and I have been through too much to muck around with sofas," he said. "One of the counsellors I've been seeing is good at getting me to decipher what's going on up here. I am getting to grips with some of the guilt." He put a hand to his head.

"Guilt that you survived?" I said slowly.

He nodded. "I don't see the faces of the men I lost in my dreams any more. But I think I need a few more sessions."

306

"Do you want me to go to the counselling with you? As soon as the holidays start I'm free."

"You'd do that?" He sounded surprised.

"Of course I'd bloody well do it." I banged the dishwasher door shut so violently that the plates crashed together in protest. "You're my husband. We're still married. I love you. I think you might still love me a bit because you choose to come and see me. I haven't exactly forced myself on you since you banished me."

He winced.

"I want to help us get back together, but —" Memories of the time he'd thrown me off the ward flooded me. I clung to the worktop. "But I've got a good job here. I've got friends, a purpose. I can't let myself be hurt again. I'm willing to do all that I can to help you — help us, I mean, I want us . . ." He moved so quickly that his mouth was over mine before I'd finished trying to say it all, his hands grabbing me and scooping me towards him. It had been nine months but my body hadn't forgotten his. His lips tasted of wine and chocolate mousse. At some point we must have moved towards the bedroom.

"What would the counsellor say?" I asked, when my mouth was free.

His answer was to push me back against the pillows. "There'll be a brief commercial break while I take this bloody thing off." He patted his prosthesis. "The physio hasn't prepared me for what I have in mind now."

I hadn't seen the stump for months and despite my attempts my muscles tightened in anticipation. He must have sensed this. "It's OK." He stroked my hair again. "Everything's healing. You don't have to be scared, Merry."

I was going to dispute the word but then I realized just how scared I had been. For months and months. And then I saw the leg, cut off just under the knee, still swollen around the stump, still pink, mottled in tone, but neater and tidier, more *sorted* than I'd thought it would be. He eyed his leg dispassionately. "It changes all the time," he said. "As the stump gets less swollen and the muscles develop. That's why they keep measuring it to make sure the socket fits properly."

I put a hand on the leg, about an inch above the stump, as though I was touching something wild and vicious. It didn't bite. "Am I hurting you?"

"No." He laughed. "Only physios and gym instructors are evil enough for that." He moved my fingers up his leg.

I wasn't frightened any longer.

CHAPTER
THIRTY-NINE

Emily

Meredith had been in her apartment all night with peg-leg. But the moment came when Charles Statton was taking assembly two days before the play was to be performed. Meredith herself was sitting with the other staff in the hall, naturally, very much the loyal daughter. Emily was supposed to attend assembly but it was easy to make an excuse about a possible clash next term between a hockey match and a rugby sevens festival. The look of horror on Jeremy's silly pink face might have made her laugh if things hadn't been so serious. "I'll sort it out, don't worry."

He'd muttered something about not being able to manage without Emily. "You didn't seem very keen on sport when you first got here," he added. "Or so I thought."

Never distrust first impressions, eh, Jezza? she'd thought.

She'd remembered Meredith's dog and had taken a couple of pieces of bacon from the morning's breakfast to distract him. Samson was large enough to make her palms sweat. He hadn't liked her much before when she'd come across him at Simon's house. The feeling was mutual.

He was standing by the door as she let herself in and he growled. She took off a boot and smacked him on the end of the nose. He retreated to the kitchen door, whimpering. Perhaps that had been a mistake. If the whimpers turned to barks someone might come over to see what was happening. Emily wasn't even sure what it was she was looking for. An email to or from Meredith was still her best hope. Perhaps she'd written down all the details and sent them to that sister of hers. *You'll never guess what I've found out about Emily . . .*

She spotted the laptop on the living room coffee table and walked slowly towards it, hoping the dog would stay where he was. Although she was in a hurry there was time enough to see how elegantly this apartment had been decorated: all off-white walls and wooden floors. No pictures on the walls, though. Meredith must be extremely plain in her tastes. There was a photograph of a man in uniform on the fireplace. The maimed husband before he'd lost his leg and fingers.

The dog was still watching her from the kitchen door, ears pricked. She switched on the laptop. No prompt for a password. Good. She went into Internet, looking at the bookmarks. There was a folder for the Czech trip, just details of flights and car hire. Prague was the only place mentioned. They hadn't downloaded any street maps or googled on particular addresses, as far as Emily could tell.

She wondered where Meredith would spend the Christmas holiday. Perhaps she'd fly somewhere sunny with the wounded hero husband. Emily had watched him enter the apartment last night and leave in a taxi only this morning, just before assembly. He was pretty hot, even with the peg leg. No wonder Meredith was looking so pleased with herself.

She went into Meredith's Internet search history. Froze. Blinked. Took a breath. Looked again. And still saw the same name. Meredith had been raking up the past. Unsuccessfully, as it happened. But that wasn't the point.

Emily sat back on her heels, shaking. Meredith might have worked it out. Emily stared at the names and felt the anger as a white-hot pulse through her bloodstream. This changed everything. The dog growled from the kitchen, obviously picking up her fury. "Shut up," she muttered at him. She would have liked to have taken one of her blades to him but she hadn't planned on doing that. When you departed from plans things went wrong. Like when she'd lost her temper before half-term and pushed Olivia downstairs.

She rocked backwards and forwards on her heels, thinking it through, trying to keep calm. *You have a choice as to how you respond, Emily,* that's what the anger management counsellor had told her a year ago. She breathed deeply, letting the breath go down into her. She made her shoulders relax. She could walk away now. Limit her actions to talking to the press, kicking up some bad publicity for the school.

As she stood up the dog barked at her, eyes blazing with fury, the fur standing up on its neck.

She changed her mind about not harming him. She opened the fridge and reached for some bacon. He stopped the noise and pricked his ears. She threw a rasher towards the back of the living room and he shot past her to retrieve it. She was at the front door a second later, by which time he'd gulped down the bacon and was running towards her again. She showed him the second rasher, tore it in half and threw one bit behind her, down the stairs to the garden. It was hard to throw accurately with her back to the stairs but when she turned to watch him he was standing by the main door, bolting down the bacon. One piece left. She threw it from halfway down the steps. It landed in the courtyard and that gave her free access to the front door.

Samson would probably hang around the courtyard waiting for someone to let him back in but there was a chance he'd wander off. The road was busy at rush hour and traffic moved quickly. She'd already seen the dog standing on his hind legs, trying to scale the fence. He'd wanted to get to the car in which she'd sat with Sofia, trying to reassure her following Meredith's visit to Bellingham. Now the dog would be free to jump onto the road if he wanted.

Emily examined her watch. Just enough time to return the key to Simon's cottage. She had his spare key, too. He hadn't noticed it was missing, Or perhaps thought that he'd given it to Meredith at some point. They were always doing one another little favours, those two. Simon hadn't asked Emily if she wanted a key to his cottage, not even after that time she'd slept with him. He was still ashamed of that event, even though she wasn't a pupil and there was nothing illegal or even particularly unethical about it. He kept muttering about taking advantage and how much younger she was. She'd been about to correct him on that score but had remembered just in time that she was supposed to be barely nineteen, not twenty-two. Thank God she'd always hated the sun and all the hearty outdoor activities New Zealanders made such a fuss about.

Tracey Johnson's lack of years hadn't put Simon off having a brief fling with her, either. Truth was, as Tracey had probably also discovered, Simon was in love with one woman only. Meredith. Adored her. Everyone else was just for fun. Meredith and the papers and photos in the history room cupboard, that was all Simon wanted. "History is my passion," he'd told Emily. For him the past meant old papers and creaky houses. For her it meant something else. Blood history.

The dog was still busy with the rasher and paid Emily no attention as she walked past him. The idea came to her like lots of her ideas: suddenly and vividly. It would take pluck. She was scared of Samson. Her hand went to the belt on her jeans and she unbuckled it. Quick, while he was still chomping. She walked up to him and willed herself to do it. She looped the belt through his collar while his head was still down, trying to be confident in her movements. "We're going for a walk." It felt better now that she had him under

313

control. She tugged at the belt and he looked at her inquiringly, licking his lips. Perhaps he thought she was a friend, after all.

"Off we go, doggy." She walked towards the woods with him. There must be somewhere she could tie him.

Her boldness with the dog had set her imagination free. If she could do this, there was more she was capable of doing. Forget just going to the newspapers and planting an embarrassing story about the head. But what?

The bell rang in the distance. Emily walked faster, the dog keeping pace in easy strides. She was due in the drama department to carry out the last alterations to costumes for the play. The play. The audience.

Waiting for something dramatic.

Like the apparently murdered baby in the history room.

That reborn doll hadn't entirely exhausted its possibilities. Only twenty or so pupils had seen it. Olivia had said she'd seen it in Charles's study.

Then the idea shot through her mind. She laughed out loud and the dog wagged his tail.

It would be a performance all right. A night nobody would forget. And all for Toby. And Mum and Dad.

She must have jerked the dog's collar; he turned his head to her. Funny to think she'd been scared of this stupid animal. There was nothing she couldn't do now.

CHAPTER
FORTY

Meredith

Most women seemed to look twice at the tall athletic man beside me in the audience in the school hall. I had to remind myself that I couldn't yet be sure he was really a permanent part of my life. One step at a time . . . I tried hard to relax, to make myself forget about Samson. It had been two days now and still there was no sign of him. He hadn't been in my flat when I'd returned at lunchtime to take him for a walk. Again I asked myself if I'd left the door open when I'd left after breakfast. Again I was pretty sure I hadn't. Where was my dog? December had continued bone-chillingly cold. I tried to push away the thought of him hurt and outdoors for the second night.

The first scenes of *The Crucible* were going well. As far as I could tell nobody had fluffed a line or forgotten a cue. Olivia entered as Mary Warren, returning from a day out at the trials and standing up against her master, John Proctor. Olivia's character gave John Proctor's wife a little doll she'd made. The calculated intent flashing over Olivia's face as she did this made me shiver. It didn't help that the object was a doll, of course, even though it was simply a small sewn-fabric object. Hugh nudged me. "Something fishy about that doll, if you ask me."

"I've had enough of dolls," I whispered back.

Jenny had made some cuts to the play, which would otherwise have run for three hours or so, but the first act still went on for just over an hour. I noticed Hugh rubbing the leg joint and wondered how long he could sit before the pain became too strong. I bit my tongue, not wanting to fuss, but seeing the relief on his face when he rose as the curtain came down for the interval. "Glass of wine, Merry?" He moved stiffly across the hall towards the table at the back where members of the parent-teacher association were selling glasses of Pinot Grigio and Merlot. "Olivia's quite chilling," he told me as we queued. "I'm impressed."

"So am I. It's not a big part but she's made something of it." Over his shoulder I saw Sofia, shyly clutching a programme. I waved to her. "Come and join us," I called. She approached, still looking cautious. "Olivia's wonderful," I told her. She gave Hugh a shy look and nodded. "This is my husband," I told her. She held out a hand, smiling.

"Your niece is making me nervous. In the best possible way," he told her.

She smiled with pride. "Thank you."

"Come on." I put a hand on his shoulder. "Let's get back to our seats."

The backstage team was obviously working hard to put things in order for the second act. I could hear scenery moving against floorboards. The curtains swished as though about to open. The audience hushed. But nothing happened for a second. I thought I made out the outline of someone running to the side. Then the curtains swung back with a jerk, the rails swaying under the force. "Whoops," Hugh muttered, "a little over-enthusiastic." We were gazing at the stage. Nobody said a word. Then a woman screamed. I stared until I thought I was going to be sick.

A baby hung by its distorted neck from a rope, looped around the top of a set of ladders. It wore the linen gown and cap — again. "It's all right," I said. "It's just a doll. It's a prank." I looked for Jenny, for my father, for someone to take control. Nobody was moving. I rose to my feet and pushed past Hugh, making for the stage, anger pulsing through me. I'd reached the steps when the voice spoke.

"Sorry for the interruption to the play. *The Crucible* will continue in a few minutes. First I'd like to take the opportunity to tell you all a story."

Emily. Speaking in a low, confident, tone. But still the stage was empty. Except for the doll swinging from the rope around its neck.

"This is the story of two men. The first man was regarded as highly successful. He had done well for himself, building up a first-rate and popular school." The back of my neck prickled. "He was married with two healthy daughters. The other man also had a respected position and two children he doted on: a girl and a boy.

"But his son was born with a rare heart defect. No surgery was available in Britain. Without treatment the

317

boy would die before his first birthday. But the father had done his research and discovered a clinic in the States where a surgeon was pioneering treatment with more than a sixty-per-cent success rate.

"The family sold their house. But still they couldn't raise the money for airfares and a long and expensive stay in Philadelphia." I was on the stage by now, looking for the source of Emily's voice. The stagehands shrugged.

"We don't know where it's coming from," one of them hissed.

"The father borrowed some money from his successful friend. The friend had promised his support. But then he brought in a third man, a retired maths teacher who fancied himself as a bit of a bookkeeper. This new arrival decided that fraud had occurred. He urged the headmaster, for that is who this friend was, our very own headmaster, to sack the father. Who now worried that the police would be involved, that he'd be charged with a crime he hadn't committed. And then what would happen to his family?"

"Draw the curtains," I hissed at the stagehands, who appeared to be paralysed. The voice seemed to be coming from above my head. Hugh was beside me now, scrutinizing the hanging doll. "The curtains," I hissed again. At last the green velvet drapes swung back together, separating us from the stare of the audience.

"Let's get that thing down," I whispered, forgetting about Hugh's leg. "Go on," I urged. Surprise flashed over his face but he clambered up the ladder and unhooked the rope from the top, letting the doll fall to the ground. Even then I found a moment to note how smoothly he was moving. Still the voice was continuing with its litany.

". . . leave the country immediately. With a baby still in desperate need of treatment. America was out of the question, they needed to go somewhere where the authorities wouldn't track them. The baby's condition was now too severe for the operation to save him. The mother was distraught and the bursar knew she wouldn't cope if he were sent to prison. That's right, the bursar. Letchford's bursar back then. Threatened with prison for taking money that the head had said he could take. But how was he to prove this? No contracts had been drawn up. It had been a gentleman's agreement.

"Eventually the family found their way to New Zealand, where doctors did their best for the baby, now very weak. He died, ladies and gentlemen." She paused. "The child who might have been saved was my brother. On the stage you see his facsimile. When the baby died, part of my mother died with him.

"Perhaps I shouldn't be telling you all this. But sadly this incident was not the only occasion on which Charles Statton has shown himself to be heartless and self-absorbed. In 1968 he was —" I stood on the doll. The voice stopped briefly. ". . . student involved in the Prague Spring," it resumed. "He abandoned a pregnant girlfriend who was unwell." It was still just about audible, but much quieter since I'd trodden on it. ". . . so that he could save his own skin, left her to the mercy of the Russian invaders, ladies and gentlemen.

And not once did he ever enquire about her and her child, not even when the Velvet Revolution had taken place and it was perfectly safe for him to return to his homeland. And now he has a granddaughter who he's never acknowledged either —"

I trod on the doll again. The voice fell silent. I pulled off its gown and ripped at the stitches in its cloth body that hid the recorder, a small black object. When I'd switched it off, I walked through the curtains and addressed the audience.

"Thank you for your patience." I gave what I hoped was a confident smile. "Our apologies for this interruption." I nodded at Jenny, standing, hand over mouth, in the wings.

"The show will now continue. Please give us a moment to set up the stage." I went back inside the curtains. Actors and backstage team were still gazing at the recorder in my hand. Finally people started moving onto the stage. The ladder was pulled to one side. I kicked the doll into the wings and threw the rope after it. Jenny was whispering to the actors. I walked off stage to find Olivia. What had she heard? Everything, probably, if she was waiting in the wings with the others. She sat, composed, hands in her lap.

"Are you all right?"

She nodded. "I always knew she was mad." She sounded dismissive. "She said she was going to do something memorable. I never thought she'd do it at the play, though."

I knelt so that I was at her level. "You should have told us, Olivia. We'd have put a stop to this."

She shook her head. "I told you, she's crazy. If it hadn't been this it would have been something worse. She pushed me down the stairs when I said I didn't want to help her." Something flickered over her pale face. "Have you found your dog yet?"

I shook my head.

"Everything's ready," Jenny whispered. "Let's make it the best we can, everyone. Let's show how professional we are."

"Break a leg," I told them in a low voice. "Sock it to them."

"We'll do it for your dad." The voice was very quiet; I had to peer into the gloom to see who had spoken. A small first-year boy, an extra in one of the courtroom scenes. I'd never heard him say anything before that wasn't in his script. I remembered his name. James Perry. The first-year who'd kicked a football through a windowpane.

No time to think about Dad now. He wouldn't want me even to look at him to make sure he was all right. The play was the thing now. If the children could carry off the second part it would be a huge vote of confidence in him and everything he had done at Letchford. Hugh shifted his prosthetic leg to let me through to my seat.

"Well done," he murmured as the curtain reopened. "You managed that excellently." Parents were still whispering but growing quieter now.

We were looking at the children on the stage, a little flustered-looking but in their positions. I nodded at them and crossed my fingers so hard they ached.

CHAPTER
FORTY-ONE

"Enough of what Emily said was true," my father said. We were in his sitting room. We'd spent some time talking to Sofia, reassuring her. Then she'd left to spend a bit of time with Olivia. "Noel and I had talked about money, about the baby being ill and the difficulties of raising the funds to take him to America. Perhaps I did casually say that I would help if I could. I meant me personally, Merry, not the school. I never meant him to take money from Letchford." He stared at the carpet. "I must just have forgotten about the conversation. He didn't mention it again. And I was over-involved in the building work."

Once again I reassured him that we knew all this. Nobody had believed every word of Emily's address. Several of the governors had come up to Dad after the play to congratulate him and to offer a quiet word of support.

As for the rest of what Emily had said, the personal details of my father's flight from Czechoslovakia, I wasn't sure how much of it could have been heard by the audience. Most of the cast and backstage crew would have heard that part of the narrative. At least they and, more importantly, Olivia wouldn't know whom Emily had meant when she referred to the granddaughter.

"I should ring Clara," I said. "Before she finds out by text, like last time." I felt in my handbag for the mobile and touched a whistle I sometimes used when walking Samson. All the time I'd been sitting here with Dad I hadn't been looking for the dog. I should have been emailing DogLost again, ringing the dog warden, friends in the village.

"I'm going out to have one last look round the grounds." Hugh must have been thinking exactly what I had been. "I'll check the cricket pavilion and the sheds. He might have got locked in."

I was about to say that nobody had been in the pavilion since August, but stopped myself. Hugh would feel better if he knew he'd looked everywhere.

"You'll find a spare set of keys in my desk drawer," my father told him.

Hugh had only just left when someone knocked on the door.

"Sofia." She seemed to have aged in the hours since the play had started. I'd assumed that she'd left the school by now.

"I start to drive home," she said. "Then I come back again." Her eyes were on my father. "There is something I must tell you."

"Please." He was already standing. "Do sit down."

I moved up on the sofa so that there was room for her to sit.

Her mouth moved as though there were words she wanted to say, but nothing came out. "You will be very angry," she said. "I did not mean to deceive you. I would never have told you that Olivia . . . that she was your granddaughter. I was just going to tell you there was a connection, that is all."

"What do you mean?" Dad frowned.

She took a deep breath. "Olivia is my daughter, not Jan's. She is Hana's granddaughter but not . . ." She shook her head.

Every fibre in me stiffened. "What?" The word came out almost as a snarl.

"Not my grandchild," said my father quietly. He didn't sound as surprised as I felt. "I see."

"How could you do this to us?" I asked her.

"I'm sorry." She hung her head. "I didn't know what to do. I thought if you knew she wasn't related to you, you might be angry with us. With her. She's happy here. I didn't want to spoil it."

"You know, when I saw her this evening on the stage there was something about her that I couldn't put my finger on." Dad was still speaking in the same quiet way. "She didn't remind me of anyone, not in our family, anyway. I thought I could see Hana in her."

"Olivia does look like Hana," Sofia said. "And a little like my former boyfriend." She paused. "He didn't die, Mr Statton. And he never married me. I just changed my name to make it look more English. He left me before I even knew I was expecting a child." She seemed to draw herself in, looking smaller and both older and younger at the same time. "I was young. I didn't know what to do."

324

"I know that feeling," Dad said softly. I thought of him alone in that forest, looking for Hana. Not knowing whether to go on alone to the border or not.

"Why did Maria tell us that Olivia was Jan's daughter?" I asked. "That's where this all started."

"Maria is becoming, how do you say, distracted." Sofia made a circular motion with her finger above her head. "Muddled in her mind. She never recovered from the death of Jan and his daughter, my niece."

"Jan's daughter died in the same accident as he did?" I asked.

She nodded. "Maria loved Irena so much. She was distraught. Then I had my baby over here in the UK. I called her Olivia because it is a good English name and I sent Maria photos. But Maria always called her Irena. The two girls looked alike. They were first cousins, so no surprises. After a while Maria forgot that Olivia was my child, not Jan's. Perhaps she was a little ashamed that I had a baby outside marriage, just like my mother."

"I see," my father said again.

"And as I started taking on various . . . jobs it was better for me just to say I had a niece not a daughter." She put a hand to her mouth briefly. "I thought it would distance Olivia from me if people here found out what I did. Otherwise they might use it against her."

"Didn't she mind having to pretend you weren't her mother?" I asked.

"I told her that the people here would look down on her for being the daughter of a housekeeper, a servant."

Dad made a sound denoting distress but said nothing.

"I am sorry." Sofia blinked hard. "When I heard you'd been to Prague and spoken to Maria, I knew she would have told you things that aren't true. And then you wanted me to tell Olivia. I didn't want to do that." She fell silent for a moment and nobody filled the silence.

"I knew I had to see Maria in person and remind her of the truth before she told Olivia the same story. But I couldn't take time off as I have to save all my leave for the school holidays." She opened her forearms in resignation. "But then these strange things happened at the play tonight."

"Strange things indeed," my father said. The ageing process he seemed to have undergone since Mum's death had accelerated tonight. He might have been ten years older. Hope had given him a temporary lift and now he was sinking again.

Shouts came from outside. I went to the window and drew back the curtain to look out. Hugh was approaching the house carrying something in his arms. Behind him trailed another person, smaller, slighter, who hesitated on the steps of the house as though uncertain whether or not to come inside. Olivia.

With a muttered explanation I ran to meet them.

CHAPTER
FORTY-TWO

Hugh laid the muddy bundle on the ground. "Not there," I called, dashing down the stairs. "The marble is freezing." Samson's tail flickered briefly as he saw me. "Bring him upstairs."

"He's very muddy."

"Dad won't mind."

Sofia was suddenly beside me. "I find towels. We put him by the radiator, yes?" She ran upstairs.

Hugh lifted the dog again.

When we reached the door to the apartment, Sofia was waiting with towels and a blanket. She acknowledged the appearance of her daughter with a quick but wide smile.

"Bring him in here, this radiator's the warmest." She pointed to the study. "But not too close." Sofia indicated a space a foot or so from the heater. "Too hot is bad for him." We laid the dog gently on the towels.

"Where was he?" I stroked his head.

"Tied to a tree in the woods. Olivia had already found him."

"I couldn't get him to walk." Olivia patted his side. "And he was too heavy for me to carry."

Samson whined gently.

"Thank you," I said.

"I'll ring the vet for advice." Hugh pulled out a mobile. I noted that he obviously still had the vet's number programmed into it. I rubbed the dog with one of the towels. Sofia appeared with a saucepan of water.

"It is lukewarm," she said. "Here, boy, you must drink." He lifted his head and managed to lap a little. He'd started to shiver. "It's good that he's doing that," Sofia said. "It will warm him up."

"Who did this to him?" Dad asked.

"Take a guess," I said. "I hope to God she's out of our lives now. If I get hold of her she'll wish she was miles away."

"I saw Emily getting into a taxi," said Olivia. "She's gone." She spoke the last words with near triumph.

"The vet says to do all we're doing," Hugh said, putting his mobile away. "Warm him up very gently and keep his fluids up. Samson is young and fit, but you can take him in first thing tomorrow if you're still worried."

The temperature had fallen below freezing the last few nights. Emily had hated us so much she was prepared to harm an animal. "I'll go and ask my housemistress if I can stay for a bit," Olivia said. "I want to make sure Samson's all right."

"Emily was the one who told me about Letchford," Sofia said, when the girl had left. She explained about the nightclub. How Emily had suggested taking on extra work to help pay the fees. How Sofia had worked at jobs she hated even more than the nightclub, relieved that her daughter was safely tucked away at boarding school and distanced by being known as her niece. "But

Emily was right. Being an escort meant I could afford Letchford." She kept her eyes on the floor as she mentioned this part of her life and did not offer details. My father looked troubled.

She composed her features. "Then Emily arrived unexpectedly at Bellingham one Saturday morning and asked if there was a parcel for her. It was that doll. The courier had just delivered it. I was angry. Mrs Smirnova would have flipped if she'd known her address was being used. And I still needed that job for when I quitted the escort work."

"She just laughed at me."

"Emily hated us so much." I felt the dog's cold coat. "It seems unbelievable that she could have planned all this." I thought of the forged email. And the note to Dad, implicating me in the doll business.

"Olivia told me that Emily was telling her strange things, encouraging her to make cuts in her arms, trying to get her to do herself serious harm. But as the play went on Olivia grew bolder. She said she wouldn't cut any more."

And Emily had pushed her down the stairs. Instead of making Olivia fear the older girl it had broken the bond. Olivia had stood firm. I felt a rush of pride in the thirteen-year-old.

"You should have told me," Dad said. "Or another teacher or housemistress."

"Emily scared me," Sofia said frankly. "She knew too much about me. She knew where I'd been working."

Then the troubled look on Dad's face reappeared. "I was worried she'd tell Olivia. Or . . . you." She looked at him. "I thought you'd be appalled. Tell Olivia to leave."

"Never." He sat straighter, his eyes blazing.

"I drove up here to beg her not to." Sofia put a hand to her forehead, as though about to beat her brow. "I feel ashamed about . . . that part of my life."

Beside me Hugh shuffled slightly. His leg must be hurting after the exertions of the evening.

"I'm sure you have nothing to feel ashamed about," Dad said. "It's the men who use these places who worry me. But perhaps I am just old-fashioned and out of touch."

"I'm going to ring for a taxi," Hugh said, his voice sounding distant and abrupt. "Would you like me to carry Samson back to your flat before I leave?" he asked me, as politely as if he were addressing a stranger.

CHAPTER
FORTY-THREE

The snowy lawn crackled under each footstep as we walked. Although I always thought I preferred Letchford in early summer, around exam time, when the herbaceous borders burst with lupins and delphiniums, there was a pared-down beauty to these winter mornings that showed off the lines of the house and grounds. All was white light, except for the stone walls, which were the colour of pale honey. Samson scampered behind us, fascinated by the feel of the snow on his paws and nose. Every year he forgot about winter and every year was a new revelation.

"Sofia sent me a Christmas card from Prague," Dad said. "She has talked to Maria about Olivia not being the same girl as Irena. She doesn't think that Maria understands though, not completely. Maria shouldn't really be living alone, she said. So Sofia's thinking of moving back to Prague, trying to find work there as a pharmacist."

"What about Olivia?" I felt Olivia's possible departure as a stab in my ribs. She might not be my niece but there was something about her that made her stand out from the other pupils. And I'd liked Sofia, too, felt a kinship for her.

"Sofia doesn't know what'll happen yet. But she can't afford the fees if she goes back to Prague. I don't know if I could put Olivia forward for a bursary."

It would do neither of them any good, I thought.

"Even though she's not a relative there's still a family tie," he said. "It wouldn't be right."

People had been sympathetic to Dad. The governors had held an extraordinary meeting and passed a vote of confidence in the head. Clara had not attended the meeting, to allow them the chance to express any doubts they felt. Few had been expressed. No parents had withdrawn their children. We'd heard nothing more of Emily and were very happy with this state of affairs. Dad had sent warnings to every school he knew. The police had told us that it would be hard to bring a prosecution against a woman who seemed, on paper, to be guilty of no more than a macabre fondness for pranks involving lifelike dolls.

"At least she didn't do anything worse to the dog," Dad had said.

I shivered, thinking of what she might have done. "How did she get a reference?" I asked. We were particular about who we took as gappies.

"A year or eighteen months ago Emily was working at a prestigious school in New Zealand as a secretary or PA. I emailed them and we worked out what she'd done." He gave me an amused glance at the mention of his use of email. "She applied as a past pupil of that school. When I sent a request for a reference to the head, she simply removed it from his post tray and used

332

school headed paper to respond on her own behalf. The head and the other staff knew nothing about it."

She'd have known which envelope to take; it would have had the Letchford school stamp on the front. She must have known she looked young for her age anyway. That marble skin. She could pass for eighteen or nineteen.

Dad fell quiet. I knew what he was thinking.

"No, Dad," I said quickly as he started to say it. "You have no responsibility to Emily. None at all. If she's so good at forging references she'll probably be sorting out another job for herself. That's what worries me. I still think we should put more pressure on the police to take this seriously."

"They said there was little evidence against her. Unless Olivia would testify about Emily pushing her downstairs."

I thought of that doll swinging on the rope and shuddered. "What about the pupils, Dad? How must they have felt when they saw that bloody doll?"

He didn't even frown at the swear word. "The pupils are fine. They are resilient young people. We educate them to bounce back."

We'd turned now, so that the blanched slopes of the Downs were before us, very clear and pure against the pale sky.

"I liked him," he said simply. I knew he was talking about Emily's father and that he would always feel deep sorrow for him and for the baby who'd died. "I wish I hadn't been so preoccupied with the wretched building

333

work and had listened to what he was saying about his son."

Dad and I had passed a quiet Christmas with Clara and family, toasting not only the season but also news of Marcus's new job. "The pressure's off," my sister had told me as we wrapped bacon round sausages to go with the turkey. "I was getting desperately worried. I know we're over-geared." She'd glanced around at the designer kitchen. "It did cross my mind that if he sold, Dad might hand on some capital from the sale of the school to you and me. It would be helpful." She put the tray of wrapped chipolatas into the oven. "But I felt terrible afterwards even mentioning it. Greedy. Selfish." She'd given me a look similar to the one she'd given me all those years ago when I'd taken all the blame for defacing the mural. I'd topped up her champagne glass again.

Hugh had vanished on a pre-skiing fitness camp and I hadn't seen him since the night of the play, although I'd received a card from him. He'd be off to the Alps tomorrow. Dad and Clara had kept their questions about the state of our marriage to themselves. I'd run through the last part of our conversation on the night of the play. We'd been talking to Sofia about her work in clubs as a hostess. She'd hinted at another job, as an escort.

I remembered what the nurse had told me about the men in rehabilitation going out together to bars and pubs. Had they extended their bonding and relaxation to visiting lap-dancing clubs? Or worse? Now I'd had time to reflect I felt I couldn't get too worked up about it. I didn't believe Hugh had been involved in anything too sleazy. But it was no great surprise to me that he might have been to these places. He was a young man in shock, relying on the comradeship of his fellow patients. And I'd accepted my banishment from his life without question, preferring the role of spurned wife.

I thought of ringing him, trying to get over to him that I wasn't dwelling on what he might or might not have done. But how would I start a conversation like that? He had to come to me.

We made a slow circle round the pitches. "That dog shouldn't really be here," Dad said. "We shouldn't make exceptions for the family, Merry. It always leads to trouble."

I couldn't hide an ironic smile. "I know." We both knew, in fact, that an exception would continue to be made for Samson during school holidays.

"There are always the Abingdon and Oxford schools," Dad went on. "I know some of them quite well. And we're near enough for the weekend."

I knew what he was thinking. He might be able to put in a word for Olivia at St Helen's, Headington or Oxford High. Perhaps there were bursaries she might apply for there. "You aren't responsible for Olivia," I reminded him, reminding myself that the same was true of me. He stopped. Turned so that his blue eyes, bright in the glasses he'd started remembering to polish, stared at me.

"I am responsible."

"But she's not —"

"My granddaughter. I know. But there's something you don't know, Merry. Something nobody, apart from Hana, possibly, knew."

"What?"

"Hana didn't leave me in that forest."

"What?" I said again, sounding as slow-witted as I felt.

"It was the other way round, Merry." He nodded at me. "I kept on looking for her. But there was nothing. No rustle in the undergrowth, no branches swaying." For a moment I was there with him in the forest, looking for a girl in a bright tunic against the dark trees. "Nothing," he said again.

"Then I heard a car coming. It slowed. The driver wound down the window. 'Heading for the border? You'd better hurry. I've heard they're about to close it. Orders from Moscow,' he said."

I pictured the driver letting out the clutch, driving on. Leaving Dad standing there alone. Unsure.

"I could return to my mother's village, ask for help with the search for Hana. There were still hours of daylight left. She must be in the trees somewhere. Once her sickness had passed and she'd rested a bit she'd feel stronger, more like the old Hana." He put a gloved hand to his throat, as though what he was saying was catching there. "But then I remembered my mother's face as she'd waved us off this morning . . ."

He wouldn't have been able to bear going through it all again: the goodbyes, the promises to write.

"It was easy to rationalize with myself. Perhaps Hana was hiding, waiting for me to go before reclaiming her bicycle and returning to the railway station. This was her way of ending things." He shrugged. "It was easy to persuade myself that she was all right. I thought about leaving a note on her bike. But what would I say? Better to leave it. I called out one last time. Waited for a minute or two for a response. Then I cycled off."

He reached the border post half an hour later, he told me. The guards were sympathetic but jumpy. They read his papers carefully before they lifted the barrier. "It won't be as easy to come back," one of them warned him. And as they lowered the barrier he wanted to shout that he'd made a terrible mistake, he'd left someone behind, he needed to go and look for her, she was just a girl, alone, ill.

But he bit his tongue and made himself push the bicycle pedals. And cycle on into the West.

"And Hana didn't tell anyone what had happened," I said. "Not Maria, not her own children, nobody." She'd kept the secret all those decades.

"She must have felt awful about being left there. She was a proud girl. She'd have felt embarrassed. Perhaps she'd tripped over and banged her head. Passed out for a while. That was why she didn't hear me shouting for her. She mightn't even have remembered what had happened. But I do."

"You don't, Dad, not really. She might well have been hiding from you, just as you said. Perhaps she lost her nerve at the last moment and wasn't able to tell you she didn't want to head for the West. If she was suffering from pregnancy sickness she might have felt so dreadful that she wasn't thinking straight." I

337

remembered how ill Clara had been with both her boys. Not just in the mornings, but all day, for weeks and months. "Perhaps she was already on her way back to the railway station."

"She left her bicycle behind, Merry. The station was miles away."

"She might have watched you cycle off. Then come out and retrieved it."

"Perhaps," he said. He turned his face away from the sun's milky rays and a shadow fell over it.

"It's hard to know," I said, "when people really do want you to leave them. And when they're just pushing you away for a moment. Regretting it later." My voice trembled slightly.

"Hugh?" he said.

"I took him at his word."

"And that of the medical staff."

"I walked out on him. I could have made an appointment with a counsellor at the rehabilitation unit. I could have pressed them. Made sure I was doing the right thing by taking him at his word." The sun was feeble but it was hurting my eyes so I turned as well. "But I slunk back here and spent months feeling sorry for myself."

"The Stastnys were always ones for retreating in dignified silence," he said. "Sulking, my mother called it."

I couldn't help laughing. He regarded me indulgently. "But not you, Merry. That's not who you really are. We named you well."

338

Samson had found an old hockey ball. He trotted towards me with it in his mouth and dropped it at my feet. I threw it towards the bushes.

"How's the painting going?" I asked. For Christmas Clara and I had bought Dad new paints and brushes and pads of beautiful white paper.

He gave a guilty smile. "I am finding it hard to devote time to school administration. All I want to do is play around with paint. I don't know what Samantha will say when she comes back."

A car I didn't recognize was driving slowly up the snowy drive. "I wonder who that is." Dad sounded weary. "I was hoping the snow would mean a few more days of peace and quiet before I start preparing for next term." I didn't think we were far away from the time when he'd tell us he was ready to think about retirement.

The small jeep stopped near the steps. A man got out: young, fit. He was taking something out of the back of the car, a parcel wrapped in Christmas paper. I stopped in my tracks. Dad wasn't paying attention to the car, obviously preferring to remain out in the grounds, off duty. Samantha was in the house if the visitor had come on school business.

"You know what," I said. "I might go in now. I want to sort out some stuff."

"What *stuff*?" He sounded amused at what he'd call my bad use of the language, but his attention was really on the turf beneath the frost. He was prodding it with a toe. "I wonder how this new grass seed will stand up to the winter."

"Ski stuff." In the loft of my apartment there was still a case with my boots and jacket in it.

"Planning a trip?"

"Perhaps."

"With Hugh?"

"Maybe. See you later, Dad."

I whistled to the dog and ran over the white lawn, heart leaping. My breath formed question marks in the clear air as I went to meet my husband. Hugh turned to look at me and the look on his face dissolved the question marks.

The dog reached him in a jumble of legs and madly wagging tail. I held my breath, fearing Hugh's balance wouldn't hold on the slippery drive. Four hours a day of intense gym work and physio wasn't enough to prepare any man for the canine welcome he was getting. I had to throw my arms around my husband to stop him from overbalancing. That was going to be my story if he pushed me away or recoiled from me.

As it happened, he did neither.

Epilogue

"Pewter curtain rails, I think." Emily stepped down from the stool and folded the tape measure. "I saw some in John Lewis. You could pick them up when you go back for the fabric."

She wrote some measurements in her notepad. "We were going for pinch pleats, weren't we? And the repeat on the material you liked was thirteen centimetres. So here's how much you need to buy." She wrote the figure. The baby crawled over towards her sewing basket. "No, sweetie, too many sharp things in there for you." She picked him up and shot an apologetic look at his mother. "Oh, sorry, do you mind? I can't resist babies."

"Not at all, he's everywhere at the moment." Jennifer Andrews was already juggling a toddler on one hip. The twins were busy pulling feathers out of one of the new cushion pads. "He's only just started crawling. No sense of danger."

"No worries." Emily smiled at the baby. He really did have a cute little face. "Hey, it's going to be hard for you to go back to the shop with all the crew, isn't it? It's just that I could actually start on the curtains tonight if I've got the material and the other bits."

"I've got the double buggy." But Jennifer sounded doubtful.

"I'll come back with you. At least that'll be two pairs of adult hands." Emily kept her eyes on the baby.

"I couldn't possibly ask you to do that."

"No trouble at all. I always need stuff from John Lewis."

"Well, it would be easier . . ." Jennifer seemed to be balancing her fear of taking advantage of an amiable New Zealand stranger with the sheer horror of escorting four under-fours into Reading again.

"Let's go, then."

Emily helped bundle infants into coats and located the baby's changing bag behind the sofa. "I just never seem to get straight." Jennifer fished her car keys out of a child's slipper. "Tim comes home at night and he doesn't say anything but I know he thinks the house is such a mess."

It was.

"Men don't realize how much effort it takes to run a house at the same time as you've got all the kids to look after," Emily offered.

Jennifer didn't say anything. Emily kicked herself. *Steady, steady, don't say anything that sounds like criticism of her husband. You're just the curtain maker. She only knows you from an ad in the corner shop.*

"We lost our au pair," Jennifer said at last. "She didn't give us any notice. It was a bit of a blow."

Emily already knew this. She'd met the au pair in the nightclub a week back and heard all about the Russian boyfriend who was going to whisk her away from all this. "Too bad," she said. "It'll be easy enough to get another one, though, won't it?" She followed with the baby as they walked to the car on the drive. New, expensive and a touch clunky. But it would need to be large with all these kids. The house was large, too.

It had been easy to track down John Andrews' nephew, Tim. He was a newspaper columnist and frequently wrote about his family: the wife who had bitten off more than she could chew, the kids and the succession of hapless au pairs and nannies. Tim had been an only child and had inherited a small but pretty house on the Thames from his Uncle John, which they'd sold at just the right time. Emily had found out most of the information herself, using the Land Registry and Internet, and asking the departing au pair some questions.

Jennifer opened the car door, executed a gentle karate chop round the waist of the toddler and manoeuvred him back into his car seat. "Four children? A house that we're still decorating?" The boy twin squeezed through to the back row of seats. "I just don't think we're an attractive proposition." The girl twin sat between the baby and the toddler in the second row. Emily checked she'd done up the baby's belt properly. She knew car seat safety was one of those things that middle-class mummies were cuckoo about.

"Wow, I know loads of people who'd love a job like this. Great house. Nice kids." She made clucking noises at the baby as she made sure the straps were right. She felt Jennifer's approving stare on her. The girl twin frowned at her. Emily'd need to watch that one.

Jennifer motioned to her take the front passenger seat. "We're not exactly overrun with applicants."

"Really? They're mad. I've worked for enough people to know a good situation."

Her eyes widened. "You've been an au pair?"

"And worked in a boarding school. Just finished there, in fact. Letchford School."

"Letchford?" Awe in her voice. "Tim's uncle taught there. He's dead now."

Emily tried not to let her lips move into a smile.

"They gave me a great reference." She squeezed her bag more tightly to her. Inside was the ivory envelope with the thick headed writing paper in it, telling whomever it concerned that Emily Collins was reliable, kind and honest. If Jennifer rang the telephone number on the reference she'd go through to the mobile of another girl Emily'd worked with at the nightclub. A girl she'd observed stealing a bottle of vodka from the club stores. The girl knew what she had to say in the persona of Samantha Evans, headmaster's PA.

"I loved Letchford but I prefer younger kids on the whole. And I missed the soft furnishing work. I'm really interested in interior design." Careful, careful, don't make it too obvious. She clenched her fingers in her lap.

"Lucky for me I saw your card in the shop."

No question of luck at all. Emily knew that Jennifer always pushed the buggy up to the corner shop on her way to collect the twins from nursery. And that she studied the cards on the board with desperation in her eyes.

Was it right to single out a mere relative of her father's old enemy? Emily had wondered. Perhaps not. But why should anyone in the extended Andrews family be allowed to live a happy and prosperous life when John Andrews had destroyed that possibility for everyone in Emily's own family? She still didn't know what she intended doing here. Nothing like the reborn doll. Perhaps nothing at all. If the family of Tim Andrews treated her well they had nothing to fear.

"I need to talk to Tim," Jennifer said. They were pulling into the car park now. "Perhaps . . ." She gave a little half-smile. "Well, let's just say you do seem to have appeared in our lives at exactly the right time."

Emily gave it ten minutes before the job was hers. She turned again to smile at the baby. The girl twin stuck out her tongue at her. Emily stared coldly at the child until her lower lip wobbled and her small face grew pale.

Acknowledgements

My particular thanks to Jill Morrow, Kristina Riggle, Becky Motew, Barbara Derbyshire, Rebecca Kingston, Danielle Schaaf and Johnnie Graham for reading various drafts of this book and commenting; and to my editor, Will Atkins.

R- 3/15